H. Freeman Wood

Egypt Under the British

H. Freeman Wood

Egypt Under the British

ISBN/EAN: 9783337230555

Printed in Europe, USA, Canada, Australia, Japan

Cover: Foto ©Andreas Hilbeck / pixelio.de

More available books at **www.hansebooks.com**

EGYPT UNDER THE BRITISH

BY

H. F. WOOD,

AUTHOR OF

"THE ENGLISHMAN OF THE RUE CAÏN," "AVENGED ON SOCIETY," ETC.

LONDON: CHAPMAN & HALL, LD.

1896.

PREFACE.

THE writer had scarcely returned from a stay in Egypt as Special Correspondent for the *Morning Advertiser* and the *Glasgow Herald,* when the decision involving an immediate military advance towards Dongola was announced in the British Parliament. He has embodied in the present volume, side by side with confirmatory or illustrative matter supplied to him at the last moment from local sources, much of the direct evidence which was collected by him, and contributed to the journals above-named, with respect to existing conditions in the New Egypt—the Egypt re-cast and re-formed as a body politic—that has arisen beneath British responsibility since 1882. Perhaps the momentous developments of influence or rule which have become a certain prospect, now, whatever the rate of the process, for both the interior of the Egyptian Soudan and the regions around its borders, may but enhance, to English-speaking peoples, the interest attaching to the success or failure of British effort within the dominions held by the Khedive.

May, 1896.

CONTENTS.

CHAPTER I.

At the threshold—The struggle of the languages—British business interests—Port Saïd no longer the "wickedest spot
on earth"—French suspicion of a British structure—An
"Evacuation speech" in England—The Port Saïd French
and English clubs   I

CHAPTER II.

Port Saïd *versus* Alexandria—Wanted, a railway—Local
grievances—The Suez Canal Company—No English
(except pilots) need apply—A missionary on the Field for
trade—British trade-marks forged—A Birmingham commercial traveller tries Egypt for the first time—Ismaïlia
a French settlement   18

CHAPTER III.

By rail through the Land of Goshen—Tel-el-Kebir—From
Bedouins to Fellaheen—Business show-cards at the Delta
railway-stations—Factory chimneys by the Nile—The
British garrison at Alexandria—A tradition of the
Gloucestershire Regiment—No outward symbols of the
Occupation   36

CONTENTS.

CHAPTER IV.

PAGE

Certain of the "people who are here to keep order"—A
British sergeant's view—At the site of Cleopatra's palace
—Association football—Native sentiment on the Occupation—The fear to declare for the British, in case they
should leave—Tactics of the French Opposition—A
policy of worry, harass, and wear-out, if possible—
British pledges 49

CHAPTER V.

Recrimination—French grievances—The British business
community at a disadvantage—Tenders for Government
contracts—British firms bid too high—The Fellaheen on
the Foreigner—An Austrian financier on the Occupation
—Probable result of a *plébiscite* 66

CHAPTER VI.

The "Anglicanization" of Cairo—Rule and Semi-Rule—
Greek money-lenders in the villages—How they evade
the law—The Fellaheen buying machinery—Two or three
wives on thirty shillings a week—An English industry
ruined by the English—Adaptability and consolation—
Under-sold again—Alexandria *versus* Port Saïd—Official
backsheesh 82

CHAPTER VII.

The Egyptian Newspaper Press—Pro-British organs—Organs
of the French, Arab, and Turkish Oppositions—Journa-
listic warfare—The programme of Hajee Abdullah Browne
—Moustafa Kamel's campaign in France—Lord Dufferin's
Organic Law—The judicial system—Reforms—Sitting of
a Native Tribunal 117

CHAPTER VIII.

PAGE

Interview with the Sheikh Ali Youssef, editor of the *Moaïad*
—The leading daily paper of the Arab Opposition—Why
the *Moaïad* allies itself with the French party—French
action in the matter of the reserve funds—Neither France,
nor England, nor the Sultan—A choice between France
and England—Egypt for the Egyptians 139

CHAPTER IX.

Dr. Nimr, of the *Mokattam*, on the programme of the *Moaïad*—
—What "Egypt for the Egyptians" means—M. Deloncle
and Moustafa Kamel : their anti-British pamphlets and
lectures—Greater freedom of the Press in Egypt, under
the British, than is enjoyed by the French Press in France
itself—Egypt envied by Syria—Fellaheen impressions—
The Year of the Blessing 154

CHAPTER X.

Another standpoint—M. Kyriacopoulo on Egypt and the
Eastern Question—The natives "recognize the benefits
of the Occupation," but "fear to manifest their sentiments:" again, "not sure that the situation will continue"—A suggestion to the British Government—
Egypt in progress—The mistakes of Gladstonian England
—What is "neutralization"? 175

CHAPTER XI.

Egypt a school of languages—The Ottoman Spy system—
Lord Cromer—Misgivings on all hands—"We have
promised"—Lord Cromer's aims and impartiality—A
parallel with 1796—Have the fellaheen short memories?
—The *plébiscite*, if secret—News for politicians who
would "give Syria to France"—The Khedive Abbas II.
—Two judgments on Great Britain 189

EGYPT UNDER THE BRITISH.

CHAPTER I.

A FRENCH polemical author and journalist, writing a volume of " Croquis de l'Occupation Anglaise," ten years ago, complained in his opening chapter that the very first individual from Egyptian territory upon whom he and his compatriots set eyes, as their steamer hove-to at Alexandria, was an Arab who did not understand French, did not understand Italian, and could not be made to understand their friendly interrogatories by signs. He understood no European language but English. He was the pilot who had come on board to bring in their Messageries Maritimes boat, from Marseilles, and already, ten years ago, " *Cet Arabe ne parlait qu'anglais !* " It seemed hard ; especially as the writer in question, together with M. Henri Le Verdier, who helped his volume with a vigorous preface, insisted at the time, and continued to insist, upon the prior, the diversified, and the preponderating claims of France. "Thanks to French capital and labour," says M. Le Verdier, "here is Egypt, one of the most important of strategical points, existing as one of the entrances to the East for the whole of Europe—and the English hold the keys of the gates!" What French capital and labour have done, in comparison with English, may be gathered from the numerous works, but better from the French than from the others, that have dealt politically with modern Egypt up to 1882. What has been the idea of thoroughness, integrity, and economy, associated in Egypt itself with the idea of any European nationality, until the system which dates from 1882 was gradually enabled to bear some fruits, we shall have opportunities of testing later on. But, *cet Arabe*, at Alexandria, which the First Napoleon himself had declared "should be the capital of the world," *ne parlait qu'anglais*, and the injustice, or the impropriety, of fate seemed quite too bad.

If any such sensitive citizen of the third republic were to push on nowadays to Port Saïd, and land at the entrance to the Suez Canal, instead of at

the city founded by Alexander, the stress of his
emotion might be sore indeed. " Here is the town
which Ferdinand de Lesseps created," he might
say,—" which sprang directly from that initial
blow of the pickaxe given by the Grand Français
at the ceremony of April 25, 1859,—here is the
seaport which ought to have been named Lesseps-
ville, after its founder, instead of receiving a mere
courtesy appellation, bestowed in compliment to
the viceroy of the day,—and the very first things
decipherable from the decks of vessels entering
the mole from the Mediterranean, are the
announcements of British commercial houses ! "
Thus fate hath willed it, for the present. The
boards of " Ship Chandlers and Stevedores,"
" Shipbrokers," a coal company, limited, and a
bank, are only a few amongst these conspicuous
business intimations that are British. When we
get to the basin, we shall find a " Bureau des
Passeports " in the group of Government offices,
but, even there, that instance stands alone. The
painted inscriptions guiding to the " Coastguard
Office," " Port Police," etc., are in English, the sole
equivalent supplied for each being in Arabic
characters. We have landed ; we have worried
through the custom-house, amid a din of Arabic,

under a hot sun ; and then, what language do we hear ?

The arrival of a British liner fills the quays and main streets with yelling and chattering Arabs, negroes, and yellow or copper-coloured nondescripts, whose medley of the English phrases will pursue the new-comer into the recesses of his hotel. The throng consists of hawkers, porters, touts, deformed and dirty mendicants, donkey-boys, and shoe-blacks, with the worst variety of sinister "guide." Costumes limited to the red or white *takía* skull-cap, and the long close-fitting blue gown, or to the ample turban and the gaudy flowing robe, or to the *takía*, the tunic, and a canvas sack for over-coat, meet the eye in every direction. Intermingled with these are dark-skinned brokers or traders, attired in either the robes and turban of their country, or in a semi-European garb, crowned with the *tarbûsh*, or fez. Levantines and negroids, Turks, and perhaps a Persian or two, or an Afghan ; Greeks, Maltese, and Italians ; British, French, and Arabs ; the concourse along the Rue du Commerce, at Port Saïd, and along the wharves, and about the *cafés*, the telegraph-office, and the banks, offers a fine picture, amid so many "make-shift" houses, in a town so evidently tentative, of

the borderland where Christendom meets Islam.
You go into the post-office, and amongst half a
dozen individuals awaiting their turn, you find
yourself to be the only European ; the others are
native merchants, agents, or *employés*, and they
are registering letters, cashing money orders, and
despatching telegrams. You take the little tramway line from the end of the Rue du Commerce,
facing the basin and the ships, and it runs you
through the centre of the town, past a square
ornamented with a bust of M. de Lesseps, and
away into the separate quarter of the squalid
local Arabs. Back again—your companions in
each trip being fairly representative of the hetero-
geneous groups along the Rue du Commerce—
and you alight at the quay in the midst of busy
negroes, native shipping clerks, and Jews, all
concerned with the processes of landing and em-
barkation. The females are few. They stay
within doors, for the most part. Here, however,
strides a gaunt, ungainly negress, bare-footed,
scarlet-robed, silver bangles around her ankles,
a silver ring through one wide nostril, and a
cigarette between her lips, who wields a baton
betokening some authority, and who actively
directs a squad of the ebon-hued carriers. In

contrast to the shining negro, the dry-skinned, dusky Arab : a specimen of the provincial middle-class Arab of Egypt, a well-to-do personage, no doubt, drives up to the Passport Office in a crowded hackney carriage, clambers out to stretch his limbs, and chats to his wives from the road-way, while the Government penmen prepare his documents. He is going to take ship, with his two wives and his little boy ; and their extra-ordinary luggage for the journey is piled up on the coachman's box, stuffed inside the vehicle, and hooked on behind. The ladies wear the usual black veil and robes, but the latter are of rich silk, whilst the *bourra*, revealing large and mis-chievous dark eyes, permits a glimpse also of complexions smooth and tolerably fair. These are coquettish wives, though veiled. A handsomely embroidered shoe, with an inch of blue silk hose, creeps forth for admiration ; and there are jewels and gold chains that flash in the sun. The costume of the lord and master consists of the *tarbûsh* ; a black frock-coat worn open over a long white night-shirt ; and old elastic-side boots, without socks or stockings. He smokes his cigarette with conscious importance ; his whole air is that of a bilious Egyptian 'Arry. His little boy, in the *tarbúsh* likewise, has been put inside an English sailor-suit, that fits him ill. The babel of dialect, with English, Italian, Greek, or French the running accompaniment, rises and falls in waves. At the two post-offices the telegraph forms are in Arabic and English ; the forms of receipt for the registered letter in Arabic and French. One of the postal clerks told me in English, with every outward mark of delighted anticipation, that he was planning a sojourn in London, as a teacher of modern Arabic. "Why not try France ?" I asked him,—"it's not so far ; the climate would be less of an ordeal for you ; and the French are very fond of the Egyptians." He laughed ; and all I need give of his response was to the effect that fewer French than English would be likely to study Arabic, and fewer English than French expected, as the matter of course, that their own language should be talked abroad. At that very moment, the street was echoing with the cries from black or swarthy touts and hawkers—"Step in and see our photographs !" " Here's the place, —here's the place for curiosities !" "Buy some views of the canal ! This is the best shop in Port Saïd !" "Walk in, walk in ! Best cigarettes !" "Christmas Cards !" "Clean your boots !"

Christmas cards appear to rank as seasonable
articles for the English all the year round at Port
Saïd ; whilst the supply of Arab boot-black boys,
incessant, irrepressible, and quite out of proportion
to any conceivable demand, whether at Port Saïd,
or Alexandria, or Cairo, may be regarded as one
of the minor marvels in Egyptian political economy.
We all know those descriptions of Lower Egypt
which present the land as one where no rain ever
falls in summer, where there is no autumn and no
spring, and where the winter resembles our month
of April, if not May.   The prevalence of the Arab
boot-black boy might reasonably lead the fugitive
visitor to doubt all this.   He infests the centre of
the town at Port Saïd, and he struggles for you,
dogs your footsteps patiently murmuring, "No
clean, you' boots, sir," or beats a tam-tam at a
distance to let you know he is within hail.   A
figure almost as familiar as that of the barefooted
little Arab, in his long dark-blue shirt and white
takía, the brushes and the box slung at his back,
is that of the Levantine skulker, in European garb,
who proffers in an undertone, at your elbow,
certain photographs he vends behind the curtain
of his bazaar.   He proffers photographs, and offers
dancing-houses.   He is an agent of a staple

industry. The byway which is his conducts to the peculiar ill-fame for which Port Saïd has been notorious. It draws the reckless into "Jibboom Street" and similar colonies, and occasionally as far as the stench-laden "Arab town" in the out-skirts. English ladies, or the friends of English ladies, in quest of reading-matter for the remainder of their journey, should be careful how they re-plenish their stock from the rows of English books at even the foremost library. The titles of the neatly bound works they glance over may be innocent enough, but innocence is not precisely what the covers enclose. Sometimes the titles alone will enlighten them sufficiently. In either case, the works have been produced in Great Britain "for exportation ;" and no doubt in quan-tities appreciable they find their way back again, from places such as Port Saïd, to the country which produced them, and where their open sale would at once lead to criminal prosecutions. I asked a member of the resident European colony whether the influence of the governing British might not be exercised with benefit on this subject. "Oh, they don't go into pettifogging things like that," was the response ; "they take broad lines ; they deal with economical and administrative reform. They are managing the whole country for its greatest good. What would be the use of meddling with a few sellers of photographs and books at Port Saïd? They are doing the best thing for every Egyptian toiler, wherever you find him, and the best thing for the world's trade."

The "wickedest spot on earth" was a description once applied to Port Saïd. I met an English resident who had just been reading in a weekly periodical, from England, an article headed with that dire sentence; and he was extremely indignant. "Absolutely the most incorrect nonsense I ever read," said he; "I am told that the description is by ——. No matter—there is scarcely a word of truth in it!" Perhaps not, at the present time. There are, nevertheless, some strange persons about: horrible accosting dwarfs from goodness knows where — villainous herculean caterers for the houses with closed shutters, the dens where the weapons are the drug, the loaded dice, the woman. The Egyptian policeman, sometimes tall, weedy, and spindle-shanked, sometimes a broad-shouldered, powerful fellow, seems to be on excellent terms with every one, and mingles with the scum of the bazaars at an easy lounge, the most amiable of mortals that ever wore a uniform as the symbol of authority, or carried in his belt a sword for somebody's defence. But, not to repeat the evidence available upon the practical efficiency of the police-force, as at present organized, would be an injustice to the men not less than to their chiefs. The gradual transformation of the system since 1882 has wrought wonders. Eye-witnesses of the changes that have taken place at Port Saïd since then state that the desperado and ferocious Arabs of the outskirts, and beyond, have not escaped the civilizing influence of the British occupation, but that they have become modified in their general character by the maintenance of law and order, as well as by the certitude of a larger outlet for the goods which they and theirs can bring in. The trade in Arab curios, woven stuffs, etc., has steadily grown with the security afforded by the altered *régime.*

On no side, however, do we perceive the slightest outward and visible sign of a British military or official occupation. If the English language confronts the eye, and continually assails the ear, the fact must be traced to the crushing predominance of British shipping in the Suez Canal. Englishmen are at the head of the local police, the custom-house, and the coastguard ; but you only hear of them—the casual visitor who actually sees one of them must be either privileged, or Caledonianly persevering. How different this would be under a similar ascendency in the grasp of certain other European nations, those who have lived among such other nationalities can readily understand. Perhaps a word of tribute may be permitted, here, to the wisdom, if we may not say the chivalry, which obtrudes no tokens or manifestations of the paramount influence, facile as the open assumption of complete authority over so mixed a population, demanding a strong and just rule, would obviously prove.

A resident who kindly rendered me much assistance in the task of forming a practical acquaintance with the town was Dr. Josiah Williams, author of " Life in the Soudan," a volume of " Adventures amongst the Tribes, and Travels in Egypt in 1881 and 1882," dedicated to Sir Samuel Baker. Dr. Williams held the post of surgeon-major in the Imperial Ottoman Army during the Russo-Turkish war ; he was afterwards medical officer to the Beira Railway ; and he now combines a private practice at Port Saïd, with the duties of medical officer at this point to the large British steamship lines. " Only those who remember what the

police was in this part of the world before 1882,"
said Dr. Williams, "can appreciate the improvement in the force since the English came in. We
have had law and order for years past, now; and
a stranger is safer at the present time in Port Saïd
than in a good many places one could name in
England." He added his own testimony to the
consensus elsewhere that the Egyptian Government *employés*, at least, are in no danger of forgetting the Slough of Despond from which the
British occupation lifted them. Every native
knows, now, that when he is employed by the
Egyptian Government he will be paid. The
officials know that their pay will be forthcoming
every month, now, and that they may positively
reckon upon receiving it on a fixed date. Formerly, they never knew when they could get it, or
whether they could get it at all.

There is the "old inhabitant," and his "grievance," even at Port Saïd, the place which, on
April 25, 1859, was but a flat sea-shore, "encore
vierge," as Monsieur L. Huard has phrased it in
his monograph upon the canal—"encore vierge
de constructions." M. Huard's pamphlet may be
purchased at the English stationery establishment
of Mr. J. Horn, Rue du Commerce; and it is an

engaging little work, not less for the candour with
which it acknowledges the long line of those, as
far back as Rameses II., who preceded M. de
Lesseps with projects for cutting the isthmus,
than for the tirades of " Oh ! il fallut encore lutter
contre l'Angleterre, dont les émissaires," etc.   At
the "end of 1859, however," writes M. Huard,
"the machinery begins to attack the soil, ten
workshops are in activity, and Port Saïd takes
birth."   Less than forty years elapse, and we have
"old inhabitants," complaining that the Suez
Canal should ever have been thrown open to traffic
through the night.   Prior to the adoption of this
measure, necessitated by the enormous increase
in the shipping, vessels remained in the port from
the afternoon, or the evening, until the morning
or noon next day.   Passengers flocked into the
town, and, as one resident put it, "£10 would be
taken where 10s. is taken now.   At present, the
vessel will be in the port and out again while
we are sleeping."   The hard times, nevertheless,
have permitted the construction of a Casino in
1896.   English capital, too, scarcely invests itself
amid unpromising conditions ; and the new
Eastern Exchange, a mart or agency for the
exhibition and distribution of manufacturers'

samples, price-lists, and show-cards, combined with an hotel and club-house, has been erected at Port Saïd by Messrs. Wills and Company (Limited), of London and Liverpool, at a cost of over £80,000. This establishment is not selected for mention with any desire to single out one undertaking more than another. It deserves notice for several reasons. In the first place, the building forms the most conspicuous feature at the business centre of the town ; in the second, its material is so largely iron that its progress during construction was watched with a daily inquisitiveness by the French who live at Port Saïd—perhaps, also, by some other French, who were brought thither to confer ; and, in the third place, it was constructed entirely with British material and by British workmen. French suspicion saw in this substantial pile a British fortress designed to command the entrance to the canal. It is not a particularly handsome work, but its storage capacity, for supplies to ships calling at the port, is prodigious ; its comforts and organization should commend it to all travellers *qui se respectent ;* and at the moment of writing it is the sole hotel in the town under English management.

I had only just re-entered the local English

Club, after an inspection of the Exchange, when
one of the members, a Roumanian, read out from
the Reuter's telegrams posted on the board a
summary of a speech by Sir Charles Dilke, in
England, against the continuance of the British
occupation. "Why cannot they leave us alone?"
exclaimed the Roumanian, whose business, like
that of many others among the local Greeks,
Maltese, Italians, French, Syrians, and Bulgarian
Jews, had sprung up or sprouted out under the
British *régime.* "A speech like that, from a man
who has held office in connection with foreign
affairs, gets talked about in the Arab broadsheets, and besides being exaggerated by the
French newspapers, unsettles the native mind.
It makes the natives fancy that, after all, you are
not to be taken seriously by them, because,
possibly, you won't stay." It was pointed out to
the speaker that Sir Charles Dilke based his
opposition, this time, not upon the interests of
the inhabitants, but upon considerations of international politics concerning Great Britain alone.
To judge by the response—indeed, the responses
—there must have been numbers of persons, not
Sir C. Dilke's fellow-subjects, who would have
rated him more highly, whether as a strategist,

a diplomatist, or a plain Briton, if he could select some different reason.

At the corner of a street somewhat farther into the town the Reuter's telegram had been perused with unqualified approval, we learnt afterwards. At the corner of that street stands the Cercle Français of Port Saïd, its membership restricted jealously to the French. The English Club, on the other hand, welcomes to its reading-rooms, billiard-rooms, and everything else, all nationalities, without distinction—the French, if they like to present themselves, equally with the rest.

C

CHAPTER II.

THE absence of direct railway communication between Port Saïd and Alexandria, the two principal channels of Egyptian trade, is one of the things which the visitor from Europe, and especially the English visitor, finds extremely difficult to reconcile with all his previous impressions of industrial developments here, upon British lines. Landed at Port Saïd, the commercial traveller, for instance, who has completed his business in that town, can get to Alexandria overland only by going most of the way to Cairo. Instead of a railway trip comparatively short—from four to four and a half hours—straight across the Delta, he must take the Suez Canal Company's narrow-gauge line, parallel with the canal itself, down to Ismaïlia, a journey of three hours and a quarter. He must wait there for the train up from Suez; proceed by the Cairo zigzag line to Zagazig and Benha; change at Benha, after three hours and ten minutes in the train ; wait an hour, and then pass two hours and three-quarters more upon the route back to Alexandria. It might be inferred that the country between the last-named place and Port Saïd presents natural difficulties. That is by no means the case. The difficulties may be natural, but they reside in Alexandria. Perhaps they will be best explained in the words of an English business man, directing an important and extensive enterprise, launched with British capital, at Port Saïd.

"Our railway communication has been thus restricted," said this gentleman, "merely because the effect of our competition is feared at Alexandria. Without asking for a route direct to that point, we should be greatly benefited by a railway connection with the Damietta line. A line already exists from Alexandria to Damietta, and it would be perfectly simple to make a railway to Damietta from Port Saïd. But the Egyptian Government have large sums invested in the Alexandria quays and docks, and they are afraid of diverting traffic to this point, for the reason that all port dues here go into the coffers of the Canal Company. If goods were to be diverted to Port Saïd the government would make nothing out of it in

that way." The pale blue domes of the Suez
Canal Company's headquarters, by the basin of
the cutting, were visible from the windows of the
office in which we were talking, and the same
thought apparently occurred to us simultaneously ;
for, before I could put the query, my informant
added, with a gesture in the direction of the
structure, " They employ no Englishmen except
a few pilots. They have some Italians, I believe,
in the administration, and the new chief engineer
is, I think, a Greek, but you will not discover a
single place in the staff, from one end to the other,
filled by an Englishmen. The concern has been
kept virtually French throughout ; but where you
do find a post that a Frenchman does not occupy,
whoever is there it is not an Englishman. No
doubt it seems extraordinary that, with British
ships forming so enormous a percentage of the
total number going through, there should not be
some local English direction ; yet, such is the
case, and it is a state of things that comes from
Paris." " Is there any alteration in the proportion
of foreign vessels, as compared with British, passing through the canal ? " " Foreign vessels are
creeping on, a little, as the latest returns show ;
but still the percentage of British shipping is so

overwhelmingly high that what difference there has been, of late, scarcely counts. The narrow-gauge railway, from Port Saïd to Ismaïlia," resumed the speaker, "is the property of the Suez Canal Company. Of course, with that gauge, two feet six inches, there can be no shunting of the carriages or waggons to the main Egyptian line, at Ismaïlia ; although, as a matter of fact, the narrow-gauge line is not allowed to receive goods. It conveys passengers, and it takes three hours and seventeen minutes to cover the forty-two miles. There is to be an attempt to run the train faster and save forty-five minutes ; but, instead of giving us this little line a couple of years ago, the government ought to have sanctioned or required a railway on the full gauge, with the ordinary facilities for the transit and transfer of goods. By the government I mean the Egyptian Government. The English are the masters, undoubtedly, but they have to consider susceptibilities and vested interests at Alexandria, and they cannot do everything they like, I suppose. What we say is, ' Give us a railway here, at Port Saïd. You will open up large tracts of land and increase the revenue, and more than recoup yourselves for anything that might be lost at Alexandria.' We think it a

short-sighted policy to prevent the expansion of
one place, or to starve it, for the sake of another.
Let each have fair play, and let the result be left
to the play of natural conditions. It would be all
the better for the prosperity of the country in
general." "What cargoes do you load at Port
Saïd now?" "There are no facilities for bringing
cargoes, except by native boats. At other ports,
when a ship discharges her cargo she reloads with
another. We cannot do that here. Ships come
here from England and discharge over a million
tons of coal per annum—from Cardiff, principally;
but when they have finished discharging, they have
no cargoes here to reload. They must reload from
Alexandria, or else put into the Black Sea and
load with another cargo there—grain, cotton, and
so forth." "Trade all round would have been
in a better condition, perhaps, and the development of the country would have been more active
and effectual, if Mr. Gladstone's Government had
acted differently in 1882?" "Of course it would!
We committed a great blunder in 1882. Mr.
Gladstone made a muddle of the position. He
tried to disguise his ignorance of things out here,
or his weakness as a statesman, by holding forth
in the vein of Egypt for the Egyptians, not for

England; whereas, the Egyptians would have been only too glad if we had taken them over definitely, and declared a protectorate, as France has done with Madagascar. I have spent most of my life in this country, and I know the people, and they appreciate all the more thoroughly at the present time, when they see what we have done for them with our hands not free, what we could and would have done if we had adopted the course which everybody looked for. After Tel-el-Kebir, we ought to have taken the country. That was what everybody expected we should do, and what any other European Power would have done. No; the French missed their opportunity at Alexandria, and we missed ours after Tel-el-Kebir. And what would happen to Egypt if we were to go out would be the break-up of all the good work we have done, and terrible anarchy—until some European power, more resolute than we in the matter, stepped in and spoke plainly. We have experience enough elsewhere to shape a pretty good estimate of the kind of scope which would be conceded to British trade under any other foreign influence."

An alternative route from Port Saïd to Alexandria is, of course, by the sea, and Egyptian,

Russian, French, Greek, and Italian vessels, plying along the Mediterranean, do at present touch at the two places. The voyage between Port Saïd and Alexandria, however, takes eighteen hours. If I have dwelt at some length upon this subject of the feeble communications, it is because of the real disadvantages under which all British capital invested at Port Saïd—the "threshold of Egypt," as one member of the English business colony defined it—obviously suffers. Capital comes here from British pockets, keen initiative and steady courage dictate and direct its employment, the British pioneer in trade shows that he can adapt himself promptly to novel conditions, detecting and utilizing openings for the people at home, and then, as if the slowness of the home manufacturer, frequently, to change his patterns for new markets were not sufficient, the British trader here must continue to be shut in artificially by a canal company on the one side, and a rival town on the other. He is cribb'd, cabin'd, and confined under a government to all intents and purposes his own, and, in particular, he is very much "cribb'd." British trade marks are forged wholesale. An English Church of England missionary, whom I met along the Suez Canal towards Ismaïlia,

told me that by far the greater portion of the
hardware goods supplied throughout this region
and in Syria are of Belgian and German make,
with British trade marks. This reverend gentleman has a twenty years' knowledge of the
Egyptian border and the adjoining Turkish provinces, he converses fluently in Arabic, and he
knows the natives well, their wants and their
ways. " They have the greatest respect throughout
the East for British workmanship," said he, " and
if they can only be sure that the article offered
to them as British is the genuine thing, they will
pay much more for it. In some cases the goods
falsely marked 'Sheffield' are selling at one-third
of the price for which Sheffield could let them go.
In consequence of the class of goods thus sold,
British marks become disparaged."

One of the passengers to Ismaïlia was an
Englishwoman who had qualified as a hospital
nurse in London, and had come out " to do some
private nursing at Cairo." She stated that there
are plenty of places for English nurses at Cairo,
and that they earn from £2 10s. to £3 per week,
plus the board and lodging. A friend who had
preceded her was one of the English governesses
appointed by the Egyptian Government at £140

per annum to teach the Arab children in the
few schools. At Ismaïlia I found a Birmingham
commercial traveller whose firm were sending to
Egypt for the first time, and who had done very
well, he said, for an initial attempt, considering
that he was relying upon "quality against lower
prices and inferior stuff." The goods he found in
possession of the market in his own line were
"cheap French and Italian products." These had
apparently satisfied most requirements, but he had
obtained orders on the strength of his better
samples, and he felt confident of quadrupling his
results the next time he came, notwithstanding the
lower tariffs of his French and Italian competitors.

He had been well received wherever he had
gone in Egypt, and he had worked from Port
Saïd to Alexandria, from Alexandria to Cairo,
from Cairo to Ismaïlia, and thence down to
Suez. Returning now from Suez to Ismaïlia, he
was to pick up an outward bound Australian liner
at Port Saïd. He believed the proportion of
British commercial travellers in Egypt to be
extremely small. There were a few travellers for
English cloths, boots, and hats, but the German
boots and French hats had the pull up to the
present. The French fancy goods, soap and

perfumery, and jewellery houses, also sent travellers, and the chief industries of Milan were
similarly represented. " If, however, we are to look
to any prospect of evacuation by the British," he
went on, "it won't be worth the while of British
houses to send travellers here." Our friend's line
was not hardware, but he listened with a good deal
of attention to what the missionary already quoted
had to say about the possibilities for hardware
hereabouts.

"Your English houses ought to commission
travellers to expose these frauds," urged the
reverend gentleman ; "you ought to go through,
and look at the commodities the people have, and
when you come to the spurious article say, ' This
is not English—that is not English. English
goods could not be sold at the price you have
paid.' It would open the eyes of the inhabitants
throughout the region." In answer to a request
for particulars as to the districts and the nature
of the trade to be developed, he admitted that
the market was poor up and down the canal, but
insisted that a great deal might be done in the
textiles as well as in hardware, from Port Saïd.
"From Port Saïd you have all the ships that
sail along the coast of Syria. You have Jaffa,

Heifa, and Beyrout as the seaports for Palestine and Syria; whilst in Damascus you have the emporium for the whole of Hauran." The reverend gentleman favoured me with much curious information anent the spies frequenting the Arab cafés; but that is a topic to be reserved for a future occasion. When I parted from him, he was bound for Port Saïd, to purchase cartridges for his revolver, and take up his passage by ship to Palestine. His destination was Jerusalem, "and," said he, in the dreamy, absent fashion which appeared to have been acquired through long residence in the East, "there is no telling what may happen. The Turkish provinces are in a very disturbed state."

The Suez Canal Company narrow-gauge railway runs parallel with the canal itself, often at a distance of a few yards only from the bank. More like toys than a serious and practical provision for a growing traffic, the little locomotive and little carriages occasionally overtake a steamship, gliding at the required low rate of speed through the blue waters of the cutting, and run a mild race. Lake Menzaleh stretches along to the right hand, past three stations; what is there to the left, on the other side of the canal? I saw

an islet-dotted expanse, fringed with palms, and
bordered towards the horizon by serrated mountain
ridges. "Is that a fresh-water lake," I asked the
Suez Canal Company official, who played at being
the guard of the train, "or is it an inlet of the
sea?" "That is a mirage," was the reply. A
bluff old British pilot, wearing the Suez Canal
Company badge, corroborated the statement, and,
difficult though it seemed to believe, in presence
of so vivid a picture and so natural a perspective,
their knowledge of the spot was of course not to
be questioned. "There is no water over there,"
the pilot added; "that's all desert." A lingering
suspicion of their good faith with the traveller was
unavoidable, but, until I should return along the
same route much later, there could be no opportunity of testing their veracity. "That's not any
scene in Egypt," added the old mariner; and
while I was thinking how admirably his portrait
would have fitted into some such interior as an
Antwerp harbour-side eating-house, with framed
inscriptions of *Rolpens* and *Paling gebakken* at his
back, or a ruddy winter parlour in Rotherhithe,
long pipes and rum upon the table, he resumed
his part in the discussion next door, with unhesi-
tating fluency and not the slightest affectation, in

three languages besides his own. The company, all local acquaintances, were debating in Arabic, Italian, and French.

Of the two stations referred to above, only the first at present bears a name—Ras-el-Ech. The other is but a topographical expression, "Kilomètres 24," marking the number of kilometers from Port Saïd. Similarly, the ensuing four halting places down to Ismaïlia, the terminus, are "Kilomètres 34," 44 (Kantara), 54, and 64 (El Ferdans), successively. At the more important of these "stations," whether from the standpoint of the Suez Canal Company, or from that of the Egyptian coastguard service, the cluster of Arab cabins is supplemented by the more substantial dwellings and the fenced gardens of Suez Canal Company *employés* or government functionaries. Between the stations, and all around, nothing but the desert—the dun, irregular, and arid waste that seems limitless, although here we are barely upon the fringe of it—meets the view when Lake Menzaleh, with the lovelier and the mocking vista that faced us from the side of Syria, have gradually receded. At Kantara the fresh-water canal which supplies Port Saïd branches away to our right, to connect with the Damietta arm of the Nile. We cross the camel-track from Lower Egypt into Syria ; we are almost on a line with El-Arish, the frontier town between Egypt and Palestine, on the other side of the canal ; and we arrive after three hours and a quarter at the point from which the British forces, conveyed along the canal, marched upon Arabi's encampment in 1882— Ismaïlia.

Dr. Josiah Williams has compressed into so convenient a compass the events of ancient history that are recalled by the site now occupied by Ismaïlia, that I venture to borrow half a dozen sentences from the work of his, already referred to, published in 1884. "The canal laid out by Rameses the Great," wrote Dr. Williams, "was between fifty and sixty miles in length, and left the Nile at Bubastis, reaching into the neighbour-hood of Lake Timsah. Upon it Rameses built his two treasure cities, Pithom and Raamses, near Ismaïlia, mentioned in the first chapter of Exodus ; and there is little doubt that the Israelites, who were then in bondage, laboured at these cities and the canal three thousand years ago. It is probable also that the canal dated far back beyond that time. . . . Pharaoh Necho took this canal in hand 500 or 600 B.C. He undertook to adapt it for

navigation, and prolong it to the head of the
Arabian Gulf. . . . He was so zealous as to perfect
the formation of a ship canal, connecting the
Nile with the Red Sea. He carried the great
work as far as the Bitter Lakes—below Ismaïlia,
and half-way towards Suez—and then abandoned
it, warned by an oracle to desist, after expending
the lives of 120,000 fellahs. Herodotus actually
saw the docks, which, as a part of the plan, he
had constructed on the Red Sea." Ismaïlia—so
named from the Khedive Ismaïl, whose dilapidated
palace forms one of the few local "sights"—now
exists as a residential settlement created by the
Suez Canal undertaking, and as a sort of stepping-
stone for travellers who prefer to land from vessels
midway along the Canal, and to at once proceed
by the main line from this point to Cairo. The
settlement radiates from the offices and workshops
of the company, and all the characteristics of the
miniature town are strikingly French. The only
British members of the permanent colony seem
to be the families of two pilots, plus an extraordinary old female who has drifted hither no
one knows how, and who earns a subsistence by
sewing. Egyptians direct the customs, coastguard, and police ; but the little engine which

brings you down the Canal Company's narrow-
gauge line from Port Saïd is from the Belfort
factory of the Compagnie Alsacienne ; the ironwork of the lock upon the fresh-water canal
between the Ismaïlia railway-station and the large
fertile oasis of the town, has been furnished by
Gouin et Cie., in France ; and the material for the
tramway line following the central avenue, and
running to a terminus on a high bank of the Suez
Canal itself, seems to have been sought exclusively
in France. It would doubtless be a waste of time
for British or other foreign contractors to tender
to the Suez Canal Company, with better material
than French firms, at the same or lower rates.
The religion of the company is France. The
bright, intelligent, and docile negroes from Berber
and adjacent tracts, who perform the menial duties
at the leading hotel and at some other of the best
establishments, are better at home in phrases of
French than of English, although the increasing
numbers of British travellers who stop at Ismaïlia
for a few days, between Port Saïd and Cairo, have
latterly scattered a counter-crop of rather superior
Anglo-Saxon.

Situated upon one bank of the salt lake,
Timsah, which is intersected by the canal,

Ismaïlia presents many attractive natural features. Enormous acacias, with branching, serpentine trunks, line the broad avenues and meet overhead. Figs and prickly pears grow wild. The walks are shaded by sycamores, palms, and pines, as well as by the ubiquitous acacia, and in the gardens the orange, lemon, and banana trees are loaded with ripening fruit. An hotel which languished under Italian management until the greater flow of British visitors impelled a well-known German caterer to purchase the building and grounds, and remodel the whole concern upon the best English lines, now easily holds the supremacy amongst the local undertakings of the kind. From the verandahs of this establishment the view embraces, in one direction, the wide expanse of blue sea water, bordered by the yellow banks of the desert; in another direction, the cutting of the Suez Canal, the course marked in the open by buoys, illuminated through the night; and, in another, the variegated houses and vegetation of the town. The disused palace of the Khedive stands on the road to the hospital founded and maintained by the company, and immediately below the hospital site, on the high bank of the canal, are the Ismaïlia "station" for the ships passing through, and the ferry for the Bedouins and their camels. From November to January, and later, a day at Ismaïlia is an English day of June, amid tropical plants, trees, and flowers.

CHAPTER III.

FOUR times a day the primitive railway station at Ismaïlia draws to its exits and its entrances the turbaned and long-robed idlers of its peaceful population. Four times a day a train arrives— two from Suez towards Cairo, two from Cairo towards Suez. The travellers are the merchants of the country, natives or Levantines ; government or Suez Canal Company officials ; and Europeans bound either for Cairo from Port Saïd, or for the latter place from Cairo. We are in the month of December, and the ebon-hued or tawny boys and girls, Arabs or negroes, who, clad in the long blue shirt or blouse which is their only garment, call their wares in Arabic as the throng around the station thickens, are offering oranges fresh-gathered at Ismaïlia itself, and water in earthen-ware jars. A cloudless sky overhead, the sun's rays tempered by the faint cool breeze from the surface of Lake Timsah ; the palm trees, acacias,

flag-leaved bananas, and sycamores bathing in
deep shadow all the roadways and the paths ; the
journey out of the desert oasis commences well.
We quickly leave the outlying fringes of the
fertile ground, however. The canal between its
high banks at this region has lessened to a
thread and vanished ; the purple expanse of Lake
Timsah, glittering in the flood of sunshine, has
dwindled to a tinsel speck ; and everything dies
presently away behind a dreadful unchanging
horizon, smooth sand and rock in illimitable
undulations—the desert. We are traversing the
Biblical Land of Goshen, at its northern boundary.

Birket-el-Timsah, the Arabic name for the salt
lake at Ismaïlia, signifies " Lake of Crocodiles," and
it is inferred from this that, at the period at which
the denomination was bestowed, the waters of the
Nile flowed as far as the point in question. The
crocodile has retired southward, and the Nile has
retired altogether. In spite of closed windows,
the parching dust penetrates everywhere. The
sight aches at the glare of white light. Beneath
this hard blue sky, and across this brown and
blinding wilderness, the Children of Israel had
marched out of the land whence Pharaoh " would
not let them go." According to the contention

of the English missionary referred to already, and according to his theory of an altered level of the Red Sea bed, it was at Ismaïlia, not at Suez, that they crossed. But, to quote the French comment upon his demonstration as we were examining the working model of the canal, at the company's offices—"*il y a longtemps que ça s'est passé!*" A locomotive engine hurries us fast towards the first few patches of swamp and bulrushes; and at the earlier halting - points, termed stations, the wealthier Bedouins, with their camels, are in wait to take the train. The ordinary tribesmen, bringing into Egypt their camels to sell, and plodding in Indian file by sun or by stars, we have overtaken from time to time or descried in the far distance; for them, as for others whom we have met, returning into Syria, their merchandise disposed of, the railway has become an object too familiar to be gazed at curiously, an outcome perhaps of magic, but a landmark fixed and convenient.

"Tel-el-Kébir!" The tattered Arab railway servants, wearing proudly as their sign of office a tin badge strapped to the arm, repeat the cry along the carriages—first, second, and third-class— "Tel-el-Kébir!" It is the first considerable

settlement at which we have stopped, and just
before entering the station we have traversed a
portion of the battle-field which French journalists
always ridicule, and which, if the graves of soldiers
ever can be ridiculous, offers to their ridicule its
simple cemetery in silence. The calls of the
water-sellers, mostly children, " Moya ! El moya ! "
("water ") mingle with those of the sugar-cane
and orange vendors, with the chatter of the local
merchants who troop into the compartments, and
with the neighing of fine Arab horses, tethered
by the forefeet, and plunging at the aspect of
the steam-engine and the sound of the steam.
But we are quitting the trackless wastes of the
Bedouins for the settled homes of the fellaheen.
The desert recedes ; the prospect changes to that
of a luxuriant country, green under the new
crops, vivid in the pure atmosphere to the far
horizon, and peaceful under golden sunlight. The
reapers and the tillers of the soil are figures
garbed like the husbandmen of Hebrew history.
They make no pauses in their earnest labour as
the train speeds by ; but when some faces turn
towards us from the wheat-sown furrows or the
waving fields of maize and sugar-cane, the expression is invariably of contentment, pleasure, hope.

No longer is the lot for each of them the lot that every adult, every man and woman of them all, can wretchedly remember. Pitiless exactions, unrequited interminable toil, drudgery, disease, and death the only outlook ever known to them, the only tale their fathers handed down—from this they have been saved. They have been saved from the scourge, and from torture, from the Pasha who possessed himself of their whole lives. The oxen yoked to the ploughs, the heavily laden camels pacing slowly along the roads, the asses bearing traders from the village to the market— none of these, no beast of burden, need be envied by the Egyptian tenant-farmer now. The Pasha cannot any longer command that the helpless fellah whom he may suspect of hoarding the fruits of his own industry shall have his flesh torn with red-hot pincers ; he cannot rob the fellah of his future harvests, nor can he take his daughters from him and sell them in the towns.

It is not so long since 1882, and the fellah does not yet perhaps believe in his good fortune. How the change has come to pass he scarcely comprehends. Those of the fellaheen who have been able to enrich themselves under the justice and the freedom with which the British rule has gradually

endowed them, no doubt can connect the new conditions with the real cause. The poorer among
them, however, seem to have small notion of the
process insensibly at work ; in the remoter districts, indeed, it is questionable whether the largest
peasant cultivator knows much more about the
origin of the reforms than the poorest of the
labourers who bend perpetually over the soil.
They hear that the English are the masters ; but
they are told that the English are monopolizing
all the profits from their industry. They are
better off, they know ; but England " despoils them
all." The French are their friends, they are
assured ; and as no human lot is without its
grievances, they visit all grievances upon the
English. Everything which in their ameliorated
circumstances might still be better is, on the other
hand, promised to them in a beautiful perfection
if only they could see the English displaced, and
dispossessed, for the French. Who tells them
this ? Everybody whose corruption, unrestrained
local power, and unjustifiable gains have suffered
under the British domination. A permanent
source of falsehood is the French press in Egypt ;
and to make doubly sure of a circulation for its
calumnies, one of the French journals here,

although necessarily aware that its articles are copied into the Arabic broadsheets, prints its attacks and so-called " information " on one of its pages in the vernacular. Another of the French organs, the *Phare d'Alexandrie,* which persistently misrepresents the attitude of Great Britain in regard to the affairs of Turkey, is reputed to be subsidized by the Egyptian Government. If public money is to be expended in any such form, it should be laid out rather in the maintenance of an Arabic journal for dissemination of the truth. But while the train runs through these bountiful and smiling plains, wooded with sycamores and palms, the air soft and fragrant, the thought hardly dwells upon the meannesses of partisan chagrin and the dishonesty of unscrupulous opposition. In this home of his, amid his meadows and cotton and cereals, the fellah tenant of the thatched mud cabin rouses to his task at dawn at length a human being. A thrill of pride may well be owned by those who can claim kindred with the nation that has wrought the miracle!

Minet-el-Gamb, the first important centre reached by the railway from Ismaïlia, has its extensive market and goods depôt in proximity to both the station and the main fresh-water canal. The latter is crowded with felucca-rigged barges, and a commercial activity prevails which prepares the traveller for the greater marts of the two junctions then following, viz. Zagazig and Benha. At Zagazig the station walls exhibited show-cards by European firms ; they were the first I had seen on the journey through the Delta, and they were the advertisements of British houses. They could scarcely have conveyed much enlightenment to the native mind, inasmuch as the one which contained an inscription in the vernacular displayed the photograph of a complicated engine that assuredly "no fellah could understand ;" whilst another consisted simply of the firm's name, with the announcement, in English, that they manufactured watches. At Benha, where it was necessary to change for the Alexandria service, with a wait of nearly an hour, the same cards were supplemented by three others, all British—the advertisement of a Scotch whisky, and the framed illustrations of agricultural machines, by competing makers. The largest of the frames enclosed five photographs of the appliances at work, a description of each being given underneath in Arabic. Benha is a centre for the cotton district ;

it was the town at which Abbas, who succeeded
Mohammed Ali in August, 1849, and to whom
Saïd succeeded in July, 1854, was strangled "in
his palace," and its catacombs have furnished the
Alexandria Museum with valuable Greek and
Roman antiquities. I shall remember it also as
the scene of a charge by a railway porter which
is probably unprecedented. For taking possession of two packages which another railway porter
had already deposited in a place of safety, and
for transferring them to the private apartment
of the booking-clerk, he requested a fee of four
shillings, not from the booking-clerk, who might
reasonably have disbursed that sum as consideration, but from the proprietor of the luggage, who
had turned his back for a diminutive cup of coffee,
and was engaged in the difficult operation of
extracting from the buffet-keeper his due amount
of change, in Egyptian coinage, for a five-franc
piece. "You give *backsheesh* me, *pour porter
bagages*, four shillings," said the wearer of the
State railway's badge when traced, and he respect-
fully urged his claim at intervals of five minutes.
"He is a foolish man," pronounced the booking-
clerk on being consulted, out of a traveller's
curiosity, as to the scale of porters' fees at Benha

Junction. Some twenty minutes before the arrival of the express for Alexandria the original porter returned to the deep window-sill in the buffet, which he had selected as the place of safety. An explanation and an argument ensued; each had his rights, the second having chatted with the traveller about the superiority of express trains over "locals." It was a knotty case; and they were assisted in solving it by the wisdom of other turbaned and tattered swarthy persons—a dozen in all—squatting on the platform in the evident companionship ascribed by Shakespeare to Sir Thomas Lucy. "It is a familiar beast to man," wrote the bard, elsewhere, "and signifieth love." Whatever they decided, the actual solution must have been prodigiously disappointing. In fact, the express had got up to a considerable rate of speed before the second of the rival badge-wearers could be induced to drop from the carriage on to the line. The backsheesh nuisance is, of course, an old story.

On leaving Benha the train for Alexandria passes over the branch of the Nile which flows down to Damietta. A second railway bridge is in course of construction across the river at this point, and the smoking factory chimneys which

cluster on the other side testify abundantly to the
expanded industrial movement. It was a surprise
to note that the locomotive engine had been
supplied by the Compagnie Franco-Belge, but
on this subject I must reproduce, later, certain
peculiar and interesting considerations obtained
from members of the English business colony at
Alexandria. Our express pulled up at Tantah,
famous for its annual fair—a generation ago as
"unspeakable" as the Turk, and to the present
day one of the world's wonders—and now a large
junction with eight platforms. The directions to
the several lines are painted upon an index-board
in Arabic and French. It was not until the next
morning, when being driven to the new museum
at Alexandria, that I discovered the English
language in any of the official notices. A dun-
coloured square building, with a spacious portico,
stood at the angle of a central street. Two inscriptions figured in plain characters upon its
walls: "*Caracol Attarine*" for the Arab—"Head-
quarters British Garrison" for the European. A
red-coated, white-helmeted sentry paced the broad
walk beneath the portico; his comrades lounged
at the guard-room windows; officers grouped at
the door. This was not my earliest glimpse of

the Army of Occupation. I had met two stripling corporals in the Place Mohammed Ali on the previous night. They were looking for the way to the Ramleh Station for their return to barracks. "Our regiment is the Gloucester, and we only came here last week from Malta," explained one of them ; "we suppose we shall stay here a twelve-month, and then go on to Cairo, to replace the regiment that has gone on there from here—the Connaught Rangers. Our barracks are in a very healthy spot, by the sea. The barracks are close to the place where our regiment, the 28th, landed in eighteen-ought-two." "Eighteen hundred and eighty-two?" "No; eighteen-ought-two, when we beat the French." "Eighteen-ought-one," corrected the other corporal, more accurate in his dates; "we were under Abercromby, and we drove the French out of Egypt. That's why we've got the right to wear the sphinx on our collar," and the speaker indicated a white metal badge, stamped with a semblance of the mysterious head. He said nothing of an incident at Rosetta in 1807, the defeat by Mohammed Ali of the British expedition despatched under General Fraser to "effect a diversion in favour of the Mamelouks as a counter-stroke to French policy." Perhaps it

was not taught. These two corporals were smart
and exemplary young fellows. They refused to
look in at any of the *cafés* or taverns where games
were being played, for the reason that the orders
to them all were to enter no premises at which
gambling went on ; and as cards, dominoes, or dice
were in the hands of the *consommateurs* everywhere, and they interpreted their orders strictly,
we parted perforce without drinking to her gracious
Majesty.

CHAPTER IV.

FROM one extreme to the other, it was less a matter of satisfaction to come upon some redcoats, fuddled and stupid, a night or two afterwards, among a score of privates in the Arab and low-class foreign quarter. A worthy British sergeant, encountered in the course of a morning constitutional towards the high ground of the Government Hospital, did not believe there was any particular harm in the "glass too much," among the lanes and dens in question. "A man can take too much," said he, "wherever he is, all the world over." "But here, don't you think it would be better for the credit of the British Occupation, in the eyes of the other European residents, if the men paid more attention to the matter?" "'Course it would! But you can't help it. The men enjoy themselves, and you can't hinder them." "No danger of affrays?" "Oh no! We're on

E

the best o' terms with 'em !" At the same time
there was the standpoint of the better-class native,
and the general European resident, as embodied
in a comment repeated to me by an acquaintance
newly arrived here from Cairo. That gentleman
had been walking in company with a Cairo
merchant when a party of British soldiers, quarrel-
ling and apparently intoxicated, drove down the
street in an open hackney carriage. Blows were
struck, and one of the men was thrown violently
out of the vehicle. He was picked up with a
broken ankle or some such injury, and, evidently
the worse for liquor, was supported either to the
hospital or to the barracks. " These are the people
who are here among us to keep order," commented
the Cairo resident—not a person of British nationality. To record such incidents is not pleasant ;
but, if they occur, a plain tale can scarcely shirk
them. If they occur, they are a part of the
full story. The British garrison at Alexandria
numbered at the time fifteen hundred men, and
doubtless such incidents were comparatively few.
But the words written in 1893 by Sir Alfred
Milner, late Under-Secretary of Finance in Egypt,
with regard to the British occupation should seem
to appeal especially to the forces themselves. " It

is as the outward and visible sign of the predominance of British influence, of the special interest
taken by Great Britain in the affairs of Egypt,"
wrote Sir Alfred Milner, "that that army is such
an important element in the present situation. Its
moral effect is out of all proportion to its actual
strength. The presence of a single British regiment lends a weight they would not otherwise
possess to the counsels of the British Consul-
General."

It might be inferred that above the " Headquarters British Garrison," if nowhere else, the
British ensign is to be seen at Alexandria. I did
not see the British ensign either there or anywhere
else until reaching Cairo, and then only at the
premises of private tradesmen and at the masthead
of Nile excursion or pleasure-boats. The absolute
"correctness" of the occupying power, in this
respect, as in others, can only be impeached by
direct travesties of the truth. The stars and
stripes floated from the summit of the American
Consulate adjacent to the English church, Place
Mohammed Ali, Alexandria; but neither upon
ordinary business structures, nor upon private
or official residences, nor upon the quarters of
the British commander at Alexandria, nor at the

headquarters of the garrison itself, was any British flag to be perceived. To discern that symbol of a foreign nationality, one must look for it where the view is confronted by the flags of all nations trading to the port, viz. amongst the ships in the busy harbour. Where any official establishment or site was surmounted by a piece of bunting, it was the emblem of the Khedivial authority, the crescent and star. I supposed that, as in the cities of the Continent where the British colonies form their clubs for outdoor recreation, the Union Jack might have harmlessly adorned the ground of the local cricket, football, and lawn-tennis club. It was not so, however. One Saturday afternoon, a British visitor to the town had an opportunity to witness an Association football match between the Alexandria Club, formed of British *employés* and employers here, and the crew of her Majesty's gunboat *Fearless*. The local team, by the way, better able, no doubt, to preserve its all-round combination by means of regular practice, against ships' crews and against the regimental elevens, won rather easily. The sunburnt tars were sturdy and nimble, but not quite clever enough. But nothing in the colours worn by either camp—red jerseys for the Alexandria Club, blue and white stripes for the *Fearless*—nothing in any of the usual decorations to a club-house or marquee, suggested the British flag. The native population of different classes who looked on, and divers of whom, the adults as well as the urchins, eagerly scrambled for the privilege or the pleasure of returning the ball back to the players from a kick into touch, might have felt that they would be better understood, and better served, if the British could but hoist their national emblem here and everywhere else in Egypt, over their playground and their workground, too. From the position of the spectator, on the side near the sea, it was but a stone's-throw to the sandy bed where Cleopatra's Needle, the obelisk of the Thames Embankment, had reposed for ages.

"What the people who concern themselves at all about the country complain of is," remarked a twenty years' business resident, in the course of a subsequent conversation, "that we don't take them over altogether and govern them altogether in our own way. They know what our ways are now, and these are juster and more honest ways than any they had ever seen or heard of. But if we won't give them our style of governing men right out, they say, 'Let us alone, and let us

govern ourselves, and then we shall know where
we are.' They don't want an administration of
mixed thievery and honesty; they want either
all honesty, which they certainly do associate
with the British, or all thievery, which they had
before the British came, and in which everybody
had a chance by being a liar and a swindler.
When they talk about their freedom, their *khou-
reah*, they mean the license which existed before
we came here by ourselves. They are fully
sensible of the increasing benefits they have enjoyed during the years of the occupation, but as
we don't assure them that those benefits are going
to be permanent, an uneasy feeling hangs about
many an Egyptian that he may make himself
obnoxious by being honest, now, under our rule,
to persons who would immediately possess the
power to persecute and injure him, if that rule
were withdrawn. They are for the most part
variable and contradictory in idea themselves, but
they can't grasp the situation. They say, ' Here
you are; what would have happened to us and to
the country if you hadn't stepped in, we shudder
to recall; you won't go away; we don't wish you
to go away—and yet we do, because something
still better might come, though what we can't

tell ; but you don't declare yourselves ; you seem
to hide yourselves ; you have never seemed quite
confident of what you would do in the face of
another foreign power ; you advised Nubar Pasha
two different ways on the same incident with the
French, and you got him to put up with humiliation ; and we hardly believe that you are so strong
as we fancied.' Bear in mind that these people
cannot get along unless they are directed. They
are willing to serve, because they are the most
comfortable when there is somebody to think for
them and guide them. But they are extremely
quick and they soon see through you if you don't
know your own mind, and shilly-shally with them."
Questioned as to the influence of patriotism upon
the inhabitants of the different classes, the speaker
quoted with emphatic confirmation the sentence of
Sir A. Milner, Under-Secretary for Finance down
to 1892 : " There are probably few countries in
which patriotic sentiment counts for less than it
does in Egypt."

The nationality which in this agglomeration of
so many obtrudes itself here, and unnecessarily
and persistently emphasizes itself, is the French.
Prior to the reforms that have rendered the
Egyptian Post Office as efficient at the present

time as any postal service of Europe, most of the
Powers maintained services of their own. The
reforms have entirely removed that need, and the
separate post-offices of the European nationalities
have disappeared—save one. France obstinately
holds to her own, and the "Postes Françaises,"
in a central thoroughfare of Alexandria — in
Alexandria as in the other large towns of the
Delta—continue as a disagreeable souvenir of the
bygone insecurity and confusion. Off the great
square which retains its original French designa-
tion, Place Mohammed Ali, a vacant plot of waste
ground, enclosed, disfigures the whole surroundings.
This is the site which the French purchased years
ago for the erection of a new consulate, and which
they refuse to build upon "until the English evacuate the country." The square terminates at one
end with the fine structure of the Stock Exchange,
and the prevalence of the French language as the
most general vehicle of business is exemplified in
the sole name painted across the *façade* in addition
to the characters in Arabic—"Bourse." But, by
the same token, it was upon this square that
the Europeans were first attacked and killed
by the Arabists in 1882, during the outbreak of
fanatical massacre and pillage which the English

were left by the French to combat and suppress
alone. The efforts of the French to "permeate,
permeate, permeate," as Sir Charles Dilke once
advised the Radicals of an extinct force, are to be
seen not less in their worthy and honourable
philanthropic and educational missions here than
in their unwearied and malignant harassing of
British authority, and their reckless and angry
opposition to whatever beneficent changes may
from time to time be introduced on British initiative. They are said to be not united in the
perversity and antagonism by which numbers of
them, at any rate, shine. British functionaries in
the Egyptian service have spoken, and still speak,
most highly of co-operation received from responsible French colleagues; but it is not the co-
operation which strikes the visitor, of no matter
what nationality, here. And in judging the French
colony as a whole, the violent, jealous, and unscrupulous as well as the moderate and impartial,
it should be remembered that they, too, "do not
know what may happen." They are naturally
sensitive to weakenings of the national prestige;
they know how easily a temperate or favourable
attitude towards the British would be misrepresented at home; they know that the Press in

France has no eyes for any but the Opposition
French journals here. All the French journals in
Egypt are "Opposition." The French colony
cannot tell when the British may not, in the phrase
current among the French and Turks, be "forced
to redeem their pledges ; " and with any revival of
French power here it would go hard with those
who might have been silently registered in the
meantime as "*mauvais Francais.*" They may feel
that they must all keep on the look-out, *ménager
la chèvre,* etc. Many who can testify to the business and the governmental methods of their own
country at home are fully aware that they could
not possibly look for, under any kind of domination
that could be substituted for the British—under
even that of their own nationality alone, were such
a contingency practicable — the freedom from
interference, and the unobstructed road to commercial success, which they have enjoyed since
1882.   I know this from conversations with French
business men themselves.   At the same time,
"what if the English, who have been here since
1882, and have never told us they would stay,
were to go ? "

Every afternoon, the *Journal Egyptien* arrives at
Alexandria from Cairo. Underneath the title of

the paper, with its motto, "*Ni provocation ni résignation,*" appears a reprint of "The Pledges of Great Britain," in French ; and this is kept standing for every issue. Thus, right across the first six columns of the paper, the first thing which confronts the reader every day is the following, translated into French : "'The policy of her Majesty's Government in regard to Egypt has no other object than the prosperity of the country, and its full possession of the liberty which it obtained by virtue of the successive firmans of the Sultan down to, and including, that of 1879. The tie which unites Egypt to the Porte is, in our conviction, an important safeguard against a foreign intervention ; and for that reason our object is to maintain that tie such as it exists to-day. Any intention on the part of the one Government or the other (France and England) to enlarge its influence would be sufficient to destroy this useful co-operation. The Khedive and his Ministers may rest assured that her Majesty's Government does not aim at any departure from the line of conduct which it has itself hitherto traced.' (Despatch of Lord Granville to Sir Edward Malet, November 4, 1881.) 'As admiral commanding the British fleet I think it opportune to repeat to your Highness

without delay that the Government of Great
Britain has no intention of making the conquest
of Egypt, or of in any way touching the religion
or the liberties of the Egyptians. Its sole object
is to protect your Highness and the Egyptian
people against the rebels.' (Letter of Admiral
Seymour to the Khedive, July 22, 1882.) 'The
Governments represented by the undersigned
pledge themselves, in any arrangement which
might be made, as the consequence of their con-
certed action, for the *règlement* of the affairs of
Egypt, to seek no territorial advantage, nor the
concession of any exclusive privilege, nor any
commercial advantage, for their subjects, other
than those which any other nation can equally
obtain.' (Thérapia, July 25, 1882. . . . The Ambassador of England : Dufferin.) 'Her Majesty's
Government have sent troops into Egypt with
the sole object of restoring the authority of the
Khedive.' (Proclamation of General Wolseley,
August 19, 1882.)" I have not observed in any
of the daily or weekly publications here, in either
the English language or the French, anything to
recall Lord Salisbury's instructions to Sir H. D.
Wolff, on the latter's return to Constantinople
in January, 1887 : "The Sultan is pressing the

Government of Great Britain to name a date for the evacuation of Egypt, and in that demand he is avowedly encouraged by one, or perhaps two, of the European Powers. Her Majesty's Government have every desire to give him satisfaction upon this point, but they cannot fix even a distant date for the evacuation until they are able to make provision for securing beyond that date the external and internal peace of Egypt. . . . The British Government must retain the right to guard and uphold the condition of things which will have been brought about by the military action and large sacrifices of this country. . . . England, if she spontaneously and willingly evacuates the country, must retain a treaty right of intervention if at any time either internal peace or external security should be seriously threatened." The failure of the Wolff negotiations at Constantinople, due to the effect upon the Sultan of the menaces by the French Ambassador, backed up by the Ambassador of the Czar, need not be recounted ; but, although the negotiations " ended in smoke, they were not without certain consequences in Egypt, both transitory and permanent." These are the words of Sir A. Milner, again placed in my hands, as the most succinct account possible,

by a prominent member of the English colony
" As long as they lasted they exercised an unfavourable and unsettling effect, as indeed do all
signs and rumours of change in a country where
public opinion is so sensitive, so unbalanced, and
so ill-informed as it is in Egypt. But this influence
was of a passing character. The permanent element
of disturbance which the Wolff negotiations have
left behind them in the Nile Valley is the presence
of the Ottoman High Commissioner. Sir Henry
Drummond Wolff came on a special and limited
mission, and went away again. But Mukhtar
Pasha, though he came on the same mission, has
remained ever since." The Ottoman High Commissioner has no intelligible attributes in Egypt.
He is not an ambassador—for a sovereign cannot
send an ambassador to a portion of his own
dominions—and the Khedive himself is the representative of the Sultan of Egypt. " Neither has
Mukhtar any part or lot in the administration of
the country. Technically, he is an anomaly ; in
practice, he is the nucleus, often the unwilling
nucleus, of the smouldering agitation of Moslem
fanaticism, or the intrigues of the old Turkish
party. His presence is thus a perpetual nuisance,
which may at any moment become a danger."

Sir A. Milner paid a warm tribute to the personal character of Mukhtar Pasha, who, whether or not he was kept at Cairo with the express aim of weakening Egypt and worrying England, disliked his errand. The British missionary whose description of a Mussulman spy system was referred to in a previous chapter, declared the headquarters of that system in Egypt to be the premises of the Ottoman High Commissioner at Cairo.

But, reverting to the daily text of the *Journal Egyptien*, which ignores every development since 1882, I never found any allusion in the local journal to the fact that on April 4, 1883, 2600 of the European inhabitants of Alexandria and other towns, representing almost all the European wealth and enterprise of the country, and comprising a few of the French, as well as the Greeks, Italians, Germans, and Austrians, presented a memorial to Lord Dufferin, praying that the British occupation might be made permanent. It has been asserted that that step sprang directly out of the exceptional feeling of relief which ensued immediately upon the panic, and that the tendency among the same classes became modified afterwards. Perhaps ; but by this time there is not much doubt about the tendency among those classes. If you ask at

this moment any European resident of commercial
Alexandria—apart from the French — what he
thinks of the general bias with respect to the
continuance of the British occupation, the most
eloquent response resides in the startled and
anxious expression with which he puts a counter-
question.   Is there anything fresh—any bad news ?
Bad news means a symptom of British lukewarm-
ness or yielding.   Does the questioner " know anything "?   Surely there has been nothing fresh in
the style of Mr. Gladstone, and Mr. Gladstone's
Foreign Ministers.   The French may be excepted ;
but with regard to the Turk, his interest in Egypt,
as one of the provinces, has become swallowed up
by his apprehensions for the safety of the Porte.
A typical anecdote of the Turk's mingled gran-
diloquence and timorousness was related to me by
an Italian merchant just " down from Cairo."   The
narrator, an old resident in Egypt, and the most
thorough of partisans for the British *régime*, was
the guest of a Turkish Pasha at the latter's palace
in Cairo a few days previously, and, the conversation turning upon politics, he asked his host and
another Turkish Pasha of the company why in
the world the Ottoman High Commissioner should
be retained here when he could serve his great

master, the Sultan, so much more effectually at home. He was retained here to keep a controlling hand upon England, replied the Pasha, solemnly. But the English were not in relations with him at all, objected the other; they esteemed him much, but he had no regular official status for them to recognize. The commissioner was retained at Cairo as a reminder to England, repeated the Pasha, of his great and powerful master, the Sultan. " You, who know the English community well," he went on, "tell me what is the English feeling with regard to events at Constantinople?" The rest shall be told in the jovial narrator's own words. " I said, 'Oh, England knows that the Turk has a big brain. England does not mean to harm or slight the Turks. You have a big brain. All shall be well, England says!' You should have seen those two Pashas looking at me, with their mouths open. I settled the Eastern Question in five minutes. . . . 'I talked the matter over with Lord Cromer this afternoon,' I said, 'and it is to be all right.' '*Inshâllâh !*' they both ejaculated in a deep voice (' May it be so, God willing! ') —'*Inshâllâh !*' "

F

CHAPTER V.

"*Qui n'entend qu'une cloche, n'entend qu'un son !*
Do not imagine that you are liked in this country,
Messieurs les Anglais. If you want to know what
they think of you here, do not say that you are
English." The observation proceeds from one of
the French gentlemen among the talkers on the
verandah. There is not a resident amongst the
company, and every one of the visitors, apart from
the writer of these lines, is a *commerçant*, a business principal or traveller—every one save, perhaps, a single individual, the personage who has
just spoken. He is a livid, furrowed, black-
bearded, bilious, furious-looking Southerner ; he
wears the Tonquin decoration, and he is well
acquainted with Algiers ; and, from a fair knowledge of the type, I have put him down, since the
day after his arrival, as a journalist from Lyons
or Marseilles. Goodness knows what farrago of
impeachment he can be sending home ! His

earliest inquiry of his neighbour at the *table d'hôte*, as soon as he appeared there at the close of a rough voyage to Alexandria from Marseilles, was dark and ominous. " *Y a t-il du mouvement?* " and he shot a savage inquisitorial glance at the other, as though to convince him that he suspected his sincerity in advance, but that dissimulation would be futile. The other happened to be a German gentleman who comes here periodically from England, and whose business negotiations are entirely on behalf of, and with, British manufacturing and commercial houses. " *Oh, non,*" replied the Teuton, " *L'Egypte est tranquille.* Wherever you go," he added, after a pause, during which the questioner's doubt and disappointment were plainly visible, "you will find nothing but perfect tranquillity." There had been movement on the sea, but there was none here. " *Et le choléra?* " demanded the new arrival, viciously. None of us could deny the cholera; some of us had traversed the districts in which its presence was reported; but the cases were few. Our Southerner received a reinforcement at the *table d'hôte* in the shape of a compatriot from Lille, a manufacturer who had journeyed to Egypt to "start a new article," as he explained when

colloquial relations had gradually established themselves. But the path was not smooth and easy
for the new article; people could not make their
minds up—they kept you "hanging on" for a
week; and the letters which ought to be arriving
from Lille did not arrive. To what could all this
be due, but the British occupation? The British
occupation causes the movement on the sea, and
maliciously represses the desired "movement" on
the land; it is answerable for the backwardness
of French residents to encourage the enterprise of
their fellow-countrymen, and for the negligence
of the French business people at home who ought
to be posting to Alexandria their promised letters.
" Let us hear of some real grievance, if you've got
any," says one, of the Englishmen amongst the
talkers on the verandah. We elict an abundance
of rhetoric in response: Mr. Gladstone's "pledges,"
which remained unfulfilled; a certain vague under-
standing as to evacuation within three years,
which could not be identified; and the inflexible
determination of France. "Well, then, instead of
talking about it so much," rejoins the same
Englishman, "let France act, and turn us out
at once." " *Oho, comme vous y allez, Monsieur
l'Anglais !* " exclaims the bilious Méridional,

almost gnashing his teeth at the sight of the three or four quiet British officers in uniform who lunch and dine at the hotel, at a separate table, every day—" We do not deceive ourselves with respect to the strength of England ; we do not suppose that France alone can drive you out." " Nobody else wishes us to go," retorts the Briton ; " I travel in a business which takes me among all the nationalities here, and I can tell you that, so far from wishing us to go, they are all anxious that we should remain. Your own countrymen, who are here with capital invested in the country, are as anxious as the rest. Of course, they won't tell you so. *Qui n'entend qu'une cloche*, as you said just now, only hears one sound. Go among the other nationalities, and inquire for yourselves. But, if you want to know what they think of France, don't tell them that you are French. But let us have some hard facts about your grievances."

Pertinacity and patience extract the following three assertions, after which the case completely collapses : (1) That the French are pushed out of government places by the British ; (2) that where they do hold places under the Egyptian Government, they are seldom at the heads of

departments ; (3) that the Egyptian authorities
favour British goods by passing them more quickly
through the custom-house.   To the last point it
is the German who replies.   If the French business men established here cannot take the trouble
which the English and the others take to get their
goods promptly through the customs, the only
people to blame are the French themselves.
With regard to the first point, the French functionaries are exceedingly numerous in the Egyptian Government departments, and it is held
by the other nationalities that, considering the
proportions of the several colonies, France is over-
represented, and by a good deal, in this direction.
With regard to the second point, which is admitted,
the fact results logically from the situation, but
would be less conspicuous if French functionaries
could be less political.   So our French friends are
informed upon the verandah; and the utmost
ingenuity and perseverance cannot draw from
them anything further in the way of "hard fact."
What is the use, however, of expending time in
argument and testimony upon folk whose anger
and prejudice lead them back invariably to the
same position, even when their silence acknowledges it to be untenable ?   Not many hours have

elapsed before we hear, from the same source, once more, " Oh, the English are in possession, and they manage that all the commercial advantages shall go to themselves. It's quite natural." The " advantages " in question—where do they lie, the seeker after information eagerly asks, and asks in vain.

What has come out, hitherto, of my own most careful and laborious inquiries is this, that numbers among the British commercial community complain of conditions which place them at a distinct disadvantage as compared with competitors belonging to the other nationalities, whether native or foreign. They say that the British authorities, in their dread of even appearing, by a stretch of excited imagination, to favour their own countrymen, again and again pass over the latter, to the detriment not alone of British industry, but, in the long run, of the public interest. A recent example furnished to me shows that a government department under English direction, inviting open tenders, declined the tender of a local English house and accepted that of a local Greek, although the latter's total exceeded the other by £150, and the Greek, a " man of straw," was obliged to fall back upon the English house to execute the contract. Another instance is that of a local British firm tendering in "open adjudication" to a government department at the rate of £22 per ton, as against £27 by a rival contractor, not British nor Egyptian. The tender of £27 per ton was accepted; whereupon the contractor applied to the British firm which had offered at £22, and entered into a sub-contract with them at £26.

It is also complained that the British functionaries do not sufficiently comprehend the extent to which official backsheesh, or jobbery, honeycombs particular branches of the administrative system, and militates against the British contractor. A third and characteristic disadvantage suffered by the resident British contractor is due to the non-pliancy of the manufacturer at home. "Tenders were invited for a large quantity of locks and keys," a member of the British colony informed me, "and I sent in an offer from England, with samples. An Arab firm underbid us, but with a greatly inferior product. We could have underbid the Arab firm with an article exactly similar to his; and, if no better article was wanted, why should we not have been content to make it? I wrote to England in that sense, but they would

not do anything on the inferior pattern, and so
the contract went to the natives, and no doubt
the stuff supplied will answer all their purposes."
A British agent in a different line of business
pointed out to me, during a journey on the suburban
line to Ramleh, that the locomotives in use upon
the Alexandria and Ramleh Railway Company, a
British enterprise, were, like those of the Egyptian
State Railway, of Belgian or Franco-Belgian make.
An English firm of engineers had tendered at $2\frac{1}{2}$
per cent. over the Belgian company, and rather
than abate their figure by $2\frac{1}{2}$ per cent. for the sake
of the footing to be acquired, they had let the
order go.*

---

* Mr. Rennell Rodd, in his report to Lord Cromer on British
commercial relations with Egypt, expresses the opinion that the
local English firms demand excessive commission-rates, and that
they consequently suffer in competition with the foreign middle-
man or broker, who—especially the German—has shown that a
safe business can be done on a very low commission. "It is a
matter for serious consideration," observes Mr. Rodd, "whether
the fact that British trade in Egypt is conducted so largely through
foreign agents on the one hand, and that English houses in Egypt,
on the other hand, are letting trade pass out of their hands by their
unwillingness to do business on a scale of profit with which other
nations are content, may not be the prelude to a considerable
falling-off in the total British import to this country. Such a
symptom has not yet manifested itself to any considerable extent,
but the fact that British metal imports have not increased in proportion to the greatly increased demand is, perhaps, a significant
warning of danger." This report, forwarded by Lord Cromer, was

With reference to the loose and facile observation quoted in the first few lines of this chapter,
to the general effect that the foreign rulers over
an uncivilized country are "not liked"—although
the speaker was scarcely justified in the parallel
which he went on to allege was the case of France
and Algeria—the attitude of the middle-class rural
population of Egypt was tersely sketched to me
by a British subject who has lived in this country
for thirty years, and who is now the postmaster
of an up-country agricultural centre. "To begin
with," he related, "no Egyptian Arab understands
the sentiment of gratitude, and every Arab is a
born liar. You dine with them, and they are full

issued by the British Foreign Office on the 16th of last month
(April). A study of the tables prepared and commented upon by
Mr. Rodd points to coals, textiles, and metals or machinery as the
three categories with which British trade is chiefly concerned in
Egypt. Whilst a general upward movement continues in the first-
named of the three, and the British share in the second still pre-
ponderates, in metals and machinery the British imports have not
augmented in proportion to the rapid advance in the Egyptian
demand. German imports, generally, increased from £64,000 in
1890 to £230,000 in 1894. Belgian imports, generally, increased
from £111,000 in 1890 to £374,000 in 1894. On the whole,
however, Mr. Rodd sums up that "if British houses will only
devote to the maintenance of their present position an energy and
enterprise similar to that which is displayed by other nations who
are now trying to secure a footing in the Egyptian market, there
need be no cause for anxiety."

of compliments about the English. You fancy you are surprising a private conversation when you catch the words, in a whisper between them, ' This Englishman is an excellent person ; what excellent people the English are ! ' They tell you that it is the grandest thing possible for the country that the English have displaced the French. The French are sons of this, that, and the other, and if they were here as the English are, they would eat up all the land. The next day they are dining with a Frenchman. They tell the Frenchman that the English are sons of this, that, and the other, and that the country is going to the dogs. ' If we could only have the French here,' they tell him, ' the country would be saved.' The day after that, they dine with one of their own people, a sheikh, and then they cry out, ' All these Christians are sons of this, that, and the other, and it's a bad thing for the land of Pharaoh that they ever came in.' "

One of the leading financiers of contemporary Egypt favoured me with an interview on the general topic of the British occupation from a non-British standpoint. " You might describe me as ex-president of a foreign Chamber of Commerce," said he ; " I am not Italian ; I am not

French ; I am an Austrian, and I am emphatically, emphatically, in favour of the British occupation. The benefits it has conferred are equal to anything that could possibly be produced. They are not equal to, but above, any that would be produced by any other state of affairs. I insist upon the point, because any other occupation, whether by a Latin or a Saxon people, whether it were German, or, I will add, even Austrian, would be a source of permanent and daily conflict between the European colony and the occupying army. And I will explain why, in my own opinion. The English army is peculiarly one that is penetrated with the civilian idea. Other armies are armies of soldiers. By that I mean professional soldiers ; the English army is one of private gentlemen. They have not the habit of military ostentation—*l'habitude de faire sonner le sabre sur le pavé*—which irritates European colonies in all countries—in all countries of the world. As evidence of this, look at what passes in Tunis—everywhere, in fact, under a Latin or a German occupation. A conquered country, on the other hand, will not cede to the civilian element alone. Now, the English, to their honour I say it, whilst preserving the order which has been indispensable for the development of

Egypt, have known how to give way to the *élément civil. Ils s'effacent.* They do not wound susceptibilities, and they never come into collision with the various colonies. In their social relations they are of an *amabilité parfaite,* and of a *discrétion extraordinaire.* So much from the point of view of our relations with the occupying army. From the point of view of the country itself, it would come to absolutely the same thing, so far as business is concerned, whether the occupying nation were England or any other. The foreign occupation amounts to a guarantee of security, for the property, or the lives, it may be, of the Europeans ; it is a guarantee, also, for the fellah— for the inhabitants in general. The natives can now be certain that their taxes will be payable at regular periods, and that they will be of settled and definite sums ; the taxation is no longer capricious and arbitrary. At the commencement of the year the natives can now make up their accounts ; they know what they have to pay. It was unfortunately not so in the past. As things now are, for the agriculturist, every one has the water on his land 'in his turn ; the rich landlord does not crush the small owner by possessing himself of all the supplies of water from the canals." After paying a tribute to the manner in which the British authorities had extended the network of irrigation cuttings, the speaker continued: "Unhappily the treaties of commerce that have existed are bad. The country cannot develop itself, either industrially or agriculturally, because of those treaties; they constitute the sore spot in Egypt. The treaties of commerce are not to be confounded with the capitulations. The Caisse de la Dette seeks to increase the customs revenue at the expense of the local resources, so that whilst the products of the country pay, in general, 9 per cent. on their entry into the towns, foreign products pay $7\frac{1}{5}$ per cent. to the customs revenue, but are liberated from the town dues, or *octroi*. Consequently, agriculture in Egypt is at a direct disadvantage. Then, the machines, which are one of the essential conditions of agriculture, must pay duty before they can come in from abroad. The Caisse de la Dette tries to augment the resources of the creditors as much as possible. Well, there is now a considerable surplus. The Egyptian Government, under the English, is begged to diminish the taxes, and they reply, 'We will, but give us the surplus of the economies,' whereupon the French Government says, 'We will consent on one condition—that you evacuate the country.' There is the financial position ; it's a *cercle vicieux.* The English will not go, and the French use their treaty power to aggravate the situation. As a result of this *histoire,* you have a serious evil for the country, because there are more than two millions sterling, as resources, in the Caisse de la Dette, which cannot be touched." A member of the great financial syndicate presided over by the speaker was present during the interview, and he interrupted with the correction, " Three millions and a quarter sterling now." " Very well—there you have a treasure which is buried in the earth—a capital which brings nothing, but which increases every day, to the detriment of the interests of the taxpayer of the country. The Caisse de la Dette, representing the bondholders, will not employ these economies in *valeurs locales,* which would be another way of aiding industry and agriculture, under the pretext that at a moment of crisis the *valeurs locales* cannot be sold."

As a Havas telegram had brought the news that Moustapha Kamel, the "leader of the Young Egypt party," had been lecturing in Paris "against the occupation of Egypt by the English," the opportunity seemed a good one to obtain an independent account of Young Egypt. In common with many others, no doubt, I had received through the post a copy of the lecturer's pamphlet, published at Toulouse. Melik was the Kamel who attempted to destroy the third pyramid of Ghizeh, at about the end of the twelfth century, and who desisted in his work of destruction only after months of almost fruitless effort ; Moustapha would appear to prefer destruction on an infinitely vaster scale.

" The detractors of the British occupation, in this country," answered the millionnaire financier, " are, in my opinion, a number of Egyptian young men (*une quantité de petits jeunes gens Egyptiens*) who ignore all idea of patriotism, and set up opposition merely to get themselves talked about, and to procure places and employments which their talent would not otherwise permit them to hope. *Ce sont des demi-savants.* They have usually been to Europe, where they have acquired very little real knowledge, but a good deal of presumption, coupled with all the defects of a foreign civilization." My informant concluded : " If the British occupation were to be replaced by any other—even if a European concert were to decide that, with the assent of the people, Egypt should become neutralized—a *plébiscite* in Egypt would result, I feel quite sure, in selection of Great Britain as the dominating influence."

CHAPTER VI.

BETWEEN busy modern Alexandria, the Cottono-
polis of the Mediterranean, and ancient Masr-el-
Kahira, the populous but much less markedly
Levantine capital of Egypt, great indeed is the
contrast. The whole movement of Alexandria
seems to tend towards the Stock Exchange and
the adjacent banks and contractors' offices, and
every coast along the entire Mediterranean has contributed to its medley population—two hundred
thousand odd in all. Among the Europeans, who
form at least 25 per cent. of the total, the Greeks
and Italians predominate. It has become not un-
common at Alexandria to see the ordinary public
notices of the town in four languages—Arabic,
French, English, and Italian,—and this is the case
not merely around the financial and shipping
centres, but on the local railway line as far out as
Ramleh. The author of " John Bull sur le Nil,"

a few years ago, related that an Italian whom he encountered at Alexandria had just returned from London, whither he had gone to "learn English in order to push his business." But French ought to suffice, he objected. " Oh no," replied the Italian, "no longer. To keep on good terms with the London houses you must write to them in their own language." "You are in commerce ? " "Yes ; my father owns a cotton press, under the style of C. H. and Co." "An English firm, no doubt ? " " No. My father is Italian, our partner is French, and we are financed by Greek bankers." " Then why not '*Cie.*' instead of 'Co.' ? " "To humour our English buyers. Indeed, the word *compagnie* is no longer *de mode* in Egypt. In business it is England that dominates."

English and French may be jostling each other for supremacy as the official spoken medium, or the official and commercial written medium ; but the prevalent spoken medium among the business men of Alexandria is probably Italian. Most of the Scotchmen and Englishmen I met in Egypt hold at command an unfinished, rough-and-ready sort of French or Italian—sometimes a little of both, if less of each—similar to the French and English heard from the average German in England. I have

not yet come across a single Scotchman or Englishman, however, resident in this country who did not
speak Arabic ; from the halting phrases, of course,
of the comparative tyro, to the fluency of the old
inhabitant, and the exceptional literary perfection
of a certain gifted or cultured few. There is one
case, not to be too particularly specified, but
recognizable by the majority of his compatriots
of anything like long residence here, in which an
Englishman, speaking Arabic better than many
Arabs themselves, turned Mussulman, married
wives, made his fortune, and preached in the
mosques. Still, the Levantine *mercantis* have
made the external business life of Alexandria
much more their own than the British have done.
It is to Cairo that the phrase " *l'Orient anglicanisé,*"
bestowed upon Alexandria by the author of
" John Bull sur le Nil," properly belongs. British
branch houses and agencies crowd so thickly one
upon another in the principal promenade and
thoroughfare, the Piccadilly of Cairo—the Esbékieh
Gardens replacing the Green Park—that the later
arrivals, or the less fortunate, have spread into
the side avenues and streets, and confront the
view at advantageous corners for some little
distance into the outskirts. The English language

turns up unexpectedly over and over again ; the
quick and imitative Arab may not yet have
mastered it in more than a fragmentary form, but
in and about Cairo he will understand and use its
phrases when, often, either French or Italian will
be as "heathen Greek" to him, and when no
variety of Greek would be intelligible. The
regular flux and reflux of the well-to-do British
and American tourist, the "winterings" here by
our valetudinarians, the great share of the British
upper classes in the determination of the fashion-
able movement, have apparently had most to do
with the production of this result. A tramway
is projected for facilitating communication between
Cairo and the Ghizeh Pyramids ; in the meantime
the coaches, breaks, private carriages, and other
vehicles which travel along the main road from
the banks of the Nile to the border of the Libyan
Desert are interspersed with British cyclists, of
whom even the ladies have ceased to dumfounder
the urban fellaheen, and to puzzle the asses or
alarm the camels. With a tone of good-breeding
and refinement substituted for a seaport grossness
and a too frequent holiday 'Arryism, the "anglicanization" of Cairo, now, may be compared in
extent to that of Boulogne-sur-Mer. And yet it

was here, in the capital, the seat of the government, the kernel of the administrative system, the
most English of all the towns, that I first discerned
pronounced misgivings as to the duration of the
British rule. " Rule," however, is not the word,
nor is it "influence ; " contact with the British
official spheres of Cairo has taught me a new
expression. The expression I have obtained with
the British official hall-mark, so to put it, is
" British semi-rule." Before touching upon the
doubts and disquietudes in question, I propose
to reproduce some general utterances by British
engineers, contractors, etc., whose business lies
directly with the rural population of Egypt, as
well as with that of the towns. This is evidence
which belongs less to Cairo than to the townships
of the districts traversed by the main line. The
railway from Alexandria to Cairo runs through
the Beherah province, of which Damanhour, with
twenty-three thousand inhabitants, is the capital,
and the Gharbiyeh province, with Tantah, thirty-
five thousand inhabitants, as its capital ; and the
excellence of the railway service decidedly deserves
mention in passing. Besides the goods trains,
laden with cotton, wheat, maize, rice, sugar, or
other agricultural produce, and besides the ordinary

slow passenger service, three "express" trains—
so-called, although they make about four stoppages
on the journey—run daily between Alexandria
and Cairo, each way, covering the entire distance
of a hundred and thirty miles in three hours and
twenty or twenty-five minutes.

"All the townships are full of Greeks," declared
one of my informants, not of British origin, but a
British subject. "The Greeks advance money to
the fellaheen ; the fellah will often be found to
have borrowed quite recklessly ; and if he cannot
pay, the Greek forecloses. That is where these
—— Greeks make their money in Egypt ; they
are just like sponges on the villages. The fellah
may be either the owner of a small piece of ground
or the tenant ; if he is the tenant only, the Greek
won't advance him anything unless he gets the
guarantee of the sheikh. The sheikh of the
village of course possesses a good portion of the
land—he would not be a sheikh unless he were a
man of some property,—and his guarantee is indispensable if you want to do business with one of
the fellahs. No one can give the fellah credit ; if
you want to conclude any agreement, you go to the
sheikh, who signs a paper of guarantee. It is the
village that answers for the fellah you are in treaty

with, and the sheikh guarantees, as the head man
of the community." "Have you found the
fellaheen quick at profiting by improved methods?
Does he buy machinery willingly?" "Willingly?
I will give you an instance that happened only this
week. I was at Alexandria about a large contract
with England. An Arab called at our agent's
office to buy an engine. He had come in from one
of the villages, and was accompanied by two or
three hundred other fellahs. They had all come in
together from the village, about this purchase; and
the Arab said he wanted an engine, with boiler, all
complete, of such and such horse-power, to drive so
many mills. I gave him a price. It was at a
figure which left us an extremely small profit; in
fact, we should not sell at that figure in England,
but as competition is so great here, and the Greeks
will sell an engine for almost no profit, we thought
we would let it go. After we had been talking to
him for hours, he said that somebody else offered
him an engine for £200 less. Well, it simply
couldn't be. No engine of the kind could be
produced at the price. We told him so, and he
threatened to go to the other people. We answered,
'All right,' and he said 'Good-bye,' and went
away. Next day he came back with all his retinue,

and began again, ' What is the price of that engine ? ' I replied, 'I told you yesterday.' 'That is too much,' he said ; 'give me your lowest figure.' I said, ' I have already given you the lowest figure.' He offered £100 less, instead of £200 the day before. I told him we could not possibly do it ; and then he promised to think it over, and went away. I will bet you that that man comes another fifty times, and sits there all day long in the office, with all his people about him, drinking coffee and smoking cigarettes, and talking about this purchase. We can't possibly reduce our quotation to him ; but in order to save time, I took that man to an engine we have in the stores, and explained to him the difference between that and the other, cheaper, engines. I showed him the construction, the fittings, all the extras that were included in our price, and everything. But he doesn't care two-pence about that. He wants an engine at £350— that's all he wants. A job like that can go on for months and months, and in the end he will buy the flimsiest thing he can get. It's the same experience all round ; the average fellah will buy the cheapest thing he can procure, and that is why there are Germans who do some business here. You see, the fellah has no needs. He eats coarse maize bread, lives in a mud hut, wears a gown, and never has to think about protection from the cold. If he makes twenty-five or thirty shillings a week, he can support two or three wives well."

The speaker went on to inveigh against the facility with which the fellah can still, as he says, rid himself of a wife of whom he has grown tired, by complaining to the *Kadi* that she "does not look after his house." The *Kadi* hears the lady's account of the matter, and tries to reconcile the spouses; if he fails, he hands the husband a certificate, and the marriage is annulled, the divorced party receiving a little pecuniary compensation. Perhaps, the *Kadi's* hands are not quite innocent of *backsheesh*. In this way, the fellah who cannot afford to maintain more than one wife is enabled to put his spouse away from him and "take a younger one." The speaker also inveighed against the Turkish pashas, both for the immorality of their lives and for their selfish and unscrupulous hostility to the true welfare of the country. He had recently been invited to the palace of a pasha for whose mills he was to supply machinery, and, while lost in admiration at the taste and sumptuousness of the interior, he could not forgive his host for possessing four legitimate wives—one of whom had brought him a great deal of property—besides a harem thirty-six strong. So angry seemed he at this fact, indeed, that if the custom of the country had permitted him access to the "ladies' household," or even to a view of it, his feelings might unluckily have got the better of him.

I asked my informant whether his firm pushed their business by means of show-cards through the country districts. He replied in the negative, asserting that the country-people did not look at show-cards, notwithstanding the fact that the illustrations of machines at work might immediately concern them, and might be accompanied by printed explanations in the vernacular. "How do you get orders from them, then?" "By reputation." "And how is a new firm to push its way into a reputation?" "Not by show-cards. By agents, who visit the districts, and by being in with the sheikhs." "What goods do you supply to the fellaheen? Agricultural implements?" "No; engines. Formerly, before the development of the irrigation by the English, and when the fellaheen had few canals for their land, engines and pumps were needed in large quantities, in order that the water should be brought up to the land. The fellaheen used portable and centrifugal pumps for

this purpose. Since the English have extended
the system of the canals, the demand for pumps
has vastly fallen off. That industry, a British
industry, has suffered; but, of course, we know
that the paramount object must be the prosperity
of the whole country, and we have nothing to say.
In another direction, more engines are wanted
now, because more mills are being put up. Flour-
mills are being put up all over the country. In
England the miller grinds the corn and sells it in
the market. The practice here is for the fellaheen
to send small quantities of corn to the miller for
their own use. The wife, for instance, buys a
bushel of corn, takes it to the mill and has it
ground, and then goes home and bakes the bread
with it. You can see fifty or a hundred of them
every day round these mills, all bringing their little
quantities of corn with them, to be ground, and
carried home. Therefore, what we have to supply
here, is a small kind of mill, not the large ones we
have at home. Another industry which has obtained a good hold in Egypt is the cotton ginning
—that is, taking the cotton seed out of the cotton
before it is shipped to England. Numbers of big
factories here, built by the most important commercial people, have done very well with the cotton

ginning, and made a lot of money. They have the electric light and everything else, and in some places you might think yourself in the district round Manchester."

With reference to the characteristics of the fellah, he insisted that the native had an apparently incurable aversion to accuracy of statement. Without being conscious or desirous of misleading, the native could not resist the pleasure of varying the facts, or the tale, as they were. The trait had extended to certain resident Europeans. "As for getting the truth out of the fellaheen, you may talk to them for twenty years, and you will never know where you are. They have no idea of ranging things straight for you. They tell lies for the sake of telling them."

The principal in an English engineering firm hurriedly summed up the results of the British occupation to me as follows: Egyptian Stock at a height which it never reached before, and which in the past would have seemed fabulous; and a cotton output of which about the same thing can be said. "And the English have ruined my business for me," he added, an Englishman himself. "I used to supply great numbers of pumps for getting the water on to the land; and the English authorities have developed irrigation to such a tune, that the pumps are no longer required." He smiled as he spoke of his ruin, and it was clear, from the dimensions of his establishment, as from the activity prevailing therein, that he had been able to adapt himself to the altered circumstances tolerably well, and to supply something else. He promised to furnish me with information more in detail; but whilst his contracts rushed him off towards one part of the country, my own errand called me in the opposite direction.

Another English business-man, adverting to the rivalry between Alexandria and Port Saïd, considered the Peninsular and Oriental Company's abandonment of the service to the former town to be a "point gained by Port Saïd." His partner observed that the withdrawal of any big passenger line from Alexandria meant a loss to British shipping. It was "said that the service to Alexandria did not pay the Peninsular and Oriental; but look at the position they have held! People who come to Egypt usually want to travel by the route Alexandria and Cairo. They have no harbour at Port Saïd; whereas we have splendid docks here." The first speaker resumed: "I am inclined to believe that there is some political

reason for the preference of Port Saïd over Alexandria From Mansourah large quantities of goods
are now shipped down the Nile to Damietta. The
bulk still goes to Alexandria, but a big amount
goes away from it now." "Do you know of any
engineering difficulties that prevent the construction
of a direct railway between Port Saïd and Alexandria ? " "It may be that the land is too swampy,"
answered one. "Oh! but it must be feasible,"
objected another ; "we have got over greater
difficulties than are to be met with across the
Delta, there." A third interposed : "The line has
been applied for several times, but it has been
refused by the Egyptian Government." "Why ?"
For all response I won the Egyptian resident's
compassionate smile. If there is one thing that
amuses the European resident of long experience,
it is the guilelessness of the new arrival, who
expects to find reasons assignable for whatever
anomalies, hard cases, and backwardnesses he
may observe under the British semi-rule in Egypt.

"We think that the British occupation is not
generally visible enough," then remarked one of
the company. "The British do not show what
they could. The natives are not impressed by
what they see. You seldom find the British

soldiers marching through the town, and when
they do march, it is usually at hours when very
few people are about. The whole thing is done
most quietly. It is extraordinary how the British
soldiery are managed. There is apparently nothing
of them." "With regard to offences against the
law," observed the first speaker, subsequently, "less
crime exists now in Egypt than perhaps, in the
proportion, in any other known country." "Do
you consider that the local French press has done
much harm?" "A great deal. But the greatest
harm was done by our own Government, in recoil-
ing from what everybody expected us to do after
Tel-el-Kébir. All the trouble has come from
that."

Inquiries elsewhere on the subject of the Belgian
locomotives employed on the State railway, led to
interesting explanations. As on the Alexandria-
Ramleh local line, so throughout the main system.
"Nearly every engine I have recently seen on the
lines up to Beni-Souef," replied a British contractor, "is of Belgian make. Last year, or the
year before, tenders were invited on an open adjudication, and the Belgian sent in a price about
2½ per cent. below the lowest English figure.
The English replied that they could not budge

from their amount, which was the lowest practicable, and orders for about ten locomotive
engines went to the French—we say 'French' and
'Belgian' indifferently, in this matter of the contracts." The speaker proceeded to describe the
" French element on the board of direction of the
railway " in terms which need not be repeated. I
learnt from another source that a contract for files
had gone to Belgium simply because, with the
heartiest intentions in the world, the English firm
communicated with could not possibly compete
at the price submitted by Belgians to the railway
board. The correspondence tells its own story.
" In reference to your inquiry for files," wrote the
English merchants and engineers, from London,
"we can quote you for these as follows: 1490
dozen files, to the Egyptian Railway Company's
specification, in best new warranted hand-cut steel
files, £1042 net cash, suitably packed and delivered
c.i.f. Alexandria. The list price of these files
would be £2850, and our price, therefore, represents a discount of 62½ per cent., and 2½ per cent.
off the list. For your information, we may say
that these orders for files were placed in the hands
of one maker in this country for something like
ten or twelve years, but for the last two years they

have been placed in Germany. From what we can gather, there appears to be some jealousy existing between the English Administrator and his French colleague on the board, which had the result of letting the German or Belgian manu- facturer step in, and take the orders which would otherwise come to this country. There is no doubt about it that the German file is neither equal in quality, appearance, or finish, to the Sheffield-made article. The price we have quoted is an extremely low one, and should, we think, enable you to secure the business. We are sending you eight sample files, stamped with our name, so that you can submit them to the authori- ties." After the reply from Egypt, with particulars as to the price at which Belgians were tendering, the firm wrote further: "On looking into the price of the files, we find that it practically amounts to something like 79 per cent. off the Sheffield list, a price at which it is impossible to supply the weight of plain crucible steel in the commonest quality, to say nothing of forging into shape, annealing, cutting, and hardening. It is evident, therefore, that Bessemer steel is being used, and we think that if you could get a chance of comparing in actual work the sample we sent you, with those being supplied from Germany, you might perhaps be able to stand a better chance of future business. We think it is more than likely that one of our files would cut one of the others in two." The order went to two different makers in Belgium. The second of the above notes was accompanied by an estimate respecting an additional matter, an "inquiry for plates and bars." The statement of prices which the firm appended was followed by the remark : "The shipbuilding strike on the Clyde is, to a certain extent, responsible for this."

"Here was a case where the English really wanted to cut out the foreigners," commented my informant, "and, on good quality, we could have done it." "Are not the people who invite the tenders capable of discriminating ? " "They ought to be. But, of course, if they are satisfied with the stuff they get for cheapness, we can't help it." The conversation ended with the final term of so many dialogues in Egypt—*backsheesh.* "I should like to know," remarked an auditor, "how it is that divers clerks, Syrians and others, are able, on their salaries, to build fine houses. One man who got into the Public Works Department, on a small salary, has just built a house costing £4000. Some of the Syrians ruin everything. They muddle up matters to such an extent that the heads of departments positively can't tell where they stand. Jobbery of all sorts is going on." "But you have lived here twenty-five years," I ventured to remind him ; "surely you can say that official *backsheesh* is diminishing ?" "It did diminish for a time after 1882," was the response ; "it diminished a good deal, naturally, under the English. But the last three years have witnessed a serious revival of it."

A local newspaper, printed in French and Arabic, contained, amongst its miscellaneous paragraphs on the front page, a complaint that the Alexandria Municipality should be ordering an air-pump from America. "Always the wretched system, dear to *nos occupants*, of purchasing abroad what can be procured in Egypt, the system which prompts them, for instance, to buy school tables in London under the pretext that the 'wood is drier in England !'" The probability is that no one ever gave any such reason as this, in the terms of the statement. Nor was it even certain, I believe, that the school tables were coming from any part of Great Britain. An English contractor told me that the Belgian firms were found to devote so much more attention than the English to orders of that class, that they would be dealt with by a natural preference. Written to for a quotation, the Englishman would as often as not leave the matter until the last moment, and then direct his clerk, off-hand, to reply with a rough estimate—" Oh, say 30*s.* each." A Belgian firm, on the contrary, would go into everything, putting down each item of cost, and presenting finally a detailed specification.

It seems surprising that the Opposition press in the French language here should omit from its regular stream of misrepresentations the plausible falsehood which would picture the British · as "getting all the best land of the country into their hands." Many of the natives in the towns may safely be reckoned upon to credit assertions much farther from the truth. The priest attached to one of the most ancient mosques in Cairo told me, as he showed me round, that the English who were in Egypt had "come from the King of Constantinople." Apparently under a mistake as to the nationality of his interlocutor, he continued that there were too many of the English people with red jackets in Egypt ; it was the will of the King at Constantinople that they should be in the land, but, personally, he disapproved of the fact. There were the "people by the Nile bridge, the

people at the Citadel, and the people at Alexandria;" all the points thus indicated are British
garrisons. He did not know why the British
remained in Egypt, nor why they had entered the
country. "Is the Arab fanatical?" I asked him.
"Yes; perhaps," he answered. The "perhaps," in
the surroundings, almost illustrated Nubar Pasha's
definition of eloquence as distinguished from
loquacity. "Loquacity," responded that statesman to a French visitor who had pressed him to
define the two, "is the art of using a great many
words to say nothing; eloquence is the inspiration
of saying a great deal in a nothing." The boy
who had fastened the slippers over the Christian's
boots at the entrance to the central court—the
usual precaution against defilement of the holy
paving—marched in the Christian's wake, repeating
verses from the Koran. Another sore-eyed boy,
crouching in an eastward corner and wagging his
head unceasingly to and fro, droned off the chapters of the Koran which he had learnt by rote.
These would be priests one day, explained my
white-robed guide. Like himself, they would
know much of the Koran by heart—and would
know nothing else, he might have added, to judge
by a certain promising look, in both, of complete

abrutissement. A priest was permitted four wives ;
he himself had four such partners to his austere
existence ; and he concluded — halting at the
threshold of the inner sanctuary, in order not to
be seen by the "blind" beggars who waited in
a cluster for their *backsheesh* at the porch—by
soliciting "*backsheesh* for the priest," and by accepting fivepence. Whilst the faithful washed their
feet, their hands, and their faces in the marble
fountain at the centre of the court—the ablution
preparatory to prayer—and whilst earlier arrivals,
on their knees towards the east, mumbled their
litany, and with their foreheads thrice touched the
ground, some notion of the frightful influence
which might be disposed of by a fanatic ignoramus
such as this Koran-crammed teacher of men, inevitably stole over the mind. He himself might
credit and disseminate any absurdity. But who is
it that is acquiring the "best land in Egypt"?
Not the British ; and not the Christians. My first
authority on the point was a practical man of
business.

"Jewish syndicates are buying up the best land
in the country," said he ; "large tracts are already
in their hands. They have bought up the Helouan
railway, and they are starting enormous factories.

They possess themselves of any good enterprise.
Most of them are in the Italian consulate ; they
are not British, but Italian and Levantine Jews.
Very nearly two-thirds of the commercial money
used in Egypt at the present time is Jewish.
Except the Crédit Lyonnais, the banks are all connected with Jews. British capitalists don't come
here ; or, if they do, they are frightened to death
of these low people who get hold of the money.
I have been in the East for more than twenty
years, and the class of Greeks and low foreigners
that flourish here are about the lowest and most
unprincipled lot you can find." "The banks at
Alexandria will not discount a single bill," put in
a bystander. "All our bills we have to keep.
You have to go to the Jews in the Serafia (the
Seraf is the money-changer). The banks will not
advance anything." In another quarter I was told
that the Alexandria bank managers complained
that the English banks restricted credits, and that,
as they could not get their bills taken up, business
suffered considerably. The present phase of the
Eastern question, however, had no doubt a great
deal to do with the reluctance and stagnation.
"Lord Cromer has stated that he cannot recommend
British capitalists to put their money into Egypt,"

remarked one of the speakers just quoted ; "he has stated it officially, in a report home." This impression appeared to be pretty confidently entertained, but I think I may say, without any fear of contradiction from official head-quarters at Cairo, that it is erroneous. Lord Cromer would be only too glad to see investments of British capital in this country.*

Here are some remarks by a British engineer and contractor, who has his workshop in the midst of the fellaheen. "My district is one of the richest in cotton and sugar-cane," he related, "and the natives agree that they never heard of better days. They don't find any fault with the Government. I am speaking of the fellaheen, not of the pashas." "Do they connect their improved condition with the British, or don't they know anything about it ?" "Oh yes, they know that the people who

---

* Mr. Rennell Rodd's report, published by the Foreign Office in April, 1896, contains the passage : "A certain want of enterprise is, indeed, noticeable as regards the attitude of British trade and capital towards Egypt. In spite, for instance, of the considerable profit and ready openings for agricultural undertakings in this country, where the sugar industry is annually assuming a more important development, next to no British capital seems to find its way to Egypt, though Englishmen are readily found to engage in far more speculative operations in countries affording far less guarantees of security."

have done the good are the English. At the same time, although they acknowledge that they are well off just now, the dislike to foreigners continues. I have noticed that they judge the Frenchman to be more suave than the Englishman, but not so straightforward. The money-lenders in the villages are mainly Greeks and Syrians; in fact, that is how the Greeks and Syrians live. There would be a good opportunity for the establishment of an English bank now, to lend money to the fellaheen. You see, every village guarantees its own people, and it would be a boon to the fellaheen to get advances at a fairly reasonable rate, instead of paying from 20 to 30 per cent., as they do now." "From 20 to 30 per cent.?" "Yes; in this way: As the law limits the rate of interest to 9 per cent., the Syrians and Greeks lend in one denomination of money, and stipulate for recoupment in another. Suppose they advance twenty louis; they exact, from the fellah borrower, a receipt for twenty sovereigns, so that they draw an interest in advance, and charge a further interest on the repayment. A State bank would be a grand thing for the fellaheen. They need the advances for buying their seed." "Do they not save money?" "Some of them. Some of them are

rich now. In Ismail's time, they used to bury
their profits in the ground, and borrow money
at high interest for the next crops. They pre-
ferred that to the suspicion of being well off,
because of the rapacity of the pachas. In my
own experience, the fellah does not often bank
his money, yet. He either hides ' it, or buys
another piece of ground, or marries another wife.
They must certainly be in a more flourishing condition of late years, because, although they have
never had any idea outside squalor, they are
furnishing their houses better now, and they
are decorating them more in the European style."
" The British have spoilt the fellah," broke in a
listener, whose familiarity with the rural population
goes back to " Ismail's time ; " "you can't talk to
the fellah now ; he is getting as 'cheeky' as
anything." "They cannot deny the good the
British have done," resumed the engineer. "I was
reminding some of them the other day of the
land near Toukh, which during Ismail's time was
offered for nothing if the recipient would under-
take to pay the taxes. It was offered, I know,
to an Englishman, and he would not accept it.
At the present day that land is worth £40 or £50
an acre." A discussion sprang up as to the

position of the British engineer in competition
with the foreigner. " The British officials favour
foreigners more than they do their own countrymen," grumbled the oldest resident in the company;
and I saw once more that this was the general
opinion of the British contractor. Profiting by
the presence of a railway surveyor, I asked for an
explanation of the fact that no direct line connected Alexandria and Port Saïd. " There are
lakes and canals to be crossed, for one thing,"
was the reply, " but another consideration relates
to the possible diversion of traffic from Alexandria.
Port Saïd would be the better port of the two,
I should say. Freights can be taken for less from
Port Saïd than from Alexandria. With respect
to the development of the local railways under
the Occupation, the passenger traffic has trebled,
right through the country, since 1882. The
fellaheen have had more money to spend, and the
fares have been reduced. A railway was projected
from Alexandria to Selhieh, and was to have been
carried into Syria; but we understood that the
scheme was abandoned partly on the score of
costliness, and partly on that of injuring the
interests of Alexandria." On the subject of the
money-lenders in the villages, it was repeated to

me from a different source that a common arrangement was for "the Greeks to lend so much in
pounds sterling, to be paid back in Egyptian
pounds, which with ordinary interest on the loan
came to 2½ per cent. per month—30 per cent. per
annum, 30 per cent. being a very moderate rate
here in Egypt." What was wanted, I heard
again and again, was a State bank.

To summarize numerous complaints, it seems
that the British officials in Cairo are liable to be
hoodwinked by the natives under them, in their
various Government departments. The Arab
engineer, for instance, expects *backsheesh*, and he
manages to favour an Arab contractor over a
British contractor, because the former understands
that *backsheesh* is to be given. If the impunity
with which the practice is maintained should,
coupled with the stress of competition, tempt a
British contractor to fight the native with his
own weapon, viz. bribes, the Government native
engineer is afraid to accept the *backsheesh* from
the British source, because he thinks he will be
reported in Cairo. The British inspectors attached
to the different circles of the Irrigation Department must necessarily rely upon their native staff;
the latter extort *backsheesh* from the contractors;

and if the contractors refuse the *backsheesh*, the reports that are made are unfavourable to them. If the inspector hears of any such case he " comes down sharp, very sharp ; " but sometimes he may feel that he is helpless. The system may be too widespread, and at the same time almost intangible. Among these distributors of official *backsheesh*, the Copts and the Syrians were especially denounced. I heard it urged that the " Cairo head-officials do not mix with the fellaheen," and that " there are two or three rings." When the British Government official from India has " gone about bullying," he is apt to suppose that he has been extremely effectual.

"When the irrigation engineers turned up here from India," commented one aggrieved personage, " all the Arabs and native Government officials were scared at them ; but during the last five or six years the natives have become accustomed to them, and they have worked back into the routine that was checked, which simply means jobbery." Proposing to close this chapter of the story from the standpoint of the English business man, I meet at the last moment with fresh grievances. The latest order for locomotives from the Egyptian State Railway went to the

Belgians "because, although their product was visibly inferior, they tendered £30 less per engine than Neilson, of Glasgow." " And if it had only been £10 less," according to another comment, " an English engine would not be ordered against a Belgian." " Why ? " " Because the railway influence is more or less French. Neilson, of Glasgow, was offering, at only £30 more, an engine that was infinitely superior." Then there are the cases of the Manouth and Ashmoune line, and the Behari railway. The contract was given out about eighteen months ago, and by this time the work should be finished. " As the firm who obtained the contract are French, the engineers of the State Railway are hobnobbing with them, and no notice is being taken of the delay ; whereas, if the firm had been English, the officials would have been down upon them at once, and their guarantee money would have been seized. The truth of the matter was that the French firm tendered at a figure at which they could not execute the work." A confirmation of this concluding statement reached me through a different channel. " A British contractor here," said my informant, " came to our bank about his tender for the Behari railway. The practice is, when tenders are invited,

to furnish schedules in which a lump sum is put
down.   The contractor may tender at above or
below that sum—put it at £60,000.   He had nearly
settled the business, I believe, but when we looked
at the schedule we saw it could not be done ; and
the contract went to a French firm."   Cannot our
Government do more for our own people ?—such
is the reiterated demand.   What can they do?   I
put the question to one of the aggrieved, a Scotchman.   "It is not that the individual wants his
Government to help him," was the response, good-
humouredly made ; "as M'Pherson of Glasgow
said, 'A M'Pherson scorns assistance.'   But we
think we are less fairly dealt with than the rest.
If the British control the government of the
country, and the Egyptian railway is a State
railway, the British ought to exert themselves
sufficiently to prevent these abuses.   We are not
strong enough here."

An anecdote of *backsheesh* in another direction
affords a curious glimpse of the life "in the villages."   A sheikh who had received certain pay-
ments, handed the total amount, from £700 to
£800, to a servant, to be placed in the safe which
he kept in a wall of his house.   The servant disappeared, and her master, on going to the safe to

withdraw a portion of the money, found that the latter had disappeared also. The superintendent of the local police, a native, expressed serious doubts as to the possibility of tracing the thief, and doubts more serious still as to the likelihood of recovering the funds. He promised, however, to devote his best attention to the inquiry. The police succeeded in tracing the fugitive, and, as the latter's facilities for expenditure had necessarily been few, in recovering nearly the whole sum. When apprised of the arrest, the native police superintendent lost no time in informing the sheikh, privately, that the search would prove a most difficult undertaking, and that the cost might "eat up," in some unexplained way, all the lost property. Nevertheless, it might be practicable for the superintendent to bring matters to a quick and satisfactory termination, by means of special industry and influence. The sheikh quite understood. "How much does he require?" asked the sheikh. "He would have well merited £200," replied the superintendent. The bargain arranged, the sheikh contentedly accepted the missing funds minus £200, *backsheesh* to "him," the native superintendent. "But give the poor soldiers £25," the superintendent then entreated, and £25 further

I

passed into his hands as *backsheesh* to the soldiers.
An English official went down from Cairo not
long afterwards, and, in the course of attendance at the *moudirieh*, snapped up little significant
morsels of dialogue which were ostensibly not
intended for his ear. "Was he not lucky to get
that £225!" observed one of the natives in
apparently a confidential communication to
another. "Oh, but the £25 was for the soldiers,"
remarked the other. "Why, you don't suppose
that he gave any of it to the soldiers!" returned
the first speaker. "He did not give them anything. He kept it all for himself." The English
effendi insisted upon an investigation, and the
£225 had to be refunded to the sheikh. As for
the defaulting servant, when interrogated before
the native judge, she argued that the money ought
properly to belong to herself. She had been
living in immoral relations with the respected
sheikh for a considerable period, and he had
never made her any present, nor paid her any
wages. "It's a great pity, and very shocking,"
remarked the native judge subsequently, to the
person from whom I have the narrative — "but
some of our people *will* lead these disgraceful
lives." "And that old judge," in the words of

the narrator, "is one of the worst of them, himself."

The difficulty of pronouncing upon the sentiments of the native population with respect to the British semi-rule is continually illustrated in the conflicting accounts by experienced British residents. The latter would doubtless agree upon one point, however, when all is said and done, viz., that to look for any definite public opinion in Egypt is absurd. There are the hot and cold fits of fanaticism, which, as at Tantah during the Riaz Pasha crisis, may be worked up into a certain effervescence by political agitators; but, outside fanaticism, the people have probably no bias, and outside money and their wives no interest. They can be induced to admit that the country has "never seen better times since the days of Pharaoh," and in the next breath they will be exclaiming, "Show us where the country is one bit the better!" An Englishman who goes into the regions up the Nile on archæological missions told me that the habitual utterances of the Bedouins with whom he treated was that they did not care "whether France or England had Egypt," but that since the English were there, they knew they would be paid for what they sold.

A Scotchman who dwells amongst the fallaheen described the latter as fully convinced that the English would "never go away now," but as wide awake to the desirability of professing discontent in order to secure indulgence and extra liberal treatment. To take a third view, that of a man whose knowledge of the natives is confined to the urban population—a man who, not a British subject, but an Anglophil trusted at head-quarters —"these people believe that England is on the eve of her ruin, and that at a puff of wind "—he blew into his hand, as if to enforce the idea— "she would collapse in pieces and in dust." I have had this last impression, by the way, from a Gladstonian also, a Yorkshire Gladstonian at an Egyptian *table d'hôte*, and he seemed to be rather gratified at the prospect.

CHAPTER VII.

IF we turn to the Egyptian newspaper press, we find that, whatever may be the conclusion to be drawn from the fact, the Opposition journals in French and Arabic largely outnumber those which appear in support of the British occupation. The particular instance of the *Journal Egyptien*, issued daily in French, with the engagements proffered by the Gladstone Government of 1882 a stereotyped feature of the front page, has already been referred to, and mention has also been made of broadsheets in Arabic which reproduce the virulent attacks and misrepresentations to be found in the French organs. With its population of about half a million, Cairo probably sees more of this newspaper warfare than all the other towns of Egypt put together, although the *Egyptian Gazette*, the single newspaper appearing daily in the English language, is published at Alexandria.

The contents of the *Gazette* are printed in French
as well as in English. It may be regarded as
the semi-official journal of the Occupation ; and
besides its authoritative character and position in
regard to all administrative matters and movements, it is a sound literary and scholarly production. But to the European non-resident the
criticism continually occurs that the *Egyptian
Gazette*, like the majority of the older British
residents, seems to assume too easily that the
extravagances and the misstatements emitted on
the other side must be notorious, and that, consequently, they can be disdained. News is not so
plentiful in Egypt that indefatigable refutations of
falsehood, and steady repetitions of all disproof
as often as the calumny turns up again, would
oust large quantities of interesting matter. There
are always the people of short memories who need
reminders, and the other people of less knowledge
who need education. The *Progrès*, an Anglophil
daily paper, published in French at Cairo, does
excellent service by occasionally tackling the
Opposition journals in quite their own tone. Add
to the *Progrès* and the *Gazette* an Arabic broadsheet, the *Mokattam*, issued at Cairo, and the
whole of the Egyptian press avowedly in the

British interest has been named. The Italian and Greek papers are left out of account.*

On the other side, that of distinct opposition, the *Echo d'Orient*, advertising itself as the only newspaper in Egypt sold for half a piastre, or a penny farthing, has reinforced the French press within the last seven months. The *Memphis*, bi-weekly, in French and Arabic, is also a new-comer, dating from eight or ten months. One piastre, "tariff," or 2½*d.*, stands as the current price of the four-page daily journal in Egypt. Among the papers printed in Arabic solely, the *Akhram*, circulating as far as Constantinople in the one direction, and Morocco in the other, should be regarded as the general Turkish Mussulman organ ; whilst the *Moaïad* heads the native Mussulman cause in Egypt proper.† Translations from

* The *Messaggiere Egiziano*, retorting upon a new prophecy to which the *Akhram* had committed itself, fairly represents the prevailing tone in the local Italian and Greek journals. The *Akhram* had announced to its readers that in six months' time—*i.e.* by the autumn of 1896—the British would be evacuating the country. "No, they will not," replied the *Messaggiere*,—"and we may inform our sanguine opponents of the reactionary party that several months beyond that period, and, indeed, several years, will elapse before this *pium desiderium* of theirs can be realized."

† Shortly after the commencement of the advance towards Dongola, the *Akhram* informed its readers that the Mahdi had re-appeared in a mosque at Omdurman, and had pronounced an anti-British harangue, in the presence of 50,000 Dervishes. This

the Arabic sheets are comprised in the contents
of the journals published in French, as the latter
are drawn upon for the polemics in the vernacular.
Thus we read in the *Echo d'Orient* that the *Moaïad*
considers the policy of England in relation to
Italy as resembling "that which succeeded so well
with Bismarck, but as stamped with more intelligence and even less probity." The *Moaïad's* notion
of the Italian difficulties in Abyssinia has been
that they result from British underhand manœuvres
directed towards the excitement of the dervishes
against the very Power which England has "played
off against France." On the first intelligence of
President Cleveland's statement with respect to
Venezuela, the *Echo d'Orient* rejoiced in both
prose and verse over the humiliation preparing for
Great Britain. "There remains only one thing

was too much, even for the *Phare d'Alexandrie,* which has never
pretended that the British occupation could be terminated by
agencies supernatural. The *Phare* reproved its colleague. For one
thing, remarked the French journal, dryly, so far as was known, no
mosque existed at Omdurman capable of containing so large a
concourse. Whereupon the *Progrès,* in the party battling of the
Egyptian newspaper press, turned the laugh against its French
contemporary with the grave rebuke that the latter had cast
profane and public doubt upon the Mahdi's power to miraculously
expand the cubic space, or, if that were not the easier course, to
wondrously withdraw the walls for the duration of his sermon, and
then put them back again.

for John Bull to do," pronounced that sapient organ, for the delectation of the native press, "and that is to accept the delimitation which will be fixed by the Washington Commission, and to hold his peace. President Cleveland has spoken too firmly and too loudly for the least doubt to be possible as to the attitude which the great nation he represents is ready to adopt." The result might not altogether bear out the forecast, but that signifies little in the quarter whence it proceeds. One fresh opportunity has presented itself for persuading Egyptians that the occupying power is weak, and can be coerced by merely a bold front. "We learn with pleasure," wrote the same journal a day or two afterwards, "that Selim Bey Hamaoui, editor of *El Felah*, has just been promoted by the Sultan to the grade of pasha (*mirmiran*). We tender our sincerest congratulations to our *confrère*." The *Felah* is an Arabic broadsheet published in Egypt in the Turkish interest. Its circulation has latterly diminished rather than augmented, and the dignity thus conferred, an extremely high one for a native editor, is construed here to mean an attempt from Constantinople to push the paper among the fellaheen by investing it with Imperial sanction.

The enlightenment that presides over its fabrication may be inferred from the slender detail that not many months ago this Hamaoui launched the statement among his readers that the English were not even Christians in religion, but, at home in England, were idolaters !

I must not omit mention of one charming publication, the *Egyptian Herald,* which "advocates the administrative autonomy of Egypt, and the interests of Islam throughout the world." This truly unique organ is further described upon its front page as "Edited by Hajee Abdullah Browne," and "published weekly." Its "weekliness" depends upon flow of funds from the Ottoman Agency at Cairo. The week becomes a month, occasionally. Mr. Browne, the editor, is a Dublin Irishman who turned Moslem, and rebaptized himself, with or without going to Mecca, the Pilgrim (*Hajee*) Abdullah. I regretted extremely to have missed him on an occasion arranged for an introduction ; his programme for the "solution of the Egyptian Question" is that of a great inventive genius, and to have heard him upon it, over a glass of whisky—there is a good deal of Scotch and Irish whisky in Egypt—would have been an intellectual ravishment. He solves the

Egyptian Question by the conversion of the British nation to Islam. He does not know, I believe, the actual fountain-head of the funds that are supplied to him ; he only knows that he draws them from the Agency of the Turkish Government.

A British official, chief of a department, commenting generally upon the Opposition press, informed me that a French citizen had been expelled from the country at the instance of his Consulate for no reason that could be discovered other than that he contributed articles to the columns of the pro-British *Progrès*. If the fact appears incredible, most of the facts which relate to the "right of extra-territoriality," conveyed by the Capitulations, would astonish persons who have fancied that "solutions" lie in such phrases as "internationalization," or "Egypt for the Egyptians." The origin of the separate treaties known as the Capitulations, and dating back to the fifteenth or sixteenth century, was natural and explicable enough ; the object primarily was to safeguard the Christians of different nationalities who desired to trade in the territories of the Porte. France, Italy, England, Germany, Austria, Russia, Holland, Spain, Portugal, Greece, Sweden,

Denmark, Belgium, the United States, and Brazil are the Powers possessing these extraordinary rights, extended during the lapse of time, rather than curtailed, by one nation after another. The same British official, speaking of the Young Egypt party, said that, while every one could understand the desire of the better-educated few to exhibit the capacity for self-government which they might have acquired under the Occupation, and while every excuse must be made for those who had begun to look upon every British functionary "as a man whose place he would like to have," yet these notions of the party's unaided competence were limited in Egypt to an extremely restricted circle, viz. Young Egypt itself. The most active and energetic members of the movement were those who were connected with the Egyptian native tribunals, and who, almost without exception, had received their education in France. I produced the text of Moustafa Kamel's assertion to a French journalist, in the course of an interview in Paris. "The English have now, by means of their instrument at the Education Department, Artin Pasha, completely suppressed the Egyptian Mission," complained Moustafa Kamel, "their object being to finish once for all with the generous country, France, *cette France généreuse*, which sends into Egypt young men whose only crime is that they have been well educated, and that they are implacable patriots." The small State educational endowment known as the Egyptian Mission simply enables a certain number of young men to prosecute their studies in a foreign country. Hitherto the greater number of them, if not all, have been sent to France; at the present time the numbers are more equally distributed over France, England, and either Germany or some other European country. As for the tale that France has been deprived of her share altogether —"there is no misrepresentation which these people will not foist upon the public," remarked my informant. " The injury they work is not so much among the Europeans, who do not believe them, but among the native population. Their articles are reproduced by the native press, and although they may be refuted, and the fellaheen may not credit them, there is this great harm involved, that the people suppose, not without reason, that the Arabic papers would never be allowed to carry on these attacks against the English in such an unscrupulous, virulent manner, unless they were supported from the very highest quarter of the country."

It may be opportune to recapitulate the main lines of the constitution, as framed by Lord Dufferin, after the military events of 1882, and dating from May in the following year. The decree which promulgated the Organic Law of Egypt, on May 1st, 1883, instituted a Council for each province; a Legislative Council; a General Assembly, and a Council of State. Of these bodies the first-named deals with local affairs in each province, and may vote extra local taxation for works of public utility within. its district, and its sittings are attended by the head-engineer of the *moudirieh* (chief town). Any act or deliberation by a provincial council relating to matters not legally pertaining to its attributes becomes "null and of no effect," the decision being rendered by a special commission created under the Organic Law. The *moudir*, or governor of the province, convenes the council and reports to the commission upon any case calling for its judgment; the members of the council have the right of appeal from the *moudir* to the Minister of the Interior. Provincial councils vary in the number of their members, Gharbiyeh possessing eight, Siout seven, and three others six each, down to Fayoum, with three. No one is eligible for membership of the provincial council if he is under thirty years of age, cannot read and write, has not for at least two years previously paid an annual land tax of five thousand piastres (the piastre equals 2½*d.*), and has not been inscribed upon the electoral roll for at least five years. Government officials and soldiers on the active list are ineligible; the term of membership extends to six years, a moiety of the councillors retiring, however, every three years by ballot; and no person may occupy a seat in more than one of these bodies.

Following the order observed in the constitu-- tion, we come to the Legislative Council. No law, nor any decree regulating public administra- tion, can be promulgated without having been presented for consideration to the Legislative Council. If the Government does not adopt the opinion emitted by the Legislative Council, the latter is made acquainted with the reasons for the decision, but no debate can take place there- upon.* The Budget must be submitted to the

* "The Council of Ministers decided to-day, in reply to the native Legislative Council, that discussion about the grant of half

Legislative Council on December 1st each year, and any opinions or desires to which the several heads of expenditure and revenue may give rise, are communicated to the Finance Minister. Ministers may attend at the sittings of the Legislative Council, and may be either assisted or represented, on special questions, by the chiefs of their departments respectively. The Legislative Council consists of thirty members, fourteen of whom are "permanent," and the remainder "*délégués.*" The president, one of the fourteen, is named directly by the Khedive ; one of the two vice-presidents and the twelve other permanent members are named by the Khedive, on the proposition of the Council of Ministers. The other vice-president and his fifteen elected colleagues are returned as follows : one for Cairo, one for the combined towns of Alexandria, Damietta, Rosetta, Suez, Port Saïd, Ismaïlia, and El-Arish, and one —elected by the Provincial Council—for each of the fourteen provinces. A pecuniary allowance is paid to the president, both the vice-presidents, and all the permanent members.

a million for the Soudan expedition was beyond their powers, as defined by the Organic Law of 1883 " (Cairo correspondent of the *Times*, April 23).

Chapter 6 of the Law declares that no new direct tax, real or personal, can be imposed in Egypt without having been discussed and voted by the General Assembly ; and this body is composed of the Ministers, the Legislative Council, and the Notables. The Notables number 46, elected by the towns and provinces in the proportions due—Cairo, 4; Alexandria, 3 ; Port Saïd and Suez, 1 ; El-Arish and Ismaïlia, 1 ; Gharbiyeh province, 4 (of which one is for the town of Tantah) ; Dakahbeh province, 3 (of which one is for the town of Mansourah), etc. For eligibility as Notable, the property qualification is limited to a yearly payment of 2000 piastres, in the shape of either taxation or licence.

By clause 1 of the second decree, bearing the date May 1st, 1883, "all Egyptians, *sujets locaux,* who have completed their twentieth year," and are not ineligible on grounds enumerated by a later section, "are electors." Clause 5 provided for the framing and posting of the electoral lists for the *toumnes* of Cairo, and the *kismes* of Alexandria, as for the towns and villages throughout the rest of the country ; and clause 11 for the annual revision, the sheikhs inscribing the new names in the case of the ordinary towns and villages, and the native committees in the case of the quarters styled

K

locally, at Cairo and Alexandria, *toumnes* and *kismes.* Clause 13 created delegate electors, and these form the constituency for the provincial councils. The illiterate vote was admitted by clause 31. By the delegate electors in the towns, and the provincial councils in the fourteen provinces, the delegate members are returned to the Legislative Council. The election of the Notables who sit as deputies in the General Assembly is by the delegate electors of Cairo, Alexandria, and six other towns, and by the delegate electors of the 14 *moudiriehs*, the latter of these two constituencies sending 35, and the former 11. The constitution has worked exceedingly well in the past, but it leaves obvious loopholes for the action of error, ignorance, and intrigue.

The judicial system embraces numerous jurisdictions, apart from all the separate Consular Courts. Thanks to one of the Appeal Court judges, who very courteously and patiently explained the most recent reforms, I am enabled to give the following account of the Egyptian tribunals as they now exist. In criminal offences, the natives are dealt with by the native Courts. Civil cases as between natives and Europeans, or between Europeans of different nationalities, are dealt with by the mixed Courts; the criminal jurisdiction over European subjects continues to reside with the Consular Courts. From the juris- diction exercised over natives by the "native Courts"—this phrase is used to designate the "new" tribunals, and only those—must be ex- cluded cases relating to marriage, divorce, and inheritance, which are still judged under the Koranic law, administered by the *Kadis* of the old native jurisdiction.

It is in the "new" tribunals that the greatest amount of interest has centred during the last few years. Their jurisdiction comprehends all civil matters between natives except those which still pertain to the *Kadis* administering the old Moslem law, and all criminal matters as between natives. The new native tribunals include what may be termed summary jurisdiction courts, consisting of a single judge; and one of Sir John Scott's im- provements a few years ago lay in the distribution of these summary courts all over the country, so that justice should be brought "near to the people." Prior to 1883 they did not exist at all; of recent years, under Lord Cromer's care, with Sir John Scott as the legal adviser to the Government, they have been enormously developed. The new tribunals are thus superposed : (1) summary courts ; (2) courts of first instance ; (3) courts of appeal. The Court of First Instance may also deal with larger cases, three or five judges sitting, according to the importance of the affair. When the sentence may be penal servitude, or hanging, the number of the judges must be five ; for offences involving a lower penalty, the number is three, as in all civil matters. From the summary judge, appeal goes to the Court of First Instance, but not higher ; appeal from the Court of First Instance, when the case has come originally before that tribunal, goes to the Court of Appeal.

As for the " cases relating to inheritance," referred to above as still judged under the old Koranic law, the following extract from the columns of the *Progrès*, in March this year, would seem to indicate that the Mehkémés, also, must now expect some sensible measures of reform : " The great suit which is being brought against the heirs of the late Ibrahim Pasha, in the Cairo Mehkémé, and in which millions were at stake, has once more raised the question whether the reform of justice in Egypt can be spoken of as accomplished, so long as these special tribunals continue as at present. For all those who know what these courts are, for all those who have been able to measure the extent of the ignorance of the judges composing them, who comprehend their vices of procedure, the denials of justice, the spoliations and other iniquities which they cloak, it is indubitable that the subject demands attention from the Egyptian Government, and merits the fullest solicitude on the part of her Britannic Majesty's Representative in Egypt. . . . As one edifying example, let us remind our readers of the worthy *Kadi*, in one of our large towns, who last year sought to terminate a lawsuit, in his court, by carrying off the young girl whose abduction was complained of, and by shutting her up in his own harem. . . . A few score years ago, all the civil and commercial suits of the Ottoman Empire were judged by the Mehkémés, according to the religious law. As their jurisdiction has already been restricted, there is no difficulty of principle in the way of a further reform. The jurisdiction of the Mehkémés should be limited to questions purely spiritual, such as sacrilege, and other *manquements aux préceptes de la religion d'Etat.*"

Very few capital sentences are passed in Egypt. For what is called here "murder simple" the maximum punishment is fifteen years' penal servitude ; for "murder with premeditation, or aggravating circumstances," the penalty is death by hanging. Clause 32, however, of the criminal law requires, basing itself on Moslem law, that before a prisoner can be condemned to death he must either have confessed his guilt, or have been found guilty on the evidence of two eye-witnesses. The vices of the French procedure, although modified by the reforms and simplifications introduced by Sir J. Scott, are easily discernible here. On the one hand, the efforts of the executive to obtain a confession, if they have grounds for being perfectly sure of the prisoner's guilt, may lead to the badgering, delay, and other modes of torture conspicuous in France ; whilst, on the other, the fact of the confession would usually be considered in mitigation when preparing sentence, because, if the man had not confessed, condemnation might not have been possible. The British have done the best they could with the criminal law as they found it, but many of its clauses are still identical with those of the code in France. A large convict prison for long terms, and "lifers," is maintained at Tura, a settlement in the desert, but not far removed from the banks of the Nile.

Afforded an opportunity of attending the weekly *séance* of the Court of First Instance, sitting with three judges, I passed a winter forenoon among native magistrates, in front of native prisoners, native counsel, and public. In the first of the two cases tried between ten o'clock and one, three prisoners were charged with uttering counterfeit coin, well knowing the same to be false. The procedure closely resembled that of the French courts, but the judges in corresponding French tribunals might have taken a salutary lesson in strict impartiality of method and demeanour. It was a picturesque scene, the brilliant sunshine falling upon an almost dazzling medley of robes and turbans in blue and scarlet, yellow, white, and black, with the crimson *tarbûsh* in abundance nearer the well of the court and the bench. The public came and went noiselessly through the wide open doors at the extremity ; through the open windows were visible the groups of gold-bedecked black-veiled women, crouching upon the ground beneath the shade of sycamores and palms ; whilst the swaying foliage of the trees themselves, sharply defined against a luminous blue sky, easily assisted fugitive impressions that we had far departed from the centre

of a city with half a million for 'its population.
Malodorous the air, however, decidedly at times ;
and an unkempt, dingy, frowsy crew, with a
mixture of physiognomical characteristics that
defied differentiation amongst the dark-skinned
races, could be descried from time to time lurking
about the courtyard, or garden, in the sunshine or
the shadow visible through window and door. The
Court heard the evidence, heard the Procureur-
Général, heard counsel for the defence, and retired
to deliberate. They eventually sentenced one of
the white-bearded Arabs charged with uttering
false coin, to three years' imprisonment, and
acquitted the other; the third prisoner, an Arab
boy, aged twelve, being let off with three months
on the ground that he had acted without discernment. As the proceedings took place wholly in
the vernacular, I was indebted to the Procureur-
Général for a running translation of their purport.
This, too, was in French. Nobody about the
premises spoke any English; and presently it
appeared—a fact which seemed stranger—that
nobody there except a sworn interpreter understood Turkish. A Turk was brought up, in
custody, on a charge of having attempted to
murder an Armenian in Cairo. The interpreter, a

negro in a drab overcoat, had to convey to the
Court that the prisoner said he had only knocked
the prosecutor down because the latter had
" insulted the Sultan." He had then to convey to
the prisoner that the successive witnesses described
him as producing a revolver from his belt when he
had knocked the Armenian down, and as having
been prevented from shooting him by interposition
alone. With respect to the prosecutor, denying
that he had insulted the Sultan, all he could state
to the Court was that the Turk had suddenly
knocked him down and stamped on him, and that
he had then lost consciousness. The Turk, a fine
brawny fellow, clad in a striped shirt, loose blue
knickerbockers, and shoes, his legs and breast
bare, swore by " Allah," and accompanied his
protestations with much persuasive gesture to the
Court, that he had done no more than he admitted.
What they took to be his drawing of a revolver
from his belt, he said, was but the movement of
clapping his right hand to his heart. Yet, if he
did not understand Arabic, how could he tell that
the Sultan was being insulted ? The witnesses,
although testifying against their co-religionist in
favour of a Christian, were too strong for the Turk.
When the case stood adjourned, his condemnation

to a term of imprisonment seemed certain. The assault had occurred in an Arab *café dansant*, known to be frequented by the friends of two Armenians who had not long previously attacked and killed a Turk. In briefly discussing the procedure, later, the presiding judge laid stress, with evident satisfaction and pride, on the fact that these cases were tried by them "in Court of First Instance sitting as Court of Assize," without a jury. They don no special garb for the appearance in their judicial character. Every Moslem of the middle and upper classes in the towns wears the *tarbûsh*, whether indoors or out-of-doors ; and the wig of the judicial Bench in England, equally with the square black hat of M. le President and his *adjoints* in France, is replaced here by the *tarbûsh*. The Khedive wears the *tarbûsh* when driving in his open carriage in state ; so does his coachman. The sole addition to the ordinary attire of the native judges for the discharge of their functions in court, consists of a broad crimson sash, passing from the right shoulder, and attached on the left side, beneath the arm, by a buckle representing the Imperial crescent and stars.

CHAPTER VIII.

THE dragoman who acted as my guide to the premises of the chief native Opposition journal, the *Moaïad*, and who was to interpret in a conversation with the Sheikh Ali Youssef, its editor and proprietor, led me through a labyrinth of teeming bazaars, through the ancient Khan-el-Khalil mart for silk and velvets, jewellery, Persian rugs and carpets, through the narrow lanes where the mosque walls and doorways, amid squalor or tinsel, astonish with their wealth of intricate decoration and sculpture, and thence out into the Sharia Mohammed Ali, the long line of main thoroughfare south-east from the centre of the town. On the hill which terminates the street at its south-eastern extremity stands El Kala'â, the Citadel, built by Saladin with the stones of the smaller pyramid at Ghizeh. The domes and minarets of the Alabaster Mosque, begun by Mohammed Ali in 1824, rise from the interior of

the fortified heights, and seem to command all
Cairo; but beyond and above El Kala'â frowns
the bare ridge of the Mokattam Mountain. It
was from the Mokattam that Mohammed Ali, the
founder of the present dynasty, obtained the
surrender of the Citadel in 1805 by means of an
artillery undreamt of in Saladin's age. We cross
the long thoroughfare, named after that destroyer
of the Mamelukes; we halt in front of a gateway
surmounted by the title of the journal, *El Moaïad*,
and the dragoman explains his business to a
blue-robed Arab messenger basking near a dust-
laden banana tree. Along Mohammed Ali Street
trudge the hawkers and the fellaheen, their
donkeys harnessed to barrows or bearing packs;
on well-groomed asses jog the native traders, in
flowing garb and snowy turban; British tourists,
in a party, pursued by the Cairo donkey-boy, who
prods the animal from behind with a stick, and
urges it on with his monotonous cry of " Ah-h-h !"
trot towards the Citadel for the regulation visit, or
for the view as far as two groups of pyramids
across the Nile, into the desert; private carriages,
preceded by the hardy *saïs*, or runners, in their
gold-embroidered vests and loose white muslin
knickerbockers, roll by from the outskirts; Arab

children play in what with a system of drainage
would be the gutters; the Arab mother in the
arcade, crouching with her infant, derives undis-
guised pleasure from the chase, and "kill;" and
the Arab policeman, tall, neat, and upright, rules
with urbanity from the middle of the road. Along
Mohammed Ali Street the British redcoat swings
on foot to unearth a comrade at the British
barracks within the Citadel. While we look out
on the whole strange scene, bathed in bright sunshine, a native compositor is setting Arabic type
at a case by the wall of the open vestibule itself.
Presently we are to be received, and I am ushered
into a sub-editors' room, where three gentlemen
wearing the *tarbûsh*, and in European habiliments,
are rapidly rewriting in Arabic characters, from
right to left, the matter before them in slips of
Arabic manuscript. The chief sub-editor parleys;
he hears, and he goes to see the sheikh. There is
a little delay, and then the chief sub-editor returns,
and escorts us most politely into the presence.

Unfortunately, the hour has been ill-chosen.
It would also be un-Oriental to despatch business
with Western celerity. Perhaps the objects of
the visit should need serious deliberation, likewise;
an ostensibly innocent call from the representative

of any inquisitive classes in far Belad-el-Inglis,
the country of the English, may conceal some
sinister design, some hostile plot.   The Sheikh
Ali Youssef motions his visitor to a seat upon the
sofa at his right hand, orders coffee, and listens
with gravity to an exposition of the visitor's wish.
He is of swart complexion, with brown expressive
eyes, short, dark, curling moustache and beard,
and agreeable features.   His manner is suave and
dignified, the voice is soft and measured, the
gestures are few.   Attired in a sober olive-green
robe, open from the throat, and showing a striped
silk vest of neutral colour that matches with the
silken under-sleeves, Ali Youssef,' in his white
turban, looks, although a comparatively young
sheikh, every inch a sheikh.   He thinks it would
be better if we called again.   The next day would
be better—not half-past ten in the morning, but
half-past three or four in the afternoon.   The
compliments that pass and are reciprocated baffle
description in cold blood.   One rises indeed to
all such efforts, but they are trying to the British
modesty, and they constitute a strain upon the
imaginative resource.   We accept our tiny cup of
the sheikh's delicate coffee ; we smoke one of the
sheikh's excellent cigarettes ; and we arrange for

the next day at four. A member of the staff
comes in with a proof of that day's leader in Arabic,
and reads it aloud for the sheikh's approbation.
It becomes an impressive process, but apparently
all goes well. We take our leave.

For the adjourned interview the services of the
dragoman proved unnecessary. I found that the
sheikh had enlisted the co-operation of a gentleman who edited the bi-weekly *Memphis*—the
Opposition journal published in the two Opposition languages—and who spoke both French and
Arabic. They explained that the *Memphis* was
printed at the *Moaïad* premises, and after a repe-
tition of courtesies and a degustation anew of the
Moaïad coffee, we entered upon the question of the
day. The editorial retreat was a spacious and
lofty apartment, comfortable, but without vain
luxury. A bookcase stood against the wall, an
Arabic calendar faced the window, and a crimson
divan opposite the sofa between the door and the
editor's table received us at our ease. The dragoman had retraced his steps, disappointed, to the
hotel, there to lie in wait for my return and solicit
backsheesh, in addition to his fee, on the ground
of " opportunities lost "—that admitted source of
income, for all classes alike, in the preposterous

days of Ismail. The later hour of the appointment, by the way, had permitted a longer stay
within doors at the hotel, where a pair of
highly respectable Hindoo jugglers and snake-
charmers had given an exhibition with the *man-
gouste*, the Indian cobra, etc., on the gaudy carpets
of the entrance-hall. They themselves had been
preceded, as it happened, by a couple of Arabs,
who had performed with the grey African cobra,
and an almost human monkey, in the full flood of
the sunshine on the pavement before the hotel.

"The Sheikh Ali Youssef says," replied the
editor of the *Memphis*, having translated to his
colleague an opening query, and having heard the
response, "that the programme of *El Moaiad* is
the programme of any journal which claims to be
the organ of the interests of the country and to
defend its independence. It approves the actions
of the Government, when those actions are in
conformity with the interests of the country, and
it opposes *une résistance, une résistance*" — the
interpreter hesitated for a word to render the
sheikh's epithet in the vernacular—"*terrible, enfin*,
when it perceives that those are contrary to the
interests of the country. But, in either case, he
preserves a proper moderation of language."

" Does it not, in judging of the interests of the country, habitually agree with France ? "

" The journal is altogether local—local to Egypt. It is a journal for our nation. Egypt is a nation which must act for itself, and must be free from foreign intervention in the administration of the country. If the reader should consider that the journal opposes its resistance over-much to England, it is because the English are those who have put their fingers in the affairs of Egypt."

" So that the Sheikh Ali Youssef and the *Moaïad* would be equally hostile to any other foreign intervention ? "

" Emphatically hostile. There would be no difference. The intervention being foreign, the journal has to safeguard the interests of the country."

Here the sheikh interposed, and thus he spoke : " It is not only the journal that would be hostile. Every native of Egypt would observe the same attitude as the *Moaïad* as long as the interest of the country requires that the foreign intervention should be removed "—*évitée éloignée, supprimée*, were the translator's successive expressions for the concluding word. " If the Egyptians were to lose all hope of independence," added Ali

L

Youssef, " if they saw that it was hopeless to think of recovering their independence, and if they had to choose between two influences, two protectors, the French or the English, my opinion is "—the guarded avowal seemed doubly significant by reason of its spontaneity—" that they would prefer the English." A pause ensued, and then the speaker resumed, with a certain vivaciousness, " That is on the hypothesis solely that all hope should be lost."

" Does the sheikh believe that the action of France has up to the present been beneficial to the country? How can he think so, with the knowledge of the veto placed by the French upon the utilization of the great reserve funds? "

" The position of France ought to be considered in connection with the evil which it is sought to remove, viz. the foreign occupation. If, however, it is considered in itself, apart from that matter, of course it is an opposition that does harm. In presence of the occupation, which is the foremost misfortune of all, the opposition by France appears in a softened light, especially when it is known to be aimed at the removal of the occupation."

" Under these circumstances, you regard it as an excusable weapon for yourselves? "

The sheikh reflected. Then said he, " A little application of this idea may be seen in what happens sometimes to a man who is eating. The morsel which the man endeavours to swallow may stop in the throat, and the man may desire that another person should come by and strike him between the two shoulders. If he is struck between the two shoulders, he may either manage to swallow the bread or the meat, or he may reject it completely, and he is willing to support the blow for the sake of the relief, one way or the other. In itself, were the bread or the meat not so arrested in the throat, the blow would be insupportable."

" You grasp the sheikh's illustration ? " queried the interpreter, as Ali Youssef gazed at us both somewhat anxiously. Satisfaction having been afforded upon that point, the sheikh pursued, " The conduct of France in not authorizing an employment of the reserve is, in itself, considered from a point of view quite independent and absolute, very hurtful to the country. But, considered as an obstacle confronting the occupation, it is deemed by the country to be a little misfortune against a big one."

" Does the sheikh differ from the opinion that the British occupation has done good ? "

"Whatever may be the good things that have been brought by the fact of the occupation, they are as nothing when compared with its ultimate object, which is to arrive at a destruction of the political life of the country. Before these last years, all Egyptians were able to look with a satisfied eye upon reforms accompanying the British occupation of Egypt, because they always had the encouragement that the English would one day keep their promise. But since three or four years, the English having shown, or perhaps having declared, that they will not evacuate the country, those reforms are not esteemed by the Egyptians. During the last three or four years the English have created, and forged to their hands, instruments for abasing the value of the Egyptian functionaries who have held high offices ; and their power to do so proves the nullity of the reforms, or detracts from their value."

What the speaker precisely meant by this, did not come out very clearly. The utterance presumably related to a warfare of individualities, upon which topic we shall hear the other side.

"Does he believe that Egypt is really ripe for self-government ? "

" I consider that the present moment is one at

which England can with confidence and safety
give to the Egyptians the administration of their
country. So long as the present state of affairs
lasts—that is to say, as long as we have the
occupation—the capacity of the Egyptians to
govern their own country will diminish."

" Why ? "

" Because the *rôle* which England has played
during the past three or four years, since the
accession of the Khedive Abbas—— "

The sheikh caught at the Khedive's name in
the translation, and interrupted, to be told exactly
what his colleague was conveying.

" A year before the accession of the present
Khedive," corrected his colleague, after their
hurried dialogue,—" since that time, because it
began before the death of the late Khedive—the
part which England seeks to fill is that of showing
to the Egyptian people that they are between
her hands. Is it to be England, or is it to be
Egypt ? There is a sort of competition betwixt
the two. Well, the continuance of the occupation
kills in us the capacity to administer for ourselves.
The capacity cannot grow ; and although it has
germinated, it will die out."

" Why, if it has been able to germinate, with

the British here since 1882, should it die now?"

"We think," said the sheikh, "that the English seek to monopolize all the administrations, and to hinder the Egyptians from being capable of governing ; and that makes us lose all hope."

"Is the majority of the native population with you, do you think?"

"Not the majority, but the totality. We are sure of it. It may happen that a nation is divided into several parties, and that some display themselves, whilst others hide their heads. But, on this question, there is not a single Egyptian who does not detest the occupation. The English use their powers and authority to gain certain categories of persons in the country to their cause, but there is not a single Egyptian who has sincerely ranged himself on their side. We claim our independence, and that is the view we stand by in the programme of our journal. The same would be the case if the French were here instead of England."

The "same" would, in all probability, not be the case, so far as *El Moaïad* might be concerned, under the hypothesis suggested. I did not learn, until too late to inform or remind the sheikh, that under the French in Algeria or Tunis no native paper in opposition is tolerated for a moment. Ali Youssef will peruse these lines, however, in the dress of his own elegant and graceful language ; and the difference in the character of the rule, the little oversight he committed in his concluding sentences, ought not to escape his perspicacity. *El Moaïad*, they explained to me, signifies *The Victor.* Several Sultans of Egypt have borne the surname ; and by one of them was erected a monumental mosque which travellers visit. A Sultan of Hama, in Syria, who also was adorned with the flattering appellation, wrote a book of history well known in Arabic literature, a history of the world from the Creation to his own day. But no such *Moaïad* as the daily journal which confronts the English in Egypt would be possible to the Sheikh Ali Youssef and his friends, "if France were here instead of England." *Ce n'est rien, ça, si vous voulez,* remarked the personage who imparted the enlightenment on the subject of the native press in Algeria and Tunis—*et c'est tout !*

The sheikh harked back to an incidental comment respecting the readiness of the Egyptian people for autonomy. He did not mean to imply, he said, that the Egyptians were as advanced in

the scale of civilization as the English or the
French, nor that they were yet as capable of
government as those two peoples.   What he
meant was that Egypt might always follow in
the road of progress, independence, and greatness
if England became her friend ; but England could
be her friend only by keeping outside her boundaries.
If Egypt could recover her independence, on such
a basis as he indicated, she would become the
leader of all the Oriental nations, and would figure
as the exemplar in the Oriental world from
the point of view of civilization and progress.
Egyptians hoped that in this sense England would
become their friend.   They knew, in fact, that in
that sense England would be the most sincere
friend they could possess, because she would do
her utmost to hinder any other country from
occupying their land.

With this remarkable utterance from the Sheikh
Ali Youssef the conversation virtually ended.   He
was extremely anxious that nothing of his remarks
should undergo modification ; and as, from an
occurrence which he narrated in detail, with names
and dates, he appears to feel that he was not quite
fairly dealt with on an analogous occasion in the
past, it is to be hoped he may be well satisfied

with the manner in which the assurances returned to him have been carried out. " Our objection to foreign occupation," ran his parting words, "applies with the same strength to Turkey, were the Turkish suzerainty to become an active force. We do not object to the suzerainty as it exists, for our vassalage is but nominal. We should object to an occupying-governing suzerainty. We say ' Egypt for the Egyptians.' If we are exhibiting an inclination towards the French, it is the English themselves who have caused it."

I believe that neither the editor of the *Moaïad* nor the members of his party who are at all well informed would dispute the assertion that the circulation of that paper attains to scarcely one-half, perhaps not one-third, of the figure which can be pointed to in the case of the *Mokattam*, the daily pro-British Arabic journal. Let us now see what are the rejoinders from the standpoint of the *Mokattam*, as from that of the ¡ *Progrès*, the pro-British daily paper published in French, and owned by an Egyptian of Hellenic origin.

CHAPTER IX.

THE Sheikh Ali Youssef told me that the first
number of his journal *El Moaïad* appeared on the
eighth day of Rabi, in the year 1306, and it would
scarcely surprise any one to learn that a newspaper of such ostensible antiquity had veered in
its political programme since the period of its
foundation. That date, however, belongs to the
Mohammedan era, not to ours. It corresponds
with December 1, 1889. Consequently, the *Moaïad*
is but between six and seven years old, and has
found its reasons for a total change of conviction
within curiously narrow limits of time. In fact,
before halfway towards what even in the East can
be regarded as the threshold of maturity, the *Moaïad*
now presents opinions, averments, and demands
which amount to a complete reversal of its original
partisanship. What said the Sheikh Ali Youssef?
He carried on his anti-British policy in this leading
organ amongst the native opposition sheets, because

it was Great Britain who occupied the country; and he was pro-French, or, rather, was the ally of the French, because the latter pursued an aim professedly identical with his own. "Egypt for the Egyptians"—those are my sentiments, the sheikh insists in Ragab, of the Moslem year 1313, forgetting Rabi, of 1306; "*L'Autonomie de l'Egypte*," reiterates M. Cogordan, the French Consul-General at Cairo, in his familiar conversations—"that is what *we* want." France did not want any such thing for several generations, and only arrived at the vague formula ventilated by M. Cogordan some years after the discovery that she had made herself impossible as one immediate obstacle, any longer, to an autonomous Egypt. As for Ali Youssef, no one, while respecting to the full the rights and worth of all true national aspiration, will expect to hear from him, or from any other member of his party, a practical definition of "Egyptian" which would satisfy all Egyptians, or a practical scheme for the application of any Egyptian definition to the matter-of-fact process of autonomy. He himself has known this well, and his friends perhaps know it as well now as ever. We will turn for a moment to Rabi, 1306. The files of the *Moaïad* are here, accessible to any

person versed in current Arabic—to any competent translator whom any person wishing to
secure the actual text for himself, may choose
to employ.

It was upon the broad proposition that Egypt
must always stand in need of the support of a
Great Power that the Sheikh Ali Youssef started
the *Moaïad;* his corollary to that proposition being
that England, by her past acts, must be considered
as the country that would "just answer the purpose." England had been tried, both before and
after the occupation, and the ablest men of Egypt
had decided that she was a country which could
not possibly be improved upon "for the purpose."
The best policy for the Egyptian Government to
adopt, therefore, should be that of co-operating
with England, and of preserving the most friendly
relations with her. All the reforms which England suggested should be put into execution ;
nothing that France suggested could weigh for a
single moment in the balance. The most violent
articles ever published in any Arabic paper against
the French and their policy in Egypt appeared
in the columns of the *Moaïad* at its commencement, and were ascribed to the Sheikh Ali Youssef
in person. No doubt the susceptibilities of a

Moslem population rendered necessary the occa-
sional hint that some day Egypt would be "fit to
rule herself," but, in order that the hint should not
be taken too seriously by England, the broad
proposition, as above, and the corollary, always
followed upon its heels. This programme flourished
until a certain event occurred which showed how
relative in politics can be men's conception of a
truth. Riaz Pasha fell. It was to Riaz Pasha that
the establishment of the *Moaïad* had been due ;
and it was he who, favourable at that time to a
British policy, had procured the reinforcement of
the *Moaïad* by an enterprise on the same lines in
a different quarter. As soon, however, as the
Riaz Pasha Ministry fell, the attitude of its chief,
in opposition, became one of antagonism to the
British policy pursued by his successor. The
Moaïad at once changed its tone.

Ali Youssef, who had gone so far in his diatribes
against the French as to pronounce a curse upon
the French language—a fearful and portentous
extreme to the Mohammedan idea—reversed his
policy with a suddenness for which he could assign
no suitable explanation. Riaz quitted office upon
the question of Sir John Scott's reforms, to which
he objected; but the embarrassment discernible

in the first few articles of the *Moaïad*, after the change, betrayed the helplessness experienced by the managers of the party in the effort to select some solid ground for their resistance. An old subscriber to the journal informed me that the vapidity and constraint in this respect may be traced on for some time past the period covered by the first few articles, and that a definite line of action became visible only when the present Khedive had succeeded to power, and when differences resulted with Lord Cromer. The advent of M. Percher, who preceded M. Deloncle, gave the Opposition Arab broadsheets their new note— the formula of " Egypt for the Egyptians." M. Deloncle is stated to have drawn £3000 or £4000 from a Moslem theocratic fund, prior to his return into France a year ago, for the purposes of his campaign against the British occupation. The positive assurances with which his parting speeches at Cairo were enamelled led the native press to look for sensational developments by the month of October. According to the popular story, he picked up a glass while speaking to the organizers of his farewell banquet, declared that, as certainly as he should shatter the glass, the English would be forced to evacuate Egypt, and then threw it down, breaking it, by a not particularly difficult feat, into the predicted fragments. But he was also reported to have committed the imprudence of fixing the date; and he fixed October 1, 1895. Persons whose business it has been to watch the symptoms of fanatical impressionability agree that a certain effervescence became perceptible as the month of September drew to its close. In the *vieux coins et recoins* there was perhaps a whisper of a "rising;" but the motives lacked force.* If any such movement had been possible, as the outcome of wild words by European agitators, it would not have been an "anti-English rising" at all; it would have been an outbreak of the Moslem against the Christian. The motives lacked force. I was talking to a travelled Egyptian upon the subject of an assertion by Moustafa Kamel, M. Deloncle's *protégé*—unless the *protégé* of the two is M. Deloncle; and I was told that even extreme fanatics had the best of reasons for an avoidance of any rising against the English, whatever might have been the case if the "semi-rule" had been vested in some other nationality. Moustafa Kamel, lecturing to a French audience, accused the English

---

* M. Deloncle afterwards fixed April, 1896, as the month during which the departure of the British would be witnessed.

of insulting the Mohammedan religion and the
Prophet. " Why," exclaimed my informant, " the
tolerance which characterizes the English has
actually turned thousands and tens of thousands
of indifferent Moslems in Egypt into devout
Moslems. A friend of ours, a prominent Mohammedan in Syria, who visited Egypt before the
occupation, was terribly grieved to notice the
religious indifference which prevailed among the
people here, and he went back bewailing that
'Islam was dead in Egypt.' He had seen a
Greek coachman lashing the crowd in the streets
of Cairo, and yelling curses on their Prophet, because they obstructed the roadway, and no one
resented by look or gesture anything he said.
Our friend wrote in an Arabic periodical, published
in Syria, that Egypt was a lost country, that the
Prophet was cursed in the streets there, and nobody
paid any heed. It would be altogether different
now," observed my informant. " The English
have taught a new freedom and a sense of right,
and I think that an equal result has been a more
general and reciprocal feeling of respect. It would
not be safe to curse their Prophet to them now ! "
I asked for an explanation of Moustafa Kamel's
coadjutancy with M. Deloncle. "When M. Deloncle

made his first appearance here to agitate in the interests of France," was the reply, "Moustafa Kamel was the young man engaged to act as his interpreter. Moustafa Kamel had failed to pass examinations in law, and I suppose he found that the lecturing offered him an easy livelihood, besides bringing him into a notoriety which he could turn to account. He has an elder brother who is a man of real acquirements, and who is greatly incensed against him for the *rôle* he has taken up."*

* If this is the brother who was court-martialled for refusing to serve on the expedition into the Soudan, the example of Moustafa has, all the same, not been without its effects. Aly Fahmy Kamel, however, officer in the Egyptian army, may be a second brother. He declined to obey orders ; was tried by court-martial ; was reduced to the ranks ; and now accompanies his regiment as private. A Paris morning paper printed a two-column "interview" which a "Correspondent at Cairo" had had with Moustafa Kamel upon this case. The Cairo correspondent, unfortunately, had the air of having arranged an interview with himself; Moustafa interrogated, and Moustafa replied ; the whole thing read like Moustafa. And the account which the interview furnished of the hard case, represented Aly Fahmy as reduced to the ranks out of sheer tyranny, Great Britain having been athirst for vengeance upon Moustafa, and having struck at him in this way through an inoffensive relative.

On March 23rd, Moustafa Kamel addressed a letter to Lord Cromer, protesting against the "punishment of a man whose sole crime is that of being my brother." He concluded : "I beg you, my lord, to act against myself, if you judge my presence or my proceedings to be injurious to the Occupation."

On March 24th, the following reply was despatched to him : "Sir,—Lord Cromer instructs me to acknowledge receipt of your

M

To return, however, to the present programme of the *Moaïad,* Dr. Nimr, one of the two gentlemen of Oriental origin who own and edit the *Mokattam,* has been kind enough to favour me with comments, from the standpoint of his journal, upon the contentions put forward by the Sheikh Ali Youssef. " No reasonable being objects to the independence of his country," said Dr. Nimr, " but when they talk about the political independence of Egypt, what do they mean by it ? Press them to explain, and you find that it simply means that they want to see the country left as Turkey is left now—free for maladministration,

letter of yesterday's date, on the subject of the judgment pronounced by court-martial upon your brother, on the 21st inst. It is contrary to the practice of his lordship to interpose in questions of military discipline ; nevertheless, and in spite of the improper terms of which you have made use in the final paragraph, Lord Cromer has instituted inquiries with respect to the case to which you drew his attention. He finds that your brother Aly effendi Fahmy was tried by summary court-martial, duly constituted, and composed of an English officer and two Egyptian officers, on the charge of having intimated that he resigned his commission when he received orders to take active service. After hearing his defence, the Court found him guilty, and sentenced him to be reduced to the ranks. This judgment has been confirmed by the Sirdar, on the instructions of his Highness the Khedive. If, therefore, you have any reasons to submit for an alleviation of the sentence, Lord Cromer is of opinion that you should address yourself to his Highness the Khedive.—I am, etc. (Signed) RENNELL RODD."

oppression, and barbarity of every sort. If we wish for independence, we wish for guarantees of that independence. But what they want is an Egypt devoid of any guarantees for either good administration, or security of property, or personal freedom. There is no question of representative Chambers. We have an absolute ruler, and a certain number of officials, and the latter are at the present time very much as they were before the occupation, when it was admitted that no independence existed whatever."

"But is not the development of representative institutions implied in the *Moaïad's* programme?"

"Did you interrogate the Sheikh Ali Youssef on that matter?"

"No; I took it for granted."

"That is one of the proofs we are always having of the Western difficulty to realize the difference there is in the Oriental atmosphere and ideas. Remember that these are people whose standard is the lives of men who lived a thousand years ago; their aim is to live up to the level of their ancient Mohammedan teachers." The remark tallied aptly with what had fallen from a British official with reference to the limitations placed upon the functions of the elected bodies by the Dufferin Constitution

which created them. But for those restrictions
the provincial councils, and the assembly, or the
assemblies above them, would be found debating
topics almost incomprehensibly foreign to their
business, and would be voting resolutions based
on antiquated theology. " The Sheikh Ali Youssef urged that the present moment was the *moment
juste* for the political independence he talked of,"
continued Dr. Nimr ; "and to answer him upon
that detail, it happens that we have a test actually
before our eyes. Two branches of Government
have been left by the English entirely in the
hands of the natives ; the one is the department
of the Wakfs, who deal with property bequeathed
for charitable purposes, and the other consists
in the tribunals administered according to the
Moslem law. Now, I believe I can say that it
is acknowledged by everybody, by the sheikh and
everybody else, that these two are a long way
behind every other department of the Government. They stand in need of the widest reforms ;
and, in order that the reforms should be carried
out, Mussulmans themselves suggest that the
English should take them in hand."

"The sheikh was of the opinion that Egypt
might now be capable of assuming the lead over
Oriental countries ? "

" As an Oriental myself, I can say to that, that
the other Orientals are really ahead of the Egyptians, because they have more backbone. Think
of what this poor nation is, and make allowance for them in everything. They have been
downtrodden for ages. The rural population do
not credit you if you tell them that there is anything higher in the world than the banks of their
canals, or such hills as they may have heard of
in their own country. They call the Nile the
' great sea of the world.' When you can once
get them to understand your English ideas of
improvement, they admit you are right. The
irrigation is a proof of this. Take Sir Colin
Scott Moncrieff's success ; the great *barrage* had
been a French failure, but when the native population saw what could be done with that work
in English hands, they said, ' Well, after all, these
Englishmen know what they are about.'. If, however, Egypt were left to herself, on the programme
of the *Moaiad*, the old Moslem education would
naturally supersede everything again ; and that
is an education consisting of religious law and
literature, logic, Arabic grammar, and commen-
taries upon the Koran. To their mind, the light
in which you look at things seems extremely

unnatural. What we call progress, the vast majority of them do not regard as progress at all. If we are to suppose that the programme of the *Moaïad* does not mean the governmental predominance of the *Moaïad* native party, but that of the existing official classes not Europeans, then I say that the career of the *Moaïad* itself would come abruptly to an end. The Sheikh Ali Youssef would not be able to bring out his paper any longer."

Both Dr. Nimr and his partner, Dr. Sarrûf, pointed out that when the native Opposition press assailed the Ministry of Public Instruction, their attacks were found to depend entirely upon the presence, or absence, of particular individuals at the head of the department, and that they would praise at one time, and blame at another, an administration and a policy which had continued unchanged in the slightest degree. Riaz Pasha, for instance, had held the portfolio of Public Instruction, and when he went out of office the native journals which supported him misrepresented the most important actions of the department under his successor. At the present time, in the interests of a single politician out of office, the *Moaïad* habitually inveighed against the Ministry of Public Instruction ; and all the criticisms were translated into the French press as though they were valid from the point of view of British administration. Anything that might be uttered in France, thereupon, was then retranslated into the Arabic journals for the sake of its effect upon the native mind.

Among the principal passages of the Deloncle-Moustafa Kamel pamphlets and lectures the following wrung expressions of disgust from several Europeans, not British, to whose notice I brought them : " The English have introduced no financial reforms whatever. They have simply suppressed the joint control by England and France, to substitute for it a single control under the supervision of an English financial adviser, who distributes amongst his compatriots the greater portion of the budget. . . . As for the state of justice in the country, everything is disorganized since the appointment of an English adviser at the Ministry of Justice." Dr. Sarrûf, who is the editor of the scientific and literary magazine, *Al-Muktataf*, published at Cairo in Arabic, replied upon the former of the two heads that the whole sum drawn by Europeans in the Egyptian services was less now than prior to the occupation, and that it was

exceedingly questionable whether the English
received, in proportion to their numbers, anything
more than the members of any other nationality.
Nor were their numbers at all so preponderating
as was implied. I read to Dr. Nimr the paragraph—"Since the appointment of an English
adviser at the Ministry of Justice, everything is
disorganized. . . . Certain Egyptian patriots have
been obliged to address a petition to the French
Chamber of Deputies, demanding in the name of
the entire Egyptian nation the benefits of the
mixed tribunals rather than that they should
remain at the mercy of the English agents."

"Poor Sir John Scott!" exclaimed Dr. Nimr;
"he worked more than any one else for the
Egyptian Moslem. They were compelled to get
in Sir John Scott to make the machine of justice
work, and it was he who developed it and
smoothed it for them."

A further paragraph complained that "last
winter the English created a special tribunal,
which is a manifest abuse of power, and dis-
honours British civilization. The constitution of
this tribunal alone should furnish an idea of England's treatment of our unfortunate country."

"That was a court which was very much needed

as a check upon what had been going on," answered Dr. Nimr. "Several cases had occurred in which English soldiers and sailors had been badly dealt with; they had been murderously attacked by the low-class population, and some of them had been killed. The special tribunal is there to see that low-class miscreants shall not escape punishment in future, in any such cases; but, as a matter of fact, it has never yet held a sitting." .

Dr. Nimr recurred to the point that if the Sheikh Ali Youssef were to obtain his "political independence" he would not be able to subsist upon his journal, the *Moaïad*, and laid great stress upon the contention. "It would not be what you understand in Europe," said he, "viz. a popular movement. Ali Youssef would have no freedom of speech. His paper would be suppressed. At the present time we have freedom of the press in Egypt greater than the French possess in France. Whether the English stay or not, their presence here has been, now is, and, as long as they do go on, must continue to be, the grandest blessing that can happen to Egypt. As things now exist, we are perfectly sure that the people in office are not the robbers of the country. We

know that every man has a fair chance to succeed
who will try to succeed. The road to progress
is open now to everybody."

" What of the education ? "

" The Minister for Public Instruction is taking
the matter earnestly in hand. But, you see, the
difficulty about popular education here is that
the Moslems who talk, and write, and guide the
rest, have not the teachers themselves, and will
not accept them from outside. There are Mohammedan primary schools, with sheikhs from
El Azhar University to teach, but the instruction
is confined to Arabic, with a little, a very little,
arithmetic. A great need exists for popular
education. The masses would still be capable of
believing what they received as gospel from the
Tantah Sheikh in 1882, viz. that during the night
he had swallowed three of the British ironclads at
Alexandria, and that he was preparing, with the
aid of the Prophet, to swallow more. With regard
to the higher classes in the towns, the incoherence
which, prior to the British occupation, despatched
a man into the law who had been studying
mechanics, or into medicine when he had been
studying law, has latterly disappeared. I remember that, before 1882, we found a man who

had been sent by the Government to Paris as a pupil in agriculture, holding the exalted Government office of toll-collector on a bridge. Since the sensible and equitable British administration has shown them that all careers are open to them if they will properly equip themselves, the natives of the towns are crowding into channels which they had previously been accustomed to regard as not for Egyptians, but for Turks and Europeans. An Egyptian who studies medicine now adopts the medical profession afterwards, instead of something else. The old Egyptians may tell you that the number of native students at the medical schools is less now than formerly; but they do not give you the reasons. One of the reasons is that the studies have a more direct bearing now upon the subsequent careers; another is that the young men are attracted by the salaries paid in the Civil Service."

" How does Egypt under the British occupation compare with Syria under Turkish rule ? "

" Since 1882 the positions have been reversed. Fifteen years ago all the Arabic newspapers were published in Syria, and had to be brought here from that province; now they are published here, and go into Syria. Syrians who visit Egypt, and

see what has been done, envy us. 'What has
come over Egypt?' they say. 'Oh, if only our
country were as Egypt is now!'"

I asked Dr. Nimr and Dr. Sarrûf for their
opinion as to the real sentiments of the fellaheen
towards England.

"The Opposition Arab sheets tell their readers
that the English have made the Mohammedans
of India a downtrodden, poor, and miserable
population," was the reply, "and the fellaheen
say to you, 'Yes, we are very happy now; but
suppose the English are not satisfied to let us
go on as we are—suppose they take our wives
and daughters, and begin to treat us as they treat
the Moslems of India!' You assure them that
they have been misled as to this, and you try to
elicit from them some expression as to the per-
manency of the English rule. 'The English must
go,' they answer you, 'because Moslems must not
be ruled by Christians.' You speak about other
matters, and they make no secret of their joy at
the altered condition of affairs, their prosperity,
their freedom from oppression, their knowledge
that if official *backsheesh* has to be given, it is not
the English who exact it, or who profit by it,
and, indeed, that the English do their best to

save the fellaheen from it. 'Ah, if we could only count upon the English keeping up this glorious era!' they say. Then you come round to your first question, and you ask whether these words of theirs are merely empty words. 'No,' they answer, 'we are truly grateful to the English; but Moslems must not be ruled by Christians.' No fanaticism or misrepresentation, however, can blind them to the vastly increased productiveness of the country since the application by the English of the irrigation methods which they introduced from India. Do you know that we raise in Egypt, now, three times more cotton per acre than is raised in America? And there are certain projects, quite feasible, for largely extending the area now under cultivation."

To go into much more of the varied, practical, and anecdotic matter contributed by both partners might perhaps weary the far-off British reader, engrossed at home, as the telegraph teaches his Egyptian friends, with sudden problems all strange to the immense Mohammedan world.

"The Egyptian Question," summed up Dr. Sarrûf, "is the difference between Turkey and Egypt before and after the British occupation."

"Many of the fellaheen in Upper Egypt," added

Dr. Nimr, " now date after the Year of the Blessing, that is, after 1883. They say, in both Upper and Lower Egypt, ' Oh, this is the time of the Blessing,' and they fix occurrences as having happened so many years after the Year of the Blessing. We have published in our columns letters of testimony and gratitude, with the many signatures, volunteered, of the correspondents—in Arabic, of course ; and the attempts which have been made in the highest quarters to persecute those poor men—fruitless attempts in every case, so far as we know—have not prevented similar tributes to the English rule from others. When we receive such communications we print them under a heading which is a text in the Koran, ' Declare aloud the blessings and the gifts that are sent to you by God.' "

CHAPTER X

ONE further document, in the same form of local
and direct evidence. M. Kyriacopoulo, the proprietor and editor of the *Progrès*, and an Egyptian
whose long experience and intimate acquaintance
with the East renders his testimony of peculiar
value, reviewed the whole subject so comprehen-
sively, in the course of a talk at his office, that
I think I cannot do better than simply reproduce
his words.

"The Egyptian Question ought to be called,
from my point of view," premised M. Kyriacopoulo, "the Question of the civilization of Africa.
The commerce of the world is necessarily concerned in seeing that the civilizing and humani-
tarian work be undertaken by that Power amongst
them all which practises free trade. Unfortunately, the general interest does not always
weigh in the balance against separate political
considerations; and so we have the Egyptian

Question subordinate to the solution which may
be arrived at in the main question of the East
centering round Constantinople. If Russia succeeded in planting herself at Constantinople, it
would not be the civilization of Africa alone, but
your British dominion in Asia, which would come
into play. Mistress of Constantinople, Russia
would be able to organize naval forces in every
sea, and she would oblige you to maintain still
larger forces always in readiness, to defend, for
instance, the Suez Canal route to your possessions
in Africa as in India. I was well acquainted with
Sir Henry Bulwer at Constantinople in bygone
years, and, at a time prior to his appointment as
Ambassador, he did me the honour of discussing
Eastern politics with me frequently. He stated
to me that if the Turks persisted in refusing to
introduce reforms into their Government, England
would detach herself completely from all interest
in the Ottoman Empire, and would occupy Egypt
as a means of securing her own national interests.
The idea made an impression upon me at that
time; but, later, when I had studied the Eastern
Question rather more minutely, I perceived that
Sir Henry Bulwer was not a great diplomatist
if he really believed that England would be

safeguarding her interests by the course he laid
down—that is, by an abandonment of the Turkish
Question, which would leave Russia free to go
to Constantinople. It became, and still is, my
opinion that the *noeud* of the British future in
Africa must be sought at Constantinople. You
will object to me that you cannot eternally
hinder a Power like Russia, a great expansive
force, from descending towards the Mediterranean.
That is true; but what are the precautions which
England has taken in presence of that eventuality?
You will scarcely argue that you must wait for
the danger to declare itself before you adopt
precautions. The help you gave to the cause of
Italian unity was an act of justice which to-day
is bearing fruit; you are rewarded for that by
the possession of an ally, and of a *point d'appui*
to the west of the Mediterranean. What are the
precautions adopted in the direction of the east
of the Mediterranean? I do not see any. Nevertheless, a maritime element exists there which
ought not to be neglected—the Greek race. The
Greek race is opposed to the Slav, is anxious to
safeguard its independence, and seeks, above
all, to avoid absorption or inclusion by Russia.
If, however, Russia arrived at a domination of

N

Constantinople, the *rayonnement* of her influence, even if Greece succeeded in preserving her independence, would be such that the Hellenic element would inevitably gravitate towards the Russian centre. The consequence would be that Russia, which is to-day a great Continental power, but not a great maritime power, would then have procured the arm now lacking to her, and would have completed her forces.

"Turning from the general question to that of Egypt internally, I say that you have for you, firstly the bondholders, and, secondly, all the Europeans who dwell in Egypt and wish for an effectual guarantee for the future. English policy, by civilizing the Egyptians, will arrive at a conciliation of two elements at present opposed, viz. the native and the European. The masses in Egypt may be fanatical, but their fanaticism would be altogether inoffensive if it were not fed by considerations of a material order. Christian peoples do not sufficiently understand, perhaps, that the Mussulman religion itself is founded upon materialism. Excitations of the fanatical feeling arise in our own epoch as much from a social inequality as from anything else. The native, who for ages has been tyrannized and despoiled, has in our own epoch seen by the side of him the European, covered by treaties, protected by his consul, and prospering upon his advantages. It was largely to the envy and hatred thus pro- duced that the rising and massacre of 1882 were due. England, by her labours to ameliorate the position of the natives, and to efface the great inequalities that have existed, as well as by her development of the public wealth, and her gift of justice and liberty to the native, will reconcile the two elements by the most practical means. There is not a native who does not recognize at heart the benefits of the British occupation. If you talk with the poorer classes, the *petit peuple*, they will tell you that never, at any period of their history, have they been as free as they are to-day ; only, they fear to manifest their senti- ments because of the instability of the situation. They are not sure that this situation will continue. I will not enumerate all the good which the English administration has accomplished in Egypt. The most conspicuous benefit resides in the vast extent of land which their system of irrigation has brought into cultivation ; but a moment must come when there will be no more new land for the Department of Irrigation to place before the

people, with the means now at its disposal. If
it should be sought to augment still more the
surface cultivable, the English administration will
find itself confronted by a difficulty considered
to be insurmountable—the absence of credit, the
poverty of the finance. The Egyptian Budget is
the Budget of a country in bankruptcy. The
engagements entered into with the bondholders
before the occupation constitute the worst fetters
now for the wider development of agriculture;
the Government cannot apply its savings to the
great works of public utility which will be requisite
for the further extension of the arable area."

Here M. Kyriacopoulo touched the one pre-
eminent topic for the fellaheen, as connected with
the future. The *Barrage,* constructed by M.
Mougelle about fifty years ago, has already been
alluded to. It consists of sluices across both
branches of the Nile at a point just below their
separation, a few miles outside Cairo; the object
being to hold the water back for irrigation purposes,
instead of permitting wasteful flow into the sea.
The credit of the undertaking is commonly conceded to the French engineer named above; but,
apart from the fact that the work remained
partially inoperative until perfected by the British,

under Lord Cromer, it was not by M. Mougelle, but by a compatriot of his who preceded him, that the scheme was laid before the Egyptian Government. And, before either of them, the idea belongs to Mohammed Ali, that "barbarian of genius," as a British official terms him ; whilst, a score of years earlier than Mohammed Ali's notion of damming up one of the two river courses, Napoleon, who uttered a good deal of fustian in Egypt, but also detected the essential in much, declared that not a drop of the Nile water ought to be allowed to reach the sea at all. The dream for the future among those of the fellaheen who know what Upper Egypt is already producing, pictures some such structure as the present *Barrage* high up along the main bed of the Nile, with sections of canals performing in those regions that which they themselves have witnessed in Middle Egypt and the Delta. There will be land to be had.*

"That would be a work preliminary to many

* Their Opposition broad-sheets tell them pretty frequently, too, of a trans-Soudanese trade that might have been retained but for England. They are reminded that there was a time when, to put the same record in the words of Sir Samuel Baker, " fifteen English steamers were plying upon the great White Nile, before the Soudan was abandoned by the despotic order of Great Britain, and handed back to savagedom and wild beasts."

others of enormous usefulness to the country,"
proceeded M. Kyriacopoulo ; "but although there
are millions sterling in the Caisse de la Dette
Publique, these savings cannot be devoted to the
purpose, cannot be applied at all, because of the
past conventions with the Powers, and because
the latter cannot all be induced to consent. A
new conversion might be executed, but the Powers
oppose. No heavier injustice could be inflicted
upon a country in full development. If the British
Government wish to spare Lord Cromer the perpetual *rôle* of Sisyphus, it ought to advise means
for disentangling the Egyptian Government from
engagements that were taken in view of a situation
now non-existent. I do not believe that diplomatic dangers would result from such a course.
The interests of the bondholders would not be in
the slightest degree injured by the proceeding ; the
public wealth would be increased. The British
Government should declare that the engagements
of Egypt having been entered into at a period of
bankruptcy, and the country being now in full
financial development, and needing to be placed
on its feet, all such engagements are suspended
for the whole duration of the occupation. This
would be all the more just, as, having assumed the

responsibility by your occupation, you are entitled to have your elbows free for your task. As there cannot be rights without responsibility, there ought not to be responsibility without rights. The highest service has been rendered to the country, again, by the separation of the judicial and the executive powers, since 1883. It is no longer competent for a Governor, a Minister, or the Khedive himself, to intervene in judicial affairs. In Europe you can scarcely conceive what that simple separation of the two functions has done. The fellaheen feel themselves to be sheltered by a safeguard they never knew until then, and they are actually in far more easy circumstances now, with cotton at less than £2 per kantar, than they were when it stood at from £10 to £11 ; at one moment it reached £12. It is the simple separation of the judicial and administrative powers, not the efficiency of the tribunals—because these are still defective—that has worked this miracle. I say they are defective, because you have passed from one extreme to the other ; you have given the native judge too much independence before he has become fitted to use it, and judgments are delivered which are in contempt of the evidence, and amount to an abuse."

Questioned on the subject of Egyptian Opposition, the speaker added: "You have the opposition of the *classes dirigeantes*. Egypt has always had two markedly distinct classes—the one that dominated, the other that was ruled. The former had been successively the Nubians, the Assyrians, the Persians, the Macedonians, the Romans, the Turks; and the natives have been the *classe dominée*. We have now families which came into Egypt with Mohammed Ali, and a large number of Turkish families which migrated from Greece when Greece was declared independent. That is the class which has supplied the officers of the army, the governors, the Ministers—public functionaries in general. They have fused to some extent with the native element, so that in their houses these families talk Arabic rather than Turkish, and their number has grown by the addition of natives who were admitted to administrative functions by Ismaïl Pasha. As soon as they become Bey or Pasha, these natives exceed the Turks in oppressiveness; they have ceased to be natives, ceased to be one with the fellah. Guerrazzi wrote, '*Non vi e tirannia peggiorè di quella del servo divenuto padrone.*' There is no tyranny worse than that of the servant become master, and it applies very well to those natives promoted under Ismaïl. At the head of the class thus formed, you have the clergy and the chief of the State ; and it seems impossible that that class should ever reconcile itself to the British occupation, because you can never give them back what they have lost. Under the old corrupt state of things fortunes were easy to make. But this class, in striving against the British occupation, are wrong if they fancy that they could recover the possession of the abuses they have lost, should the *Maison Britannique* give way. If the English went away from here, all the people of that class would find themselves overrun or overthrown by the mass of the natives. Should the English yield, and leave us, there would be for a brief interval the strange phenomenon of a *chef d'Etat*, who is Turkish, using Egyptian instruments for a tyranny over the Egyptian people. But the first ambitious officer who, like Arabi under Tewfik Pasha, should raise the standard of revolt, would see the whole of the fellaheen group themselves around him. That would be so at the present moment, without the army of occupation. The presence of the British troops, and of Lord Cromer, acts as the counterweight to the absolute power of the

Khedive, and as a check upon it. You must not
talk `of evacuation unless you have lost your
reason, or unless you are satisfied with merely
making money, under no matter what *régime*,
and are indifferent to what happens beyond that.
Of course, the French understand the sentiments
of the *classe dirigeante*, and turn them to account,
but if the country could be told that the existing
situation is not provisional, your difficulties would
diminish as if by magic. You see, the native
population has the impression that the English
intend to go away at some time or other, and
they feel it to be a matter of life and death to
them to put themselves on good terms with those
who would then come into power, viz. the *classe
dirigeante* I have described. It is not a question
of patriotism ; the editors of the Opposition Arabic
sheets know that as well as I do, but they have
learnt to use the phrases which have a patriotic
ring. The harm is the consequence of Mr. Gladstone's repeated pledges. That man, by his shallow
conception of Egyptian conditions, and by his
never-failing talk, did more to wrong the fellah,
and more to retard the progress of the country,
than anything else that dates from the events in
1882,—or, I ought to say, not Mr. Gladstone, but

England under his influence. You were wrong,
too, in assuming when you came here that you
ought to govern through the governing class, and
limit yourself to the control. You ought to have
understood that the governing class is antipathetic
to the people. If you did it to gain the goodwill
of that *classe dirigeante*, you made so prodigious
a blunder that "—the speaker broke into a laugh—
" I can hardly characterize it." Adverting to the
scanty but invariable grounds of the opposition
by the French themselves, M. Kyriacopoulo ended :
" The French come and tell you such absurd
things that you might well marvel where they
have left their senses. For instance, they will say
that agriculture and the finances are in a terrible
state, when you know that the exact contrary is
the case, and they ought to know it, too. In fact,
they do know it. They have too much intelligence
to believe what they come and tell you. I wager
that among themselves they laugh at what they
have said. As for the 'neutralization' of Egypt,
you cannot *trancher une question* by a word.
We have to look at internal government here,
and what is 'neutralization'? If it signifies anything, it is 'internationalization,' which is precisely
the *régime* of privilege, confusion, bribery, and

hopelessness, of which the country had a bitter experience prior to 1882—of which the capitulations are a visible reminder—and from which you partially rescued the Egyptian people by the fact of your occupation in 1882."

CHAPTER XI.

RETURNING to Ismaïlia by the main line from Cairo, the traveller whose own term of sojourn in the country has reached its close feels for the first time, perhaps, at the spectacle of leisured people about to follow the road he is relinquishing, the force of the strange charm which Egypt exerts. These people may be the men of commerce for whom the certitude of a settled Egypt, insensitive to European diplomatic rumours, would mean the investment of capital at present holding aloof, though wanted ; or they may be mere cyphers in social distractions, contributing their share to a common useful end, unwittingly ; or they may be new eager Egyptologists, bound for the latest wonders of the recovered past. While still beneath the cloudless skies, and still within the spell, the traveller returning would perhaps wish to change his place with one of these ; even the invalid, semi-comatose, and " condemned " elsewhere, seems for an instant enviable, as he departs upon his way towards the calm, the rest, the magic air, the peaceful panoramas of the stately Nile in Upper Egypt. But Ismaïlia, as the half-way settlement along the Suez Canal, brings us into touch, however faintly, with all that lies outside. When the Oxford tutor of the present Khedive, Abbas, took his leave of Egypt after a twelve months' residence, he wrote of the pang with which, despite all motives for the contrary, he "turned to face the dreariness of Europe." Fifteen years have elapsed. At Ismaïlia, now, the visitors into Egypt from England are mingled with Australian colonists and British Indians, deviating from their homeward or their outward routes to pay their honours to the land in Occupation, and to see for themselves what their countrymen have done; and the relation of the news from Europe to the circumstances and the case of Egypt becomes, under the stress of recent developments, a topic for them all. Mr. A. J. Butler was probably thinking of England, solely, when he wrote of the dreary outlook in 1881. His pupil, Abbas, then seven years old, has since succeeded to his father, Tewfik Pasha; and if the present Khedive has not altogether borne out his tutor's description

of him, as "remarkable for his sweetness of dis-
position," he has eventually shown that he can
learn. Men have come, and men have gone. The
situation has altered. There were three years of
British rule, immediately after 1883, "based on
the principle of doing no good, and suffering all
evil ; " but neither in England itself, nor in Europe
generally, can there be said to be much dreariness
of prospect just now for the British subject or the
colonist, looking forth from Egypt. "We know
that we have stronger hands at home now," remarked one of the last of the business men with
whom I talked at Cairo — a Scotch engineer ;
"Rosebery was an improvement upon what we
had had before from the same party ; he was not
too weak ; he was just strong enough ; but, even
with Rosebery, we never knew what was going to
happen. As soon as the present Government
succeeded to the Rosebery Administration, the
Egyptian Question in Egypt—*in* Egypt—became
quite quiet." Some of the warmest expressions
of pride with respect to the task pursued by the
British in this country, proceeded from Australians.
One of the latter proved to be so little accessible
to the notion of any dreariness as connected with
"home" that he consulted me repeatedly as to

the likelihood of his arriving in England in time
to witness a snowfall. He had heard of snow-
storms on the Derby Day, and later. "Ah, it
evidently doesn't appeal to you in the same
manner," said he; "but I haven't seen snow for
ten years, and there's something so cosy about it!"

The wretched nature of the railway communication between Ismaïlia and Port Saïd was referred
to in the earliest of these chapters. As we crawled
onward I had ample opportunity of verifying
certain assurances not credited on the occasion
of the journey in the inverse direction. When
travelling from Port Saïd to Ismaïlia, I had been
told that the beautiful islet-dotted expanse, fringed
with palms, which stretched away to the horizon
on our left across the canal, was not a lake, but
mirage. "There is no water over there," had stated
the Suez Canal Company's British pilot; "that's all
desert." And desert I found it to be, on returning
along the same ground. Desert on the one side as
on the other; and at the bare line which had thus
been clothed in illusion the rim of the sun would
peer, and rise to-morrow, just as at this moment
it neared the bare line opposite to the west, and
dropped out of sight. In the gloom, the flashing
of the electric light from vessels advancing at their

snail's pace through the canal gives to that turnpike road of the world a mysterious and, indeed,
imposing character which it is far from possessing
under the light of day. Another of the three or
four British pilots employed by the Suez Canal
Company sat in the adjoining compartment of the
pinched carriage, and the sound of his voice, sometimes in one language, sometimes in another,
recalled the accents of his comrade, and the
linguistic proficiency of that comrade, on the
occasion when the vista of brown desert towards
Syria had been veiled in the counterfeit "due to
refractions of light."

Instances of the ease with which the British in
general who are scattered up and down the Levant
sustain their share in the polyglot conversations
thereabouts, became all the more noticeable from
the fact that a present neighbour was one of the
overrated linguistic Germans who are met with
abroad as travelling representatives of English
commercial houses. This gentleman, with good
English, but quite inferior French, and with no
other language apart from his own, intimated that
he travelled for his English firm from Spain to
Morocco, and from Morocco through Algiers, Tunis,
and Egypt. Another German, whom I came

O

across at Cairo, and who represented an extremely
important English manufacturing firm, had a
boisterous inaccurate kind of English, a lumbering,
irritating sort of French that must have cost his
employers many orders from French-speaking
customers, but good Spanish, which he required
for business tours through South America. The
managers of English hotels, too, were usually
Germans who had learnt their business, as they
acknowledged—when they did not boast of it—in
subordinate situations in London. " We work for
little, so long as we are learning," I heard an hotel-
manager say rather vengefully, to an Englishman
who had levelled the reproach that the Germans
underbid,—" but, when we know, we exact our
terms." The two particular cases above mentioned,
however, are types of several.   Both those gentlemen appeared to be in receipt of liberal salaries,
but I could not discover that they possessed any
special business gifts. On the contrary, the tedious-
ness of their explanations, a lack of real discernment
and tact, with an insistence upon their personal
opinions where they were clearly but half-informed,
seemed to ruffle and annoy some of the very people
with whom they hoped to conclude agreements ;
and no amount of suppleness or flattery, afterwards,

would succeed in removing the irritation they had unconsciously aroused. That they should be found filling such excellent situations for English houses must convey to numbers among their customers a poor idea of the capabilities to be reckoned upon among the English themselves. The strong points to be perceived in them were steadiness, and a martinet attention to their business. As a linguist the average German commercial traveller in the East is, of course, far outshone by the Levantine ; and if the latter's title to a responsible firm's confidence needs a great deal of guarantee, there are Englishmen and Scotchmen out here who have been born in the Levantine's own latitudes. A Briton has come out in the past, and has married into the nationality amidst which he has settled, and the children grow up to speak the languages that are all around them. I was introduced at Alexandria to a British non-commissioned officer attached to the staff at Cairo who was reputed to speak five languages. That seemed a respectable total, but on meeting him again accidentally at Cairo, and on inquiring whether it were the fact, I learnt from him that the figure should have been, not five, but eight. He was the son of an English

missionary who had gone out to Syria ; he had
been born in Syria ; and his languages were Russ,
Greek, Italian, German, French, English, Turkish,
and Arabic. The British authorities at Cairo are
well supplied with such cases. Egypt alone is a
school for Italian and modern Greek, to say
nothing of Arabic, French, and English. There
being small domestic and no parochial politics in
and about Egypt, international affairs are talked
by everybody, and many of us were asked, during
the recent "strained relations" with Germany,
why, with the German press and public adopting
towards England so unexpected a tone, Germans
were retained in any responsible English situations.
German sentiment was supposed to have exhibited
the greatest ingratitude towards a country which
formed the most secure and most profitable outlet
for hosts of industrious Germans, ultimately serving
the Fatherland. However this may be, the young
men who compete for scanty clerkships in the
towns of Great Britain can reconquer ground lost
to foreigners, and considerably embellish their
prospects, if they will take the trouble to acquire
—not in literary perfection, nor for nonsensi-
cal ostentation, but for practical use, as far as
the comparatively narrow bounds of commercial

intercourse—two foreign languages. It has not always been pleasant to hear a would-be patronizing German traveller, "manager" of a "foreign department" in England, talk in a lofty style about " my shorthand clerks," *i.e.* the English clerks who are placed under him by English employers, and who appear usually to be satisfied with the accomplishments of shorthand and type-writing, in which they can be undersold now by women.

Since the previous journey along the Suez Canal Company's foolish little line, fitful disturbances had continued in the Turkish provinces to be visited by the English missionary whose acquaintance I made at that time. When I parted from him, he was bent on purchasing cartridges for his revolver; I could glean no subsequent news of him. The recollection of the acquaintance brought to the memory his queer account of the Ottoman spy system in Egypt. The tale of a secret organization of which the members recognize one another by the fashion of wearing or carrying a rose, or of clasping the hand when walking in pairs, had a ring of the fantastic, nor did the useful purpose to be answered by the system become readily apparent. But futile things are, no doubt, what the Porte does habitually. The reverend gentleman in question stated that he had been in Arab *cafés*, discoursing with the native Moslems upon the Armenian grievances, when the entrance of a single individual, not differing outwardly from the rest, would either at once divert the conversation to topics entirely irrelevant, or empty the establishment.   At other times, said he, " men come in and relate stories, and after a while they give out a sign.   The ordinary people gradually disappear, until the only persons remaining are those who have received the sign, and who have information to lodge, or to exchange."   One of my informants in responsible quarters at Cairo put the total of such spies through the Turkish provinces at ten thousand.   The system is hollow enough in Egypt at the present time, but under a less wholesome *régime*, or under any new fanatical incentive, it might assume the character of a very stern reality indeed.   These are Ottoman spies, reporting in Egypt to the non-official agency which the Sultan set up at Cairo with Mukhtar Pasha—a reluctant representative of such business — at its head. What have they to report, I asked.   The " current thought of the country," was the missionary's response ; and under the existing *régime*, peaceful and prosperous, the reply seemed rather absurd.

"Any stuff they can concoct," was the response of my informant at Cairo. The latter quoted one of his own friends, a known Turkish spy—to be a spy for the Sultan is to be a great man—as avowing that "the bigger the lie, the better it is for us." It may be wondered by the reader whether any Intelligence Department devotes attention to such matters, in the British occupation. The answer to be met with everywhere in Egypt is, "Lord Cromer knows everything that goes on."

Allusions to the British Consul-General have hitherto been few in these pages. If Lord Cromer himself were consulted as to any narrative of benefits conferred upon Egypt by the British, he might confidently be expected to stipulate for no mention whatever of his name. The subject cannot be so dismissed. The onerous part he has sustained in this guidance of a country towards order, solvency, strength, and the brightest of outlooks, moral and material, may be well enough known within the country itself, and within every Governmental sphere in Europe, but is hardly understood at home among his compatriots in general. The frightful complexities and arduousness of the task, its peculiar delicacy, the sensitiveness of the whole undertaking to all sorts of influences unconnected with Egypt herself, must await the deliberate historian for an adequate measure of justice ; but they ought not to escape the popular attention altogether, while the man who has wrought so much for both England and Egypt continues at his post. These are no lines due to suggestion, interest, or favour. The attempt to portray broadly the Egypt of the day, Egypt at a stage of evolution, will have never departed from the completest independence of official opinion or bias, if any such there be. As a matter of fact, the opinion of a British official in Egypt is about as hard to elicit as anything can be in this world.

The sincerest testimony to Lord Cromer's value resides perhaps in the dread with which his eventual retirement is contemplated by all classes. Even the French and Turkish opposition can scarcely be described as pining for the day when Lord Cromer will be no longer in Egypt; for the successor might prove less tolerant. The mixed European community fear the departure of Lord Cromer, for the reason that his successor might prove less strong ; whilst the masses of the fellaheen look to the same prospect with anxiety

because his successor might prove less "paternal"
for them, and less equitable. If we consult the
British, whether they have settled in the country
before or since the occupation, we discover that
both the older type of resident, who thinks the
courbash ought never to have been abolished, and
deems the Arab incorrigibly ungrateful and men-
dacious, and the newer generation, who hold to
the virtues of a gentle and humane rule for the
native population, view the contingency with mis-
giving. The simple rumour that Lord Cromer
has been studying Turkish of late suffices to
depress the friends of the British occupation. Why
should the "King of Egypt," as he is currently
styled, need the Turkish language, unless he were
proposing to exchange Cairo for Constantinople?
So runs the argument, among supporters and
opponents alike; and the pessimistic fringe of
the British official circles at Cairo nourish their
gloomy forebodings upon reiterations of the in-
disputable fact that "we have promised to go,"
and upon stories of the difficulty experienced in
obtaining British candidates for the Egyptian civil
service. "So-and-So, just the man for such-and-
such a place, would not come out, because he sees
no guarantee for a career;" and somebody else of

exceptional fitness, who would have been well
inclined to disregard the " career," could not really
afford to accept, " being a poor man, and not convinced that it would last." We have promised ;
now comes the question, as Lord Cromer might
say, "whether we *can* go." It may be laid down
without fear of contradiction that Lord Cromer
himself does not see how England possibly can go
out of Egypt. Looking at the enormous interests
involved, it is in the highest degree improbable
that the whole machine would ever be allowed to
collapse ; but nobody—"nobody on earth" was
the phrase used to myself—has hitherto been able
to guarantee to British capital that the English
would stay ; and the investors who have held back
have been outrun by bolder or more sagacious men
of Continental nationalities.

British capital would be welcomed in Egypt by
the British authorities; but it must go there on
a large scale, and those who despatch it must not
imagine that they can reap a great deal by diplomatic means. Lord Cromer's answer to the complaint that tenders from home are shelved for
those of Belgian, French, or German origin would
be that the English must suit themselves to their
customers, and that when they offer a certain

article, and something else is wanted, they must either endeavour to supply the article required, or put up with defeat at the hands of people who do what the English either cannot or will not do. The contracts given out to foreign firms by Government departments are defended on the ground that the only general basis upon which such business can be transacted must be that of accepting the tender which is lowest. The British manufacturer at home is sometimes found by the representatives of his Government in Egypt to be a personage who wants a great deal of help, and yet to be very hard to help ; he is slow in adapting himself to a diversity of requirements, and he is bad at taking advice. In the matter of the locomotive engines, the grievance of the British contractors at Alexandria and Cairo, the case is regarded in official circles as merely one of underselling with a Belgian product which, although it would not have satisfied the people at home, satisfied the people here, viz. those who framed the specification and were going to pay the money. Lord Cromer cannot interfere to specially protect British industry. He pursues one aim—the development and happiness of Egypt. His answer to the charges that official *backsheesh* still flourishes, and, indeed, has increased during the past three years, would be, firstly, that no definite instances of any such bribery are brought forward ; secondly, that *backsheesh* cannot be eradicated by a stroke of the pen ; and, thirdly, that the British authorities in Egypt are "trying to do what Lord Cornwallis did in India in 1796," viz. to pay the Government officials upon a scale which will enable them to subsist without accepting bribes.   In this way, with prompt punishment when any such cases are discovered, the corruption should diminish by degrees, and should die out as far as human frailty may permit. " Until our time in Egypt," a British functionary at Cairo said to me, " a man could not live without receiving bribes.   Jobbery became inevitable ; and it existed everywhere." Lord Cromer's comment, again, upon the fact that the greatly·extended irrigation by the British since 1883 had virtually ruined a branch of British industry in Egypt, ought to be served up as often as possible by the three journals which champion the Occupation, to the unscrupulous French and Arabic press of the other side.   "Instead of having to buy pumps, the fellaheen get water now by a system of gravitation," said he ; "it is possible that the English may have suffered by the decline in the demand,

but that is part of our work in Egypt—that is the
testimony to what we have done." There are six
millions of fellaheen who know at the present time
not only that the irrigation cuttings bring the
precious Nile to the soil itself, but that the rich man
can no longer monopolize the water, or take it out
of his turn. Lord Cromer has been asked whether
he thinks that the fellaheen understand that good
has been wrought for them. "They understand
water and justice," he replied.*

⁻ Have the fellaheen short memories for the good
that has been done ? I have frequently heard the
point debated, and it ought never to be lost sight
of by the *Mokattam*, the *Progrès*, and the *Egyptian
Gazette.* They have not short memories for the

* An anecdote of the British Consul-General, in the midst of
divers recent diplomatic pre-occupations, has been retailed through
the polyglot gossip of Egypt with universal relish for an instance of
characteristic imperturbability. Lord Cromer is a player of lawn-
tennis ; and he was accustomed to meet three other followers of the
game, for a "four," every afternoon. The diplomatic situation
suddenly became acute. One only of the four attended at the daily
rendezvous. The other three, penetrated with a sense of the grave
difficulties in which British interests ought to consider themselves
all at once involved, deemed it the more seemly course, or the
more delicate attention to the chief of the *Maison Britannique*, to
stay away. Lord Cromer, who alone attended, was exceedingly
surprised, the story goes, that any one should break an appointment,
and exceedingly disappointed that he should lose his "afternoon
set."

performances by the French at the commencement
of the century.   They have not forgotten that the
French under Napoleon stabled their horses in
the mosques, and that when the French military
occupation collapsed, Napoleon's troops put up to
auction the Egyptian women and girls whom they
had appropriated.   When at the capital, I repeated
to a personage well situated to follow popular
sentiment throughout the country, the assertion
by the well-known Austrian financier at Alexandria
that a *plébiscite* through Egypt would certainly
yield a majority in favour of the British occupation.   " He might have gone farther," was the
response ; "he might have added that if the vote
could be secret, it would yield, not a majority, but
unanimity."

And what will be said of this, by way of testimony to the progress achieved under the British—
that a movement has latterly arisen in Syria for
union with Egypt !   A Syrian gentleman of independent position, and of the remarkable culture
which is the splendid fruit of the work done in
that province by the American Missionary Society,
admitted the existence of the movement to me
in the cautious words : " Many Syrians would be
ready, on a partition of Turkey, to propose to the

Khedive that Syria should be annexed to Egypt."
We have discussed the gratitude of the fellaheen ;
we cannot tell what gratitude is to be expected
from the Khedive. The latter is a young man ;
" we were none of us very wise, I suppose, when
we were his age," observed M. Kyriacopoulo, I
remember ; and in some things he is growing to
resemble his grandfather, Ismaïl. Those who can
speak of Ismaïl Pasha from direct cognizance,
assert that the resemblance can be traced in
personal appearance as well as in particular
attributes. He has had a tendency towards
dictation, however, which is all his own, unless
we seek for it still further back in the dynastic
progeniture. But, in the first place, the Khedive
Abbas II. is not popular in Egypt—the family
itself, being Turkish, is not popular,—and, in the
second place, his frame of mind appears to have
undergone a material change since his visit to
Constantinople last year. The story current in
Cairo is that, apart from the half-million sterling
which he was reported to have offered the Sultan
as an inducement towards joint action against
England, he addressed himself to the Porte in the
character of a useful ally. On arriving at Constantinople, he found that he was nothing but a

vassal there. The Sultan kept him in attendance day after day before he would grant an audience, then received him most haughtily, and, next, forbade him to quit Constantinople until he had received permission. For two months the Khedive was kept hanging about. At length, after an interval which had taught him *de visu* the real proportions of British power, he was allowed by his suzerain to return ; and, in order to conceal the fiasco, the Opposition Arabic sheets in Egypt represented to their readers among the fellaheen that he had been yachting in the Mediterranean, and had passed some time upon an island in the Archipelago which belongs to the Khedivial house. He has abilities, and up to the present he has exhibited a good deal of pertinacity. People say in Egypt : "The Khedive is under Lord Cromer; Lord Cromer is king." * At the

* The phrase has travelled as far as the columns of anti-British Continental journals, where its reproduction has been so managed as to convey the idea that Lord Cromer's compatriots are the people who bestow that appellation upon him, or that his lordship himself has usurped the title. Behind those columns are opponents whom the popular colloquialism unavoidably displeases. The man the least likely to be pleased with it, however, is the British Consul-General. No one who has been present at a meeting of the British Consul-General with the Khedive can have failed to observe the studious deference of his lordship's bearing towards the Sovereign of the State.

same time they are not altogether proof against
the little surprises which the Khedive occasionally
seems to arrange. Not to dwell upon the incidents
of a moment only, there is for numerous persons
a marked significance in his exclusive encouragement of the French at the Cairo Opera-house.
This public establishment is the property not of
the State, nor of private individuals, but of the
Khedive. It has a French manager; French
plays are performed there by a French company;
and the Khedive pointedly supports it by an
almost nightly attendance. I was told at Cairo—
the speaker was not of British nationality—that,
however inferior the French art might be that he
got there, the Khedive was determined to keep
out the English. A ridiculous detail in the
situation had been the attitude of the manager
on the arrival of the troupe. He displayed the
tricolour, assembled the company, and addressed
them in solemn terms to the effect that they were
here not merely to illustrate French art, but to
" uphold the *prestige* of the French flag."

A tribute must be paid, once more, to all those
British administrators who have severally succeeded in doing various things that had previously
been deemed impossible. Their most conspicuous

achievements we have seen.   But, quietly, without
self-advertisement, or airs of superior claim to
recognition,—in plain devotion to the work before
them for the time—they have done other useful
things, both in detail and in large breadth of plan.
They have to a great extent cured the native
Egyptian of his aversion to military service; the
conscription has now become almost popular.
They have organized an efficient police force;
have set up a coinage which substitutes for the
previous chaos a currency combining the pound
sterling with the decimal system; and they are
only debarred from pushing on a large scheme of
education by the absence of funds.

I have presented many witnesses in the course
of this inquiry; and, not in any instance, although
the evidence has not invariably been of identical
purport, have the depositions been in the smallest
degree warped or modified.   The conclusion shall
still be in the words of others: " I do not know
if the English govern everywhere as they govern
in Egypt," summed up at Cairo a native of high
and responsible position — a gentleman whom
Mr. Chamberlain saw and questioned very minutely,
when he was in Egypt—"but if they do, then I
say that they are sent by God to rule the world."

The Arabesque of language, and the Oriental decorativeness, may be pardoned in a man who has lived beneath the miseries of the misrule in the past. For an utterance in a different tone, and from a different source, but not less vigorous in corroboration, I may quote the verdict of a somewhat cynical Hellene, who closed a survey of human liberties and international politics with this paraphrase of a *mot* long famous—" *Si l'Angleterre n'existait pas, il faudrait l'inventer.*"

THE END.

PRINTED BY WILLIAM CLOWES AND SONS, LIMITED, LONDON AND BECCLES.

April, 1896

A

GENERAL CATALOGUE

OF BOOKS

PUBLISHED BY

CHAPMAN AND HALL, Ld.

LONDON

11, HENRIETTA STREET, COVENT GARDEN, W.C.

AGENTS FOR

THE SCIENCE AND ART DEPARTMENT, SOUTH KENSINGTON, AND

MESSRS. JOHN WILEY & SONS OF NEW YORK

FOR LIST OF DIFFERENT CATALOGUES ISSUED, SEE PAGE 47

NOTICE.

MESSRS. CHAPMAN & HALL NOW HOLD THE EXCLU-SIVE AGENCY FOR THE SALE IN THIS COUNTRY, ON THE CONTINENT, AND IN THE COLONIES, OF THE IMPORTANT SCIENTIFIC, EDUCATIONAL, AND TECHNI-CAL WORKS PUBLISHED BY MESSRS. WILEY & SONS, OF NEW YORK, AN AGENCY HITHERTO DISTRIBUTED AMONG SEVERAL OF THE CHIEF LONDON PUBLISHERS. THE VARIOUS PUBLICATIONS OF MESSRS. WILEY & SONS DEAL WITH MILITARY AND NAVAL ENGINEERING, ASTRONOMY, CHEMISTRY, ASSAYING, CIVIL AND MECHANICAL ENGINEERING, METALLURGY AND MINERALOGY, AND PHYSICS.

MESSRS. CHAPMAN & HALL HAVE A SPACIOUS AND WELL-APPOINTED BOOK ROOM ON THE GROUND FLOOR OF THEIR PREMISES IN HENRIETTA STREET, COVENT GARDEN, WHERE ANY OF THE BOOKS NAMED IN THIS CATALOGUE CAN BE INSPECTED, AS WELL AS THOSE PUBLISHED BY MESSRS. JOHN WILEY & SONS, OF NEW YORK, TOGETHER WITH A VARIED DISPLAY OF MODELS, DIAGRAMS, DRAWING EXAMPLES, INSTRU-MENTS, MECHANICAL AND OTHER APPARATUS, &c., &c.

A LIST OF SPECIAL CATALOGUES WILL BE FOUND ON PAGE 47, COPIES OF WHICH WILL BE FORWARDED TO ANY ADDRESS ON APPLICATION.

BOOKS

PUBLISHED BY

CHAPMAN & HALL, Limited.

ABOUT (Edmund).—*HANDBOOK OF SOCIAL ECONOMY;* or, The Worker's A B C. From the French. With a Biographical and Critical Introduction by W. FRASER RAE. Second Edition, revised. Crown 8vo, 4*s*.

ADAMS (Henry), M.I.C.E., &c.—*MACHINE CONSTRUC-TION AND DRAWING:* A Key to the Examinations of the Science and Art Department (Subject II.). Elementary. With numerous Illustrations. Crown 8vo, 2*s*. 6*d*.

———— Advanced. With Illustrations. Crown 8vo, 2*s*. 6*d*.

———— *BUILDING CONSTRUCTION.* Key to Examinations of Science and Art Department (Subject III.). With Numerous Illustrations. Crown 8vo, 4*s*.

AFLALO (F. G.) and PASKE (Surg.-Gen.).—*THE SEA AND THE ROD.* With Illustrations. Crown 8vo, 4*s*. 6*d*.

AGRICULTURAL SCIENCE.—*LECTURES ON AGRI-CULTURAL SCIENCE,* and other Proceedings of the Institute of Agriculture, South Kensington, 1883-4. Crown 8vo, sewed, 2*s*.

AÏDÉ (Hamilton).—*ELIZABETH'S PRETENDERS.* A novel. Second Edition. Crown 8vo, 6*s*.

ANDREWS (T. N.).—*A COMPLETE AND COMPREHEN-SIVE COURSE OF SCALE DRAWING.* For Students, Civil Engineers, and others. Crown 4to, 7*s*. 6*d*.

ANGEL (Henry).—*PRACTICAL PLANE AND SOLID GEOMETRY.* A Key to the Examinations of the Science and Art Department (Subject I.). Crown 8vo, 3*s*. 6*d*.

ASHTON (John).—*IN THE DAYS OF WILLIAM THE FOURTH.* With Illustrations. Crown 8vo.

AVELING (Edward), D.Sc.—*MECHANICS AND EXPERI-MENTAL SCIENCE.* As required for the Matriculation Examina-tion of the University of London.
MECHANICS. With numerous Woodcuts. Crown 8vo, 2*s*. 6*d*.
Key to Problems in ditto, crown 8vo, 1*s*. 6*d*.
CHEMISTRY. With numerous Woodcuts. Crown 8vo, 2*s*. 6*d*.
Key to Problems in ditto, crown 8vo, 1*s*. 6*d*.
MAGNETISM AND ELECTRICITY. With numerous Woodcuts. Crown 8vo, 2*s*. 6*d*.
LIGHT AND HEAT. With numerous Woodcuts. Crown 8vo, 2*s*. 6*d*.
Keys to the last two vols. together. Crown 8vo, 1*s*. 6*d*.

BAILEY (Captain H.).—*CONGO FREE STATE AND ITS BIG GAME SHOOTING, TRAVEL AND ADVEN-TURES.* Illustrated from the Author's sketches. Demy 8vo, 14*s*.

BAILEY (John Burn).—*FROM SINNER TO SAINT;* or, Character Transformations. Crown 8vo, **6***s.*

————— *MODERN METHUSELAHS;* or, Short Biographical Sketches of a few advanced Nonagenarians or actual Centenarians. Demy 8vo, **10***s.* **6***d.*

BAKER (W. L.).—*THE BEAM;* or, Technical Elements of Girder Construction. Crown 8vo, **4***s.*

BEATTY-KINGSTON (W.). — *A JOURNALIST'S JOTTINGS.* 2 vols. Demy 8vo, **24***s.*

————— *A WANDERER'S NOTES.* 2 vols. Demy 8vo, **24***s.*

BELL (James), Ph.D.—*THE CHEMISTRY OF FOODS.* With Microscopic Illustrations.
> PART I. *TEA, COFFEE, COCOA, SUGAR, &c.* Large crown 8vo, **2***s.* **6***d.*
> PART II. *MILK, BUTTER, CHEESE, CEREALS, PREPARED STARCHES, &c.* Large crown 8vo, **3***s.*

BENTLEY (H. Cumberland).—*SONGS AND VERSES.* Illustrated by FINCH MASON, and dedicated to J. G. WHYTE MELVILLE. Crown 8vo, **4***s.*

BINGHAM (Capt. the Hon. D.).—*RECOLLECTIONS OF PARIS.* 2 vols. Large crown 8vo, **18***s.*

BILLINGTON (Mary Frances).—*WOMAN IN INDIA.* Dedicated by permission to H.R.H. the Duchess of Connaught. With an Introduction by the MARCHIONESS OF DUFFERIN AND AVA, C.I., and numerous Illustrations by HERBERT JOHNSON and others. Demy 8vo, **14***s.*

BIRDWOOD (Sir Geo.), C.S.I.—*THE INDUSTRIAL ARTS OF INDIA.* With Map and 174 Illustrations. New Edition. Demy 8vo, **14***s.*

"BLACK AND WHITE," STORIES FROM. By GRANT ALLEN, Mrs. LYNN LYNTON, J. M. BARRIE, Mrs. OLIPHANT, W. CLARK RUSSELL, THOMAS HARDY, W. E. NORRIS, and JAMES PAYN. With numerous Illustrations. Crown 8vo, **3***s.* **6***d.*

BLOOMFIELD (Lord).—*MEMOIR OF BENJAMIN LORD BLOOMFIELD'S MISSION TO THE COURT OF BERNADOTTE.* With Portraits. 2 vols. Demy 8vo, **28***s.*

BONVALOT (Gabriel). — *THROUGH THE HEART OF ASIA OVER THE PAMIR TO INDIA.* Translated from the French by C. B. PITMAN. With 250 Illustrations by ALBERT PÉPIN. 2 vols. Royal 8vo, **32***s.*

BOS (Dr. J. Ritzema). — *AGRICULTURAL ZOOLOGY.* Translated by Professor J. R. AINSWORTH DAVIS, B.A., F.C.P. With an Introduction by MISS E. A. ORMEROD, F.R.Met.S., F.R.M.S., &c. With 149 Illustrations. Crown 8vo, **6***s.*

BOYLE (Frederick).—*FROM THE FRONTIER:* Sketches and Stories of Savage Life. Crown 8vo, **3***s.* **6***d.*

————— *ABOUT ORCHIDS.* A Chat. With Coloured Illustrations. Large crown 8vo, **8***s.*

————— *THE PROPHET JOHN.* A Romance. Cr. 8vo, **5***s.*

BOYLE (F.) and RUSSAN (A.). — *THE ORCHID SEEKERS*: A Story of Adventure in Borneo. Illustrated by ALFRED HARTLEY. Crown 8vo, 7*s*. 6*d*.

BRACKENBURY (Col. C. B.). — *FREDERICK THE GREAT.* With Maps and Portrait. Large crown 8vo, 4*s*.

BRADLEY (Thomas). — *ELEMENTS OF GEOMETRICAL DRAWING.* In two Parts, with Sixty Plates. Oblong folio, half bound, 16*s*. each Part.

BREWER (J. J.). — *CONJUGATIONS OF FRENCH VERBS, AUXILIARY AND REGULAR.* 2*d*.

———— *CONJUGATIONS OF IRREGULAR AND DEFECTIVE FRENCH VERBS.* Classified. With Notes. Limp cloth, 6*d*.

BRIDGMAN (F. A.). — *WINTERS IN ALGERIA.* With 62 Illustrations. Royal 8vo, 10*s*. 6*d*.

BROCK (Dr. J. H. E.). — *ELEMENTS OF HUMAN PHYSIOLOGY FOR THE HYGIENE EXAMINATIONS OF THE SCIENCE AND ART DEPARTMENT.* Crown 8vo, 1*s*. 6*d*.

BROMLEY-DAVENPORT (W.). — *SPORT:* Fox Hunting, Salmon Fishing, Covert Shooting, Deer Stalking. With Numerous Illustrations by General CREALOCK, C.B. New Cheap Edition. Post 8vo, 3*s*. 6*d*.

BUCKLAND (Frank). — *LOG-BOOK OF A FISHERMAN AND ZOOLOGIST.* With Illustrations. Sixth Thousand. Crown 8vo, 3*s*. 6*d*.

BUFFEN (F. F.). — *MUSICAL CELEBRITIES:* Portraits and Biographies. Second Series. Crown 4to, 21*s*.

BURCHETT (R.). — *LINEAR PERSPECTIVE*, for the Use of Schools of Art. New Edition. With Illustrations. Post 8vo, cloth, 7*s*.

———— *PRACTICAL GEOMETRY:* The Course of Construction of Plane Geometrical Figures. With 137 Diagrams. Eighteenth Edition. Post 8vo, cloth, 5*s*.

BURTON (Lady Isabel). — *THE LIFE OF SIR RICHARD FRANCIS BURTON.* With Portraits, numerous Coloured and other Illustrations, and Maps. 2 vols. demy 8vo, 42*s*.

CARLYLE (Thomas). — *THOUGHTS ON LIFE.* Selected by ROBERT DUNCAN. With a Photogravure Portrait. Crown 8vo, 1*s*. 6*d*. ; in paper covers, 1*s*.

    A limited edition on Hand-made Paper, 5*s*.

———— *THE CARLYLE BIRTHDAY BOOK.* Compiled by C. N. WILLIAMSON. Second Edition. Small fcap. 8vo, 3*s*.

*** For detailed list of the different editions of Carlyle's Works, see page 31.

CARSTENSEN (A. Riis). — *TWO SUMMERS IN GREENLAND:* An Artist's Adventures among Ice and Islands in Fjords and Mountains. With numerous Illustrations by the Author. Demy 8vo, 14*s*.

CERVANTES.—*THE LIFE OF MIGUEL CERVANTES SAAVEDRA:* A Biographical, Literary, and Historical Study, with a Tentative Bibliography from 1585 to 1892, and an Annotated Appendix on the "Canto de Caliope." By JAMES FITZMAURICE KELLY. Demy 8vo, 16s.

CHARACTER IN THE FACE. Physiognomical Sketches. Our Looks and what they mean. Crown 8vo, 5s.

CHAPMAN'S MAGAZINE OF FICTION. Monthly. 6d. Volumes bound in decorative cloth, in colours and gold, gilt top, 4s. Cases for binding, 1s. 6d. See page 48.

CHAPMAN'S STORY SERIES. A Series of Short Novels of Adventure, Action and Incident. Each Volume contains a Frontispiece and will be of about 216 pages in length. Small crown 8vo.

    1. *THE LONG ARM.* By MARY E. WILKINS, and other Detective Stories by GEO. IRA BRETT, ROY TELLET and Professor BRANDER MATTHEWS. With a Frontispiece by ADOLPH BIRKENRUTH. 3s. 6d. in cloth; 2s. 6d. in paper.

    2. *IN A HOLLOW OF THE HILLS.* By BRET HARTE, with a Frontispiece by ST. MAR FITZGERALD. 3s. 6d. in cloth; 2s. 6d. in paper.

    3. *AT THE SIGN OF THE OSTRICH.* By CHARLES JAMES. With a Frontispiece by ADOLPH BIRKENRUTH. 3s. 6d. in cloth; 2s. 6d. in paper.

    4. *THE WHITE FEATHER:* and Other Stories. By OSWALD CRAWFURD, with a Frontispiece by ADOLPH BIRKENRUTH. 2s. 6d. in cloth; 2s. in paper.

Other Volumes by well-known Writers to follow.

CHARLOTTE ELIZABETH.—*LIFE AND LETTERS OF CHARLOTTE ELIZABETH,* Princess Palatine and Mother of Philippe d'Orléans, Regent of France, 1652-1722. With Portraits. Demy 8vo, 10s. 6d.

CHURCH (Prof. A. H.).—*FOOD GRAINS OF INDIA.* With numerous Woodcuts. Small 4to, 6s.

———— *ENGLISH PORCELAIN.* A Handbook to the China made in England during the Eighteenth Century. With numerous Woodcuts. Large crown 8vo, 3s.

———— *ENGLISH EARTHENWARE.* A Handbook to the Wares made in England during the 17th and 18th Centuries. With numerous Woodcuts. Large crown 8vo, 3s.

———— *PLAIN WORDS ABOUT WATER.* Illustrated. Revised Edition. Crown 8vo, sewed, 6d.

———— *FOOD:* Some Account of its Sources, Constituents, and Uses. A New and Revised Edition. Large crown 8vo, 3s.

———— *PRECIOUS STONES:* considered in their Scientific and Artistic Relations. With a Coloured Plate and Woodcuts. Second Edition. Large crown 8vo, 2s. 6d.

COLLINS (Wilkie) and DICKENS (Charles).—*THE LAZY TOUR OF TWO IDLE APPRENTICES; NO THOROUGH-FARE;* and *THE PERILS OF CERTAIN ENGLISH PRISONERS.* With 8 Illustrations. Crown 8vo, 5s.

COOKERY.—

COOKERY UP TO DATE. By Mrs Humphry ("Madge," of *Truth.*) Crown 8vo, 3*s.* 6*d.*

ST. JAMES'S COOKERY BOOK. By Louisa Rochfort. Crown 8vo, 3*s.* 6*d.*

DINNERS IN MINIATURE. By Mrs. Earl. Crown 8vo, 2*s.* 6*d.*

HILDA'S "WHERE IS IT?" OF RECIPES. Containing many old CAPE, INDIAN, and MALAY DISHES and PRESERVES; also Directions for Polishing Furniture, Cleaning Silk, &c.; and a Collection of Home Remedies in Case of Sickness. By Hildagonda J. Duckitt. Sixth Thousand. Crown 8vo. 4*s.* 6*d.*

THE PYTCHLEY BOOK OF REFINED COOKERY AND BILLS OF FARE. By Major L——. Fifth Edition. Large crown 8vo, 8*s.*

BREAKFASTS, LUNCHEONS, AND BALL SUPPERS. By Major L——. Crown 8vo, 4*s.*

OFFICIAL HANDBOOK OF THE NATIONAL TRAINING SCHOOL FOR COOKERY. Containing Lessons on Cookery, forming the Course of Instruction in the School. Compiled by "R. O. C." A New and Cheaper Edition. (Twenty-fourth Thousand.) Large crown 8vo, 3*s.* 6*d.*

BREAKFAST AND SAVOURY DISHES. By "R.O.C." Ninth Thousand. Crown 8vo, 1*s.*

THE ROYAL CONFECTIONER: English and Foreign. By C. E. Francatelli. With Illustrations. Sixth Thousand. Crown 8vo, 5*s.*

COOPER-KING (Lt.-Col.) — *GEORGE WASHINGTON.* With Portrait, Maps, and Plans. Large crown 8vo, 6*s.*

COURTNEY(W. L.), M.A., LL.D.—*STUDIES AT LEISURE.* Crown 8vo, 6*s.*

—————— *STUDIES NEW AND OLD.* Crown 8vo, 6*s.*

—————— *CONSTRUCTIVE ETHICS:* A Review of Modern Philosophy and its Three Stages of Interpretation, Criticism, and Reconstruction. A New and Cheap Edition. Demy 8vo, 3*s.* 6*d.*

CRAIK (George Lillie).—*ENGLISH OF SHAKESPEARE.* Illustrated in a Philological Commentary on "Julius Cæsar." Eighth Edition. Post 8vo, cloth, 5*s.*

—————— *OUTLINES OF THE HISTORY OF THE ENGLISH LANGUAGE.* Eleventh Edition. Post 8vo, cloth, 2*s.* 6*d.*

CRAWFURD (Oswald). — *LYRICAL VERSE FROM ELIZABETH TO VICTORIA.* Edited by Oswald Crawfurd. With Copious Notes, Index of Writers, and Index of First Lines. Small crown 8vo, cloth, gilt top, 3*s.* 6*d.* net.

A limited edition of 50 copies, on large paper, numbered, levant morocco, gilt top, £1 1*s.*

CRAWFURD (Oswald), *cont.*—*THE WHITE FEATHER:* and Other Stories. **Chapman's Story Series.**

———— *DIALOGUES OF THE DAY.* Edited by OSWALD CRAWFURD, and written by ANTHONY HOPE, VIOLET HUNT, MARION HEPWORTH DIXON, and others. With 20 full-page Illustrations. Crown 4to, **5s.**

———— *A YEAR OF SPORT AND NATURAL HISTORY.* Shooting, Hunting, Coursing, Falconry, and Fishing. With Chapters on Birds of Prey, the Nidification of Birds, and the Habits of British Wild Birds and Animals. Edited by OSWALD CRAWFURD. With numerous Illustrations by FRANK FELLER, CECIL ALDIN, STANLEY BERKELEY, G. E. LODGE, etc. Demy 4to, **21s.** net.

———— *ROUND THE CALENDAR IN PORTUGAL.* With numerous Illustrations. Royal 8vo, **18s.**

CRIPPS (Wilfred Joseph), **M.A., F.S.A.**—*COLLEGE AND CORPORATION PLATE.* A Hand-book for the Reproduction of Silver Plate. With numerous Illustrations. Large crown 8vo, cloth, **2s. 6d.**

CUMBERLAND (Stuart).—*WHAT I THINK OF SOUTH AFRICA, ITS PEOPLE AND ITS POLITICS.* With Portraits and Illustrations. Crown 8vo, **5s.**

DAIRY FARMING—

DAIRY FARMING. To which is added a Description of the Chief Continental Systems. With numerous Illustrations. By JAMES LONG. Crown 8vo, **9s.**

DAIRY FARMING, MANAGEMENT OF COWS, &c. By ARTHUR ROWLAND. Edited by WILLIAM ABLETT. Crown 8vo, **5s.**

DALY (J. B.), **LL.D.**—*IRELAND IN THE DAYS OF DEAN SWIFT.* Crown 8vo, **5s.**

DAS (Devendra N.).—*SKETCHES OF HINDOO LIFE.* Crown 8vo, **5s.**

DAUBOURG (E.).—*INTERIOR ARCHITECTURE.* Doors, Vestibules, Staircases, Anterooms, Drawing, Dining, and Bed Rooms, Libraries, Bank and Newspaper Offices, Shop Fronts and Interiors. Half-imperial, cloth, £2 12s. 6d.

DAWSON (B., B.A.).—*JULIUS CÆSAR* (The University Shakespere Series). With Notes, Introduction and Glossary. Cloth limp, round corners, **1s.**

DAWSON (William Harbutt).—*GERMANY AND THE GERMANS:* Social Life, Culture, Religious Life, &c., &c. In 2 vols. Demy 8vo, **26s.**

DAY (William).—*THE RACEHORSE IN TRAINING.* With Hints on Racing and Racing Reform. Fifth Thousand. Demy 8vo, **9s.**

D'ORLEANS (Prince Henry).—*AROUND TONKIN AND SIAM.* Translated by C. B. PITMAN. With 28 Illustrations. Demy 8vo, **14s.**

DE BOVET (Madame). — *THREE MONTHS' TOUR IN IRELAND.* Translated and Condensed by Mrs. ARTHUR WALTER. With Illustrations. Crown 8vo, **6**s.

DE CHAMPEAUX (Alfred).—*TAPESTRY.* With numerous Woodcuts. Cloth, **2**s. **6**d.

DE FALLOUX (The Count).—*MEMOIRS OF A ROYALIST.* Edited by C. B. PITMAN. 2 vols. With Portraits. Demy 8vo, **32**s.

DE KONINCK (L. L.) and **DIETZ** (E.).).—*PRACTICAL MANUAL OF CHEMICAL ASSAYING*, as applied to the Manufacture of Iron. Edited, with notes, by ROBERT MALLET. Post 8vo, cloth, **6**s.

DELILLE (Edward).—*SOME FRENCH WRITERS.* Crown 8vo, **5**s.

DE WINDT (H.).—*SIBERIA AS IT IS.* With numerous Illustrations. Demy 8vo, **18**s.

———— *FROM PEKIN TO CALAIS BY LAND.* With numerous Illustrations by C. E. FRIPP from Sketches by the Author. New and Cheaper Edition. **7**s. **6**d.

———— *A RIDE TO INDIA ACROSS PERSIA AND BELUCHISTAN.* With numerous Illustrations. Demy 8vo, **16**s.

DICKENS (Charles).—*THE ADVENTURES OF OLIVER TWIST*; or, The Parish Boy's Progress. An *Edition de Luxe.* With Twenty-six Watercolour Drawings by GEORGE CRUIKSHANK. Royal 8vo, **42**s. net.

———— *THE CHARLES DICKENS BIRTHDAY BOOK.* With Five Illustrations. In a handsome fcap. 4to volume, **12**s.

———— *THE DICKENS DICTIONARY.* A Key to the Characters and Principal Incidents in the Tales of Charles Dickens. New Edition. Large crown 8vo, **5**s.

———— and **COLLINS** (Wilkie).—*THE LAZY TOUR OF TWO IDLE APPRENTICES; NO THOROUGHFARE; THE PERILS OF CERTAIN ENGLISH PRISONERS.* A New Edition. With fresh Illustrations. Crown 8vo, **5**s.

*** For detailed list of the various editions of Dickens's Works, see page 33.

DICKENS (Mary A.). — *CROSS CURRENTS.* A Novel. Third Thousand. Crown **3**s. **6**d. In boards, **2**s.

DILKE (Sir Chas.), Bart.—*THE BRITISH ARMY.* Demy 8vo, **12**s.

———— *THE PRESENT POSITION OF EUROPEAN POLITICS.* Demy 8vo, **12**s.

DILKE (Lady).—*ART IN THE MODERN STATE.* With Facsimile. Demy 8vo, **9**s.

DIXON (Charles). — *THE MIGRATION OF BRITISH BIRDS.* Including their Post-Glacial Emigration as traced by the application of a new Law of Dispersal; being a contribution to the study of Migration, Geographical Distribution, and Insular Faunas. With six Maps. Crown 8vo, **7s. 6d.**

——— *THE NESTS AND EGGS OF NON-INDIGENOUS BRITISH BIRDS,* or such species that do not Breed within the British Archipelego. With Coloured Frontispiece. Crown 8vo, **6s.**

——— *THE NESTS AND EGGS OF BRITISH BIRDS:* When and Where to Find Them. Being a Handbook to the Oology of the British Islands. Crown 8vo, **6s.**

Large Paper Edition, with 157 Coloured Illustrations. Demy 8vo, **15s.** net.

——— *JOTTINGS ABOUT BIRDS.* With Coloured Frontispiece by J. SMIT. Crown 8vo, **6s.**

——— *THE GAME BIRDS AND WILD FOWL OF THE BRITISH ISLANDS.* With Coloured Illustrations by A. T. ELWES. Demy 8vo, **18s.**

——— *THE MIGRATION OF BIRDS:* An Attempt to Reduce the Avian Season-flight to Law. Crown 8vo, **6s.**

——— *THE BIRDS OF OUR RAMBLES :* A Companion for the Country. With Illustrations by A. T. ELWES. Large Crown 8vo, **7s. 6d.**

——— *IDLE HOURS WITH NATURE.* With Frontispiece. Crown 8vo, **6s.**

——— *ANNALS OF BIRD LIFE :* A Year-Book of British Ornithology. With Illustrations. Crown 8vo, **7s. 6d.**

DOUGLAS (John).—*SKETCH OF THE FIRST PRINCIPLES OF PHYSIOGRAPHY.* With Maps and numerous Illustrations. Crown 8vo, **6s.**

DRAYSON (Major-General A. W.).—*THIRTY THOUSAND YEARS OF THE EARTH'S PAST HISTORY.* Large Crown 8vo, **5s.**

——— *EXPERIENCES OF A WOOLWICH PROFESSOR* during Fifteen Years at the Royal Military Academy. Demy 8vo, **8s.**

DUCKITT (Hildagonda J.).—*HILDA'S "WHERE IS IT?" OF RECIPES.* Containing many old CAPE, INDIAN, and MALAY DISHES and PRESERVES ; also Directions for Polishing Furniture, Cleaning silk, etc. Sixth Thousand. Crown 8vo, **4s. 6d.**

DUCOUDRAY (Gustave).—*THE HISTORY OF ANCIENT CIVILIZATION.* A Handbook based upon M. Gustave Ducoudray's " Histoire Sommaire de la Civilisation." Edited by REV. J. VERSCHOYLE, M.A. With Illustrations. Large crown 8vo, **6s.**

——— *THE HISTORY OF MODERN CIVILIZATION.* With Illustrations. Large crown 8vo, **9s.**

DUNCAN (Robert).—*THOUGHTS ON LIFE.* By THOMAS CARLYLE. Selected by ROBERT DUNCAN. With a Photogravure Portrait of CARLYLE. Crown 8vo, **1s. 6d.** ; in paper covers, **1s.** A Limited Edition on Hand-made paper, **5s.**

DYCE (William), **R.A.** — *DRAWING-BOOK OF THE GOVERNMENT SCHOOL OF DESIGN.* Fifty selected Plates. Folio, sewed, **5s.** net; mounted, **18s.** net.

———— *ELEMENTARY OUTLINES OF ORNAMENT.* Plates I. to XXII., containing 97 Examples, adapted for Practice of Standards I. to IV. Small folio, sewed, **2s. 6d.** net.

———— *SELECTION FROM DYCE'S DRAWING-BOOK.* 15 Plates, sewed, **1s. 6d.** net; mounted on cardboard, **6s. 6d.** net.

———— *TEXT TO ABOVE.* Crown 8vo, sewed, **6d.**

EARL (Mrs.).—*DINNERS IN MINIATURE.* Crown 8vo, **2s. 6d.**

ELLIOT (Frances Minto).—*OLD COURT LIFE IN SPAIN.* 2 vols. Demy 8vo, **24s.**

ELLIS (**A. B.**).—*THE YORUBA-SPEAKING PEOPLES OF THE SLAVE COAST OF WEST AFRICA:* their Religion, Manners, Customs, Laws, Language, &c. With an Appendix and Map. Demy 8vo, **10s. 6d.**

———— *HISTORY OF THE GOLD COAST OF WEST AFRICA.* Demy 8vo, **10s. 6d.**

———— *SOUTH AFRICAN SKETCHES.* Crown 8vo, **6s.**

ENGEL(Carl).—*MUSICAL INSTRUMENTS.* With numerous Woodcuts. Large crown 8vo, **2s. 6d.**

ESCOTT (**T. H. S.**).—*POLITICS AND LETTERS.* Demy 8vo, **9s.**

———— *ENGLAND:* Its People, Polity, and Pursuits. New and Revised Edition. Eighth Thousand. Demy 8vo, **3s. 6d.**

FANE (Violet).—*AUTUMN SONGS.* Crown 8vo, **6s.**

———— *THE STORY OF HELEN DAVENANT.* Crown 8vo, **3s. 6d.** In boards, **2s.**

FISHER (**W. E. Garret**).—*THE TRANSVAAL AND THE BOERS:* a Brief History. Crown 8vo.

FISKE (John).—*LIFE AND LETTERS OF EDWARD LIVINGSTONE YOUMANS.* Comprising Correspondence with Spencer, Huxley, Tyndall, and others. Crown 8vo, **8s.**

FITZGERALD (Percy), **F.S.A.**—*HENRY IRVING:* A Record of Twenty Years at the Lyceum. With Portrait. Demy 8vo, **14s.**

———— *CHRONICLES OF BOW STREET POLICE OFFICE.* New and Cheaper Edition.

———— *THE HISTORY OF PICKWICK.* An Account of its Characters, Localities, Allusions and Illustrations. With a Bibliography. Demy 8vo, **8s.**

FLEMING (George), **F.R.C.S.** — *ANIMAL PLAGUES:* Their History, Nature, and Prevention. 8vo. cloth, **15s.**

———— *PRACTICAL HORSE-SHOEING.* With 37 Illustrations. Fifth Edition, enlarged. 8vo, sewed, **2s.**

———— *RABIES AND HYDROPHOBIA:* Their History Nature, Causes, Symptoms, and Prevention. With 8 Illustrations. 8vo, cloth, **15s.**

FORSTER (The Rt. Hon. W. E.).—*THE LIFE OF THE RIGHT HON. W. E. FORSTER.* By Sir T. WEMYSS REID. With Portraits. Sixth Edition, with Gilt Edges. Demy 8vo, 6s.

FORSTER (John).—*WALTER SAVAGE LANDOR:* A Biography. A New Edition, with Portraits. Demy 8vo, 7s. 6d.

—————— *THE LIFE OF CHARLES DICKENS.* Uniform with the Illustrated Library Edition of Dickens's Works. 2 vols. Demy 8vo, 20s.

Uniform with the "C. D." Edition. With Numerous Illustrations. 2 vols. 7s.

Uniform with the Crown Edition. Crown 8vo, 5s.

Uniform with the Household Edition. With Illustrations by F. BARNARD. Crown 4to, cloth, 5s.

Uniform with the Pictorial Edition. With 40 Illustrations by F. BARNARD and others. Royal 8vo, 3s. 6d.

FORTNIGHTLY REVIEW (The). Published Monthly, 2s. 6d. See page 48.

FORTNUM (C. D. E.), F.S A.—*MAIOLICA.* With numerous Woodcuts. Large crown, 8vo, cloth, 2s. 6d.

—————— *BRONZES.* With numerous Woodcuts. Large crown 8vo, cloth, 2s. 6d.

FOSTER (A. J.), M.A.—*ROUND ABOUT THE CROOKED SPIRE.* With Illustrations. Crown 8vo, 5s.

FOUQUÉ (De la Motte).—*UNDINE:* a Romance translated from the German. With an Introduction by JULIA CARTWRIGHT. Illustrated by HEYWOOD SUMNER. Crown 4to, 5s.

FRANCATELLI (C. E.).—*THE ROYAL CONFECTIONER:* English and Foreign. A Practical Treatise. With Illustrations. Sixth Thousand. Crown 8vo, 5s.

FRANKS (A. W.).—*JAPANESE POTTERY.* Being a Native Report, with an Introduction and Catalogue. With Numerous Illustrations and Marks. Large Crown 8vo, cloth, 2s. 6d.

FRÖBEL (Friedrich).—*A SHORT SKETCH OF THE LIFE OF FRIEDRICH FRÖBEL.* Together with a Notice of Madame von Marenholtz Bülow's Personal Recollections of F. Fröbel. A New Edition, including Fröbel's Letters from Dresden and Leipzig to his Wife, now first Translated into English. By EMILY SHIRREFF. Crown 8vo, 2s.

FYLER (Colonel).—*THE HISTORY OF THE 50th (THE QUEEN'S OWN) REGIMENT.* From the Earliest Date to the Year 1881. With Coloured Illustrations, Maps, and Plans. Crown 4to, 15s. net.

GARDNER (J. Starkie).—*IRONWORK.* From the Earliest Time to the End of the Mediæval Period. With 57 Illustrations. Large Crown 8vo, 3s.

GASNAULT (P.) and GARNIER (E.).—*FRENCH POTTERY.* With Illustrations and Marks. Large crown 8vo, 3s.

GILLMORE (Parker).—*THE HUNTER'S ARCADIA.* With numerous Illustrations. Demy 8vo, 10*s.* 6*d.*

GINGELL (Julia R.). — *APHORISMS FROM THE WRITINGS OF HERBERT SPENCER.* Second Edition, revised, with Photogravure Portrait of Herbert Spencer. Cr. 8vo, 3*s.*

GONNER (E. C. K.,) M.A.—*POLITICAL ECONOMY.* Crown 8vo, 2*s.*

GORDON (General).—*LETTERS FROM THE CRIMEA, THE DANUBE, AND ARMENIA.* Edited by DEMETRIUS C. BOULGER. Second Edition. Crown 8vo, 5*s.*

GORE (J. E.,) F.R.A.S.—*PLANETARY AND STELLAR STUDIES.* Illustrated. Crown 8vo, 5*s.*

——— *THE SCENERY OF THE HEAVENS.* New Edition. With many very beautiful Illustrations, Photographs, &c., of Star Clusters and Nebulæ, from the Original Photographs, taken at the Paris Observatory. Crown 8vo, 6*s.*

——— *ASTRONOMICAL LESSONS.* Profusely Illustrated. Cloth, 2*s.*

GORST (Sir J. E.), Q.C.—*AN ELECTION MANUAL.* Containing the Parliamentary Elections (Corrupt and Illegal Practices) Act, 1883, with Notes. Third Edition. Crown 8vo, 1*s.* 6*d.*

GOWER (A. R.).—*AN ELEMENTARY TEXT-BOOK OF PRACTICAL METALLURGY.* With Illustrations. Crown 8vo, 3*s.*

GRESWELL (W.), M.A.—*OUR SOUTH AFRICAN EMPIRE.* With Map. 2 vols. Crown 8vo, 21*s.*

GREVILLE-NUGENT(Hon. Mrs.).—*A LAND OF MOSQUES AND MARABOUTS.* Illustrated. Demy 8vo, 14*s.*

GRIFFIN (Sir Lepel).—*THE GREAT REPUBLIC.* Second Edition. Crown 8vo, 4*s.* 6*d.*

GRIFFITHS (Major Arthur). — *CRIMINALS I HAVE KNOWN.* With Illustrations by G. GULICH. Crown 8vo, 6*s.*

——— *CHRONICLES OF NEWGATE.* A New and Revised Edition. With Illustrations. Crown 8vo, 6*s.*

——— *SECRETS OF THE PRISON HOUSE.* With Illustrations by G. D. ROWLANDSON. 2 vols. Demy 8vo, 30*s.*

——— *FRENCH REVOLUTIONARY GENERALS.* Large crown 8vo, 6*s.*

GRINNELL (G. B.).—*THE STORY OF THE INDIAN.* With Illustrations. Crown 8vo, 6*s.*

GUNDRY (R. S.).—*CHINA, PRESENT AND PAST.* Foreign Intercourse, Progress and Resources, the Missionary Question, &c., &c. With Map. Demy 8vo, 10*s.* 6*d.*

HALL (Sidney).—*A TRAVELLING ATLAS OF THE ENGLISH COUNTIES.* Fifty Maps, coloured. New Edition including the Railways. Demy 8vo, in roan tuck, 10*s.* 6*d.*

HARPER (Charles G.).—*THE DOVER ROAD:* Annals of an Ancient Turnpike. With numerous Illustrations from Drawings by the Author, and from old-time Prints. Demy 8vo, 16*s.*

———— *THE PORTSMOUTH ROAD AND ITS TRIBU-TARIES TO-DAY AND IN DAYS OF OLD.* With 85 Illustrations from Drawings by the Author and from old-time prints. Demy 8vo, 16*s.*

———— *THE MARCHES OF WALES:* Notes and Impressions on the Welsh Borders, from the Severn Sea to the Sands o' Dee. With 114 Illustrations. Demy 8vo, 16*s.* ·

———— *A PRACTICAL HANDBOOK OF DRAWING,* for modern methods of Reproduction, with many Illustrations showing comparative results. Crown 8vo, 7*s.* 6*d.*

HARRISON (John).—*THE DECORATION OF METALS, CHASING, REPOUSSÉ AND SAW PIERCING.* With 180 Illustrations. Crown 8vo, 3*s.* 6*d.*

HARTE (Bret). — *IN A HOLLOW OF THE HILLS.* Chapman's Story Series.

HARTINGTON (E.)—*THE NEW ACADEME:* An Educational Romance. Crown 8vo, 5*s.*

HASTINGS (Warren). — *THE LIFE OF WARREN HASTINGS.* First Governor-General of India. By COLONEL G. B. MALLESON, C.S.I. With Portrait. Demy 8vo, 18*s.*

HATTON (R. G.).—*GUIDE TO THE ESTABLISHMENT AND EQUIPMENT OF ART CLASSES AND SCHOOLS OF ART.* With Estimates of probable Cost, &c. Paper Wrapper, 1*s.*

———— *FIGURE DRAWING AND COMPOSITION:* Being a number of hints for the student and designer upon the treatment of the human figure. With numerous Illustrations. Large crown 8vo, 9*s.*

———— *ELEMENTARY DESIGN:* being a Theoretical and Practical Introduction in the Art of Decoration. With 110 Illustrations. Second Edition Enlarged. Crown 8vo, 2*s.* 6*d.*

HAY (Rev. James).—*SWIFT:* The Mystery of his Life and Love. Crown 8vo, 6*s*

HENRY (Re).—*QUEEN OF BEAUTY:* or, The Adventures of Prince Elfreston. Illustrated by JOHN JELLICOE. Square 8vo, 6*s.*

HILDEBRAND (Hans).—*INDUSTRIAL ARTS OF SCANDINAVIA IN THE PAGAN TIME.* With numerous Woodcuts. Large crown 8vo, 2*s.* 6*d.*

HOLBEIN. — *TWELVE HEADS AFTER HOLBEIN.* Selected from Drawings in Her Majesty's Collection at Windsor. Reproduced in Autotype, in portfolio. £1 16*s.* net.

HOLMES (G. C. V.).—*NAVAL ARCHITECTURE AND SHIPBUILDING.* [*In the Press.*

———— *MARINE ENGINES AND BOILERS.* With Sixty-nine Woodcuts. Large crown 8vo, 3*s.*

HOPE (Andrée).—*THE VYVYANS;* or, The Murder in the Rue Bellechasse. Crown 8vo, 3*s.* 6*d.*

HOPE (Anthony) and others.—*DIALOGUES OF THE DAY.* Edited by OSWALD CRAWFURD, and written by ANTHONY HOPE, VIOLET HUNT, CLARA SAVILLE CLARKE, MARION HEPWORTH DIXON, SQUIRE SPRIGGE, Mrs. CRACKANTHORPE, Mrs. ERNEST LEVERSON, GERTRUDE KINGSTON, the EDITOR, and others. With 20 Full-page Illustrations. Crown 4to, 5s.

HOUSSAYE (Arsene).—*BEHIND THE SCENES OF THE COMÉDIE FRANCAISE, AND OTHER RECOLLECTIONS.* Translated from the French. Demy 8vo, 14s.

HOVELACQUE (Abel).—*THE SCIENCE OF LANGUAGE:* Linguistics, Philology, and Etymology. With Maps. Large crown 8vo, cloth, 3s. 6d.

HOZIER (H. M.). — *TURENNE.* With Portrait and Two Maps. Large crown 8vo, 4s.

HUDSON (W. H.), C.M.Z.S.—*BIRDS IN A VILLAGE.* Square Crown 8vo, 7s. 6d.

——— *IDLE DAYS IN PATAGONIA.* With numerous Illustrations by J. SMIT and A. HARTLEY. Demy 8vo, 14s.

——— *THE NATURALIST IN LA PLATA.* With numerous Illustrations by J. SMIT. Third Edition. Demy 8vo, 8s.

HUDSON (Prof. W. H.).—*THE PHILOSOPHY OF HER-BERT SPENCER.* (An Introduction to). With a Biographical Sketch. Second Edition. Crown 8vo, 5s.

HUEFFER (F.).—*HALF A CENTURY OF MUSIC IN ENGLAND.* 1837—1887. Demy 8vo, 8s.

HUGHES (W. R.).—*A WEEK'S TRAMP IN DICKENS-LAND.* With upwards of 100 Illustrations by F. G. KITTON, HERBERT RAILTON, and others. Second Edition. Demy 8vo, 7s. 6d.

HUMPHRY (Mrs.).—*COOKERY UP TO DATE.* Crown 8vo, 3s. 6d.

HUNT (Violet).—*A HARD WOMAN.* A Story in Scenes. Second Edition. Crown 8vo, 6s.

——— *THE MAIDEN'S PROGRESS:* A Novel in Dialogue. Crown 8vo, 6s.

HUNTLY (Marquis of). — *TRAVELS, SPORTS, AND POLITICS IN THE EAST OF EUROPE.* With Illustrations. Large crown 8vo, 12s.

HUTCHINSON (Rev. H. N.).—*CREATURES OF OTHER DAYS.* With a Preface by SIR W. H. FLOWER, K.C.B., F.R.S., and numerous Illustrations by J. SMIT and others. A Cheaper Edition. Large crown 8vo, 6s.

——— *EXTINCT MONSTERS.* A Popular Account of some of the larger forms of Ancient Animal Life. With numerous Illustrations by J. SMIT and others. A Cheaper Edition. Revised and Enlarged. Large crown 8vo, 6s.

INDUSTRIAL ARTS: Historical Sketches. With numerous Illustrations. Large crown 8vo, 3s.

IRVING (Henry).—*A RECORD OF TWENTY YEARS AT THE LYCEUM.* By PERCY FITZGERALD, M.A., F.S.A. With Portrait. Demy 8vo, 14s.

JACKSON (F. G.). — *THEORY AND PRACTICE OF DESIGN:* An Advanced Text Book on Decorative Art. With 700 Illustrations. Large crown 8vo, 9s.

———— *DECORATIVE DESIGN.* An Elementary Text Book of Principles and Practice. With numerous Illustrations. Fourth Thousand. Crown 8vo, 7s. 6d.

JAMES (Charles).—*AT THE SIGN OF THE OSTRICH.* Chapman's Story Series.

JAMES (H. A.).—*HANDBOOK TO PERSPECTIVE.* Crown 8vo, 2s. 6d.

———— *PERSPECTIVE CHARTS,* for Use in Class Teaching. 2s.

JEAFFRESON (J. Cordy). — *MIDDLESEX COUNTY RECORDS.* Indictments, Recognisances, Coroners' Inquisitions Post Mortem, Orders, Memoranda, and Certificates of Convictors of Conventiclers, *temp.* 19 Charles II. to 4 James II. With Portraits, Illustrations, and Facsimiles. 4 vols. Demy 8vo, 25s. each.

JEANS (W. T.).—*CREATORS OF THE AGE OF STEEL.* Memoirs of Sir W. Siemens, Sir H. Bessemer, Sir J. Whitworth, Sir J. Brown, and other Inventors. Second Edition. Crown 8vo, 7s. 6d.

JOKAI (Maurus).—*PRETTY MICHAL.* Translated by R. NISBET BAIN. Crown 8vo, 3s. 6d. In boards, 2s.

———— *'MIDST THE WILD CARPATHIANS.* Translated by R. NISBET BAIN. Crown 8vo, 3s. 6d.

JOPLING (Louise).—*HINTS TO AMATEURS.* A Handbook on Art. With Diagrams. Crown 8vo, 1s. 6d.

JUNKER (Dr. Wm.).—*TRAVELS IN AFRICA.* Translated from the German by Professor KEANE.

> *DURING THE YEARS* 1879 *to* 1883. Containing numerous Full-page Plates, and Illustrations in the Text and Map. Demy 8vo, 21s.

> *DURING THE YEARS* 1882 *to* 1886. Containing numerous Full-page Plates and Illustrations in the Text and Maps. Demy 8vo, 21s.

KELLY (J. F.).—*THE LIFE OF MIGUEL DE CERVANTES SAAVEDRA :* A Biographical, Literary, and Historical Study, with a Tentative Bibliography from 1585 to 1892, and an Annotated Appendix on the "Canto de Caliope." Demy 8vo, 16s.

KEMPT (R.).—*CONVIVIAL CALEDONIA :* Inns and Taverns of Scotland, and some Famous People who have frequented them. Crown 8vo, 2s. 6d.

KENNARD (H. Martyn).—*THE VEIL LIFTED:* A New Light on the World's History. With Illustrations. Demy 8vo.

LACORDAIRE (Pere). — *JESUS CHRIST; GOD: AND GOD AND MAN.* Conferences delivered at Notre Dame in Paris. Eighth Thousand. Crown 8vo, 3*s.* 6*d.*

LAING (S.).—*HUMAN ORIGINS:* Evidence from History and Science. With Illustrations. Fourteenth Thousand. Demy 8vo, 3*s.* 6*d.*

———— *PROBLEMS OF THE FUTURE AND ESSAYS.* Thirteenth Thousand. Demy 8vo, 3*s.* 6*d.*

———— *MODERN SCIENCE AND MODERN THOUGHT.* Twenty-first Thousand. Demy 8vo, 3*s.* 6*d.*

———— *A MODERN ZOROASTRIAN.* Ninth Thousand. Demy 8vo, 3*s.* 6*d.*

LAMENNAIS (F.).—*WORDS OF A BELIEVER, AND THE PAST AND FUTURE OF THE PEOPLE.* Translated from the French by L. E. MARTINEAU. With a Memoir of Lamennais. Crown 8vo, 4*s.*

LANDOR.—*WALTER SAVAGE LANDOR:* a Biography. By JOHN FORSTER. New Edition, with Portraits. Demy 8vo, 7*s.* 6*d.*

LANIN (E. B.).—*RUSSIAN CHARACTERISTICS.* Reprinted, with Revisions, from *The Fortnightly Review.* Demy 8vo, 14*s.*

LAVELEYE (Emile de).—*THE ELEMENTS OF POLITICAL ECONOMY.* Translated by W. POLLARD, B.A., St. John's College, Oxford. Crown 8vo, 6*s.*

LE CONTE (Professor J.).—*EVOLUTION:* Its Nature, its Evidences, and its Relations to Religious Thought. A New and Revised Edition. Crown 8vo, 6*s.*

LEE (Fitzhugh). — *GENERAL LEE OF THE CONFEDERATE ARMY.* With Portrait. Crown 8vo, 6*s.*

LEFEVRE (André).—*PHILOSOPHY,* Historical and Critical. Translated, with an Introduction, by A. W. KEANE, B.A. Large crown 8vo, 3*s.* 6*d.*

LE ROUX (H.).—*ACROBATS AND MOUNTEBANKS.* With over 200 Illustrations by J. GARNIER. Royal 8vo, 16*s.*

LEROY-BEAULIEU (A.).—*PAPACY, SOCIALISM, AND DEMOCRACY.* Translated by Professor B. L. O'DONNELL. Crown 8vo, 7*s.* 6*d.*

LESLIE (R. C.).—*A WATER BIOGRAPHY.* With Illustrations by the Author. Large crown 8vo, 7*s.* 6*d.*

———— *THE SEA BOAT:* How to Build, Rig, and Sail Her. With numerous Illustrations by the Author. Crown 8vo, 4*s.* 6*d.*

———— *LIFE ABOARD A BRITISH PRIVATEER IN THE TIME OF QUEEN ANNE.* Being the Journals of Captain Woodes Rogers, Master Mariner. With Notes and Illustrations by ROBERT C. LESLIE. A New and Cheaper Edition. Large crown 8vo, 3*s.* 6*d.*

LETOURNEAU (Charles). — *SOCIOLOGY.* Based upon Ethnology. Large crown 8vo, 3*s.* 6*d.*

———— *BIOLOGY.* With 83 Illustrations. A New Edition. Demy 8vo, 3*s.* 6*d.*

LILLEY (A. E. V.) and **MIDGLEY** (W.).—*A BOOK OF STUDIES IN PLANT FORM:* With some Suggestions for their Application to Design. Containing nearly 200 Illustrations. Large crown 8vo, 4*s.*

LILLY (W. S.).—*THE CLAIMS OF CHRISTIANITY.* Demy 8vo, 12*s.*

———— *ON SHIBBOLETHS.* Demy 8vo, 12*s.*

———— *ON RIGHT AND WRONG.* Second Edition. Demy 8vo, 12*s.*

———— *A CENTURY OF REVOLUTION.* Second Edition. Demy 8vo, 12*s.*

———— *CHAPTERS ON EUROPEAN HISTORY.* With an Introductory Dialogue on the Philosophy of History. 2 vols Demy 8vo, 21*s.*

———— *ANCIENT RELIGION & MODERN THOUGHT.* Second Edition. Demy 8vo, 12*s.*

LINEHAM (Ray S.). — *A DIRECTORY OF SCIENCE, ART, AND TECHNICAL COLLEGES, SCHOOLS, AND TEACHERS IN THE UNITED KINGDOM.* Including a brief Review of Educational Movements from 1835 to 1895. Demy 8vo, 2*s.* 6*d.* net.

———— *THE STREET OF HUMAN HABITATIONS.* Fully Illustrated. Crown 8vo, 6*s.*

LINEHAM (W. J.).—*A TEXT-BOOK OF MECHANICAL ENGINEERING.* With 700 Illustrations and 18 Folding Plates. Second Edition. Revised. Crown 8vo, 10*s.* 6*d.* net.

LITTLE (Canon Knox). — *THE WAIF FROM THE WAVES:* A Story of Three Lives, touching this World and another. Fifth Thousand. Crown 8vo, 3*s.* 6*d.* and 1*s.* 6*d.*; boards, 1*s.*

———— *THE CHILD OF STAFFERTON:* A Chapter from a Family Chronicle. Twelfth Thousand. Crown 8vo, boards, 1*s.*; cloth, 1*s.* 6*d.*

———— *THE BROKEN VOW.* A Story of Here and Here- after. Eighteenth Thousand. Crown 8vo, boards, 1*s.*; cloth, 1*s.* 6*d.*

LLOYD (W. W.).—*ON ACTIVE SERVICE.* Printed in Colours. Oblong 4to, 5*s.*

———— *SKETCHES OF INDIAN LIFE.* Printed in Colours. 4to, 6*s.*

LONG (James).—*DAIRY FARMING.* To which is added a Description of the Chief Continental Systems. With numerous Illustrations. Crown 8vo, 9*s.*

LOW (William).—*TABLE DECORATION.* With 19 Full-page Illustrations. Demy 8vo, 6*s.*

LÜTZOW (Francis, Count).—*BOHEMIA:* An Historical Sketch. With Maps. Crown 8vo.

MACDONALD (A. F.)—*OUR OCEAN RAILWAYS;* or, The Rise, Progress, and Development of Ocean Steam Navigation, &c., &c. With Maps and Illustrations. Large crown 8vo, 6s.

McCOAN (J. C.).—*EGYPT UNDER ISMAIL:* a Romance of History. With Portrait and Appendix of Official Documents. Crown 8vo, 7s. 6d.

MAITLAND (Ella Fuller).—*PAGES FROM THE DAY-BOOK OF BETHIA HARDACRE.* Fourth Edition. Crown 8vo, 5s.

MALLESON (Col. G. B.), C.S.I.—*THE LIFE OF WARREN HASTINGS, FIRST GOVERNOR-GENERAL OF INDIA.* With Portrait. Demy 8vo, 18s.

—— *PRINCE EUGENE OF SAVOY.* With Portrait and Maps. Large crown 8vo, 6s.

—— *LOUDON.* A Sketch of the Military Life of Gideon Ernest, Freicherr von Loudon. With Portrait and Maps. Large crown 8vo, 4s.

MALLOCK (W. H.).—*THE HEART OF LIFE.* Fifth Thousand. Crown 8vo, 6s.

—— *A HUMAN DOCUMENT.* Eighth Thousand. Crown 8vo, 3s. 6d.

MARCEAU (Sergent).—*REMINISCENCES OF A REGICIDE.* Edited from the Original MSS. of SERGENT MARCEAU, Member of the Convention, and Administrator of Police in the French Revolution of 1789. By M. C. M. SIMPSON. With Illustrations and Portraits. Demy 8vo, 14s.

MARMERY (V.).—*THE PROGRESS OF SCIENCE:* Its Origin, Course, Promoters, and Results. With an Introduction by SAMUEL LAING. Demy 8vo, 7s. 6d.

MASKELL (Alfred).—*RUSSIAN ART AND ART OBJECTS IN RUSSIA.* A Handbook to the Reproduction of Goldsmiths' Work and other Art Treasures. With Illustrations. Large crown 8vo, 4s. 6d.

MASKELL (William).—*IVORIES:* Ancient and Mediæval. With numerous Woodcuts. Large crown 8vo, 2s. 6d.

—— *HANDBOOK TO THE DYCE AND FORSTER COLLECTIONS.* With Illustrations. Large crown 8vo, 2s. 6d.

MASPERO (G.).—*LIFE IN ANCIENT EGYPT AND ASSYRIA.* Translated by A. P. MORTON. With 188 Illustrations. Third Thousand. Crown 8vo, 5s.

MAUDE, (Col. F. C.), V.C., C.B.—*FIVE YEARS IN MADAGASCAR.* With a Frontispiece Portrait of Queen Ranavalona III. Crown 8vo, 6s.

MEREDITH (George). — *LORD ORMONT AND HIS AMINTA.* Crown 8vo, 6s.

A Uniform Edition. Crown 8vo., 3s. 6d. each.

ONE OF OUR CONQUERORS.
DIANA OF THE CROSSWAYS.
EVAN HARRINGTON.
THE ORDEAL OF RICHARD FEVEREL.
THE ADVENTURES OF HARRY RICHMOND.
SANDRA BELLONI.
VITTORIA.
RHODA FLEMING.
BEAUCHAMP'S CAREER.
THE EGOIST.
THE SHAVING OF SHAGPAT; and FARINA.

The 6s. Edition is also to be had of above.

MIDGLEY (W.) and LILLEY (A. E. V.). — *A BOOK OF STUDIES IN PLANT FORM:* With some Suggestions for their Application to Design. Containing nearly 200 Illustrations. Large crown 8vo, 4s.

MILLS (John). — *ADVANCED PHYSIOGRAPHY (PHYSIO-GRAPHIC ASTRONOMY).* Designed to meet the Requirements of Students preparing for the Elementary and Advanced Stages of Physiography in the Science and Art Department Examinations, and as an Introduction to Physical Astronomy. Crown 8vo, 4s. 6d.

———— *ELEMENTARY PHYSIOGRAPHIC ASTRO-NOMY.* Crown 8vo, 1s. 6d.

———— *ALTERNATIVE ELEMENTARY PHYSICS.* Crown 8vo, 2s. 6d.

MILLS (J.) and NORTH (B.). — *QUANTITATIVE ANALYSIS (INTRODUCTORY LESSONS ON).* With numerous Woodcuts. Crown 8vo, 1s. 6d.

———— *HANDBOOK OF QUANTITATIVE ANALYSIS.* Crown 8vo, 3s. 6d.

MITRE (Gen. Don B.). — *THE EMANCIPATION OF SOUTH AMERICA.* Being a Condensed Translation, by WILLIAM PILLING, of "The History of San Martin." Demy 8vo, with Maps, 12s.

MOLTKE (Count Von). — *POLAND:* An Historical Sketch. With Biographical Notice by E. S. BUCHHEIM. Crown 8vo, 4s. 6d.; in Paper, 1s.

MUDDOCK (J. E.). — *THE STAR OF FORTUNE:* A Story of the Indian Mutiny. Crown 8vo, 3s. 6d.

MUNTZ (Eugene). — *RAPHAEL:* His Life, Works, and Times. A New Edition Revised, corrected, and condensed from the large original work, containing 108 illustrations. Royal 8vo, 7s. 6d.

MURRAY (Andrew). — *ECONOMIC ENTOMOLOGY.* APTERA. With numerous Illustrations. Large crown 8vo, 3s. 6d.

NECKER (Madame). — *THE SALON OF MADAME NECKER.* By VICOMTE D'HAUSSONVILLE. 2 vols. Cr. 8vo, 18s.

NELSON (W.).—*WOOD-WORKING POSITIONS.* 12 Illustrations by HERBERT COLE. Royal 4to, 2s. 6d. net Large size, 6s. net.

NESBITT (Alexander).—*GLASS.* With numerous Woodcuts· Large crown 8vo, 2s. 6d.

NEWEY (H. F.).—*ELEMENTARY DRAWING:* A Few Suggestions for Students and Teachers. Illustrated. Cr. 8vo, 2s. 6d.

NORMAN (C. B.).—*TONKIN:* or, France in· the Far East. With Maps. Demy 8vo, 14s.

O'CONNOR (T. P.).—*SOME OLD. LOVE STORIES.* With a Portrait of the Author. Third Thousand. Crown 8vo, 5s.

OLIVER (D.), F.R.S., &c.—*ILLUSTRATIONS OF THE PRINCIPAL NATURAL ORDERS OF THE VEGETABLE KINGDOM,* prepared for the Science and Art Department, South Kensington. New Edition, revised by Author. With 109 Plates. Coloured, royal 8vo, 16s.

OLIVER (E. E.).—*ACROSS THE BORDER:* or, Pathan and Biloch. With numerous Illustrations by .J. L. KIPLING, C.I.E. Demy 8vo, 14s.

OTWAY (Sir · Arthur). — *AUTOBIOGRAPHY AND JOURNALS OF LORD CLARENCE E. PAGET, G.C B.* With Portraits and other Illustrations. Demy 8vo, 16s.

PAGET (Lord Clarence). — *AUTOBIOGRAPHY AND JOURNALS OF LORD CLARENCE E. PAGET, G.C.B.* Edited by Sir ARTHUR OTWAY, Bart. With Portraits and other Illustrations. Demy 8vo, 16s.

PEEK (Hedley).—*NEMA:* and other Stories. Illustrated by C. E. BROCK. Crown 8vo, 6s.

A Limited Large Paper Edition with Photogravure Illustrations. Demy 4to, 21s. net.

PERROT (G.) and **CHIPIEZ** (C.).—*A HISTORY OF ART IN PRIMITIVE GREECE (MYCÆNIAN).* With 553 Illustrations and 20 Coloured Plates. 2 vols. Imperial 8vo, 42s.

———— *A HISTORY OF ANCIENT ART IN PERSIA.* With 254 Illustrations, and 12 Steel and Coloured Plates. Imperial 8vo, 21s.

———— *A HISTORY OF ANCIENT ART IN PHRYGIA, LYDIA, CARIA and LYCIA.* With 280 Illustrations. Imperial 8vo, 15s.

PERROT (G.) and CHIPIEZ (C.), *cont.—A HISTORY OF ANCIENT ART IN SARDINIA, JUDÆA, SYRIA, and ASIA MINOR.* With 395 Illustrations. 2 vols. Imperial 8vo, **36s.**

—————— *A HISTORY OF ANCIENT ART IN PHŒNICIA AND ITS DEPENDENCIES.* With 654 Illustrations. 2 vols. Imperial 8vo, **42s.**

—————— *A HISTORY OF ART IN CHALDÆA AND ASSYRIA.* With 452 Illustrations. 2 vols. Imperial 8vo, **42s.**

—————— *A HISTORY OF ART IN ANCIENT EGYPT.* With 600 Illustrations. 2 vols. Imperial 8vo, **42s.**

PETERBOROUGH (Earl of).—*THE EARL OF PETER-BOROUGH AND MONMOUTH* (Charles Mordaunt) : A Memoir. By Colonel FRANK RUSSELL, Royal Dragoons. With Illustrations. 2 vols. Demy 8vo, **32s.**

PILLING (Wm.).—*LAND TENURE BY REGISTRATION.* Third Edition. Revised. Crown 8vo, **5s.**

POLLEN (J. H.).—*GOLD AND SILVER SMITH'S WORK.* With numerous Woodcuts. Large crown 8vo, **2s. 6d.**

—————— *ANCIENT AND MODERN FURNITURE AND WOODWORK.* With numerous Woodcuts. Large crown 8vo, **2s. 6d.**

POLLOK (Colonel).—*INCIDENTS OF FOREIGN SPORT AND TRAVEL.* With Illustrations. Demy 8vo, **16s.**

POOLE (Stanley Lane).—*THE ART OF THE SARACENS IN EGYPT.* Published for the Committee of Council on Education. With 108 Woodcuts. Large crown 8vo, **4s.**

POYNTER (E. J.), R.A.—*TEN LECTURES ON ART.* Third Edition. Large crown 8vo, **9s.**

PRATT (Robert).—*SCIOGRAPHY;* or, Parallel and Radial Projection of Shadows. Being a Course of Exercises for the use of Students in Architectural and Engineering Drawing, and for Candidates preparing for the Examinations in this subject and in Third Grade Perspective conducted by the Science and Art Department. Oblong quarto, **7s. 6d.**

PUCKETT (R. C.).—*SCIOGRAPHY;* or Radical Projection of Shadows. Third Edition. Illustrated. Crown 8vo, **6s.**

PUSHKIN (A. S.).—*THE QUEEN OF SPADES,* and Other Stories. Translated from the Russian. With a Biography by Mrs. SUTHERLAND EDWARDS. Illustrated. Crown 8vo, **3s. 6d.**; in boards, **2s.**

RAE (W. Fraser). — *AUSTRIAN HEALTH RESORTS THROUGHOUT THE YEAR.* A New and Enlarged Edition. Crown 8vo, **5s.**

RAMSDEN (Lady).—*A BIRTHDAY BOOK.* Containing 46 Illustrations from Original Drawings. Royal 8vo, 21s.

RAPHAEL: His Life, Works, and Times. By EUGENE MUNTZ. A New Edition, revised, corrected, and condensed from the large original work, containing 108 Illustrations. Royal 8vo, 7s. 6d.

——— *PORTFOLIO OF TWENTY SELECTED COLLO-TYPE REPRODUCTIONS OF DRAWINGS AND CAR-TOONS OF RAPHAEL SANZIO.* 5s. net.

REDGRAVE (R.), R.A.—*MANUAL OF DESIGN.* With Woodcuts. Large crown 8vo, 2s. 6d.

——— *ELEMENTARY MANUAL OF COLOUR*, with a Catechism on Colour. 24mo, cloth, 9d.

REDGRAVE (Samuel).—*A DESCRIPTIVE CATALOGUE OF THE HISTORICAL COLLECTION OF WATER-COLOUR PAINTINGS IN THE SOUTH KENSINGTON MUSEUM.* With numerous Chromo-lithographs and other Illustrations. Royal 8vo, £1 1s.

REID (G. A.).—*THE PRESENT EVOLUTION OF MAN.* Crown 8vo, 7s. 6d.

REID (Sir T. Wemyss).—*THE LIFE OF THE RIGHT HON. W. E. FORSTER.* Sixth Edition, in one volume, gilt edges, with new Portrait. Demy 8vo, 6s.

RENAN (Ernest).—*RECOLLECTIONS OF MY YOUTH.* Translated from the French, and revised by MADAME RENAN. Second Edition. Crown 8vo, 3s. 6d.

RIANO (Juan F.).—*THE INDUSTRIAL ARTS IN SPAIN.* With numerous Woodcuts. Large crown 8vo, 4s.

RIBTON-TURNER (C. J.).—*A HISTORY OF VAGRANTS AND VAGRANCY AND BEGGARS AND BEGGING.* With Illustrations. Demy 8vo, 21s.

ROBERTS (Morley). — *IN LOW RELIEF:* A Bohemian Transcript. Crown 8vo, 3s. 6d. In boards, 2s.

ROBINSON (J. F.).—*BRITISH BEE-FARMING.* Its Profits and Pleasures. Large crown 8vo, 5s.

ROBINSON (J. C.).—*ITALIAN SCULPTURE OF THE MIDDLE AGES AND PERIOD OF THE REVIVAL OF ART.* With 20 Engravings. Royal 8vo, cloth, 7s. 6d.

ROBSON (George). — *ELEMENTARY BUILDING CON-STRUCTION.* Illustrated by a Design for an Entrance Lodge and Gate. 15 Plates. Oblong folio, sewed, 8s.

ROCK (Rev. Canon).—*TEXTILE FABRICS.* With numerous Woodcuts. Large crown 8vo, 2s. 6d.

ROLAND (Arthur).—*FARMING FOR PLEASURE AND PROFIT.* Edited by W. ABLETT. 8 vols. Crown 8vo, 5s. each.
DAIRY-FARMING, MANAGEMENT OF COWS, &c.
POULTRY-KEEPING.
TREE-PLANTING, FOR ORNAMENTATION OR PROFIT.
STOCK-KEEPING AND CATTLE-REARING.
DRAINAGE OF LAND, IRRIGATION, MANURES, &c.
ROOT-GROWING, HOPS, &c.
MANAGEMENT OF GRASS LANDS, LAYING DOWN GRASS, ARTIFICIAL GRASSES, &c.
MARKET GARDENING, HUSBANDRY FOR FARMERS AND GENERAL CULTIVATORS.

ROOSEVELT (Blanche).—*ELIZABETH OF ROUMANIA:* A Study. With Two Tales from the German of Carmen Sylva, Her Majesty Queen of Roumania. With Two Portraits and Illustration. Demy 8vo, 12s.

ROSS (Mrs. Janet).—*EARLY DAYS RECALLED.* With Illustrations and Portrait. Crown 8vo, 5s.

RUSSELL (W. Clark).—*MISS PARSON'S ADVENTURE:* and other Stories by W. E. NORRIS, JULIAN HAWTHORNE, MRS. L. B. WALFORD, J. M. BARRIE, F. C. PHILIPS, MRS. ALEXANDER, and WILLIAM WESTALL. With 16 Illustrations. One volume. Crown 8vo, 3s. 6d.

RYAN (Charles).—*EGYPTIAN ART.* An Elementary Handbook for the use of Students. With 56 Illustrations. Crown 8vo, 2s. 6d.

SANDEMAN (Fraser).—*ANGLING TRAVELS IN NORWAY.* With numerous Illustrations from Drawings and Photographs by the Author, and Coloured Plates of Salmon Flies. Demy 8vo, price 16s.
Large Paper Edition, with an extra Plate of Salmon Flies. 30s. net.

SANDERS (Amanda).—*BENT IRONWORK FOR BEGINNERS AND PROFICIENTS*, With 55 Illustrations by the Author. Crown 8vo, 2s. 6d.; in paper wrapper, 1s. 6d.

SCHAUERMANN (F. L.).—*WOOD-CARVING IN PRACTICE AND THEORY, AS APPLIED TO HOME ARTS.* With Notes on Designs having special application to Carved Wood in different styles. Containing 124 Illustrations. Second Edition. Large crown 8vo, 5s.

SCOTT (John).—*THE REPUBLIC AS A FORM OF GOVERNMENT;* or, The Evolution of Democracy in America. Crown 8vo, 7s. 6d.

SEEMANN (O.).—*THE MYTHOLOGY OF GREECE AND ROME,* with Special Reference to its Use in Art. From the German. Edited by G. H. BIANCHI. 64 Illustrations. New Edition. Crown 8vo, 5s.

SETON-KARR (H. W.).—*BEAR HUNTING IN THE WHITE MOUNTAINS;* or, Alaska and British Columbia Revisited. Illustrated. Large crown, 4s. 6d.

SETON-KARR (H. W.), *continued.—TEN YEARS' TRAVEL AND SPORT IN FOREIGN LANDS;* or, Travels in the Eighties. Second Edition, with additions and Portrait of Author. Large crown 8vo, 5*s.*

SEXTON (A. H.).—*THE FIRST TECHNICAL COLLEGE :* a Sketch of the History of "The Andersonian," and the Institutions descended from it 1796-1894. With Portraits and Illustrations. Crown 8vo, 3*s.* 6*d.*

———— *HOME WORK IN INORGANIC CHEMISTRY:* A Series of Exercises with Explanations and Worked Examples. Third Edition. Crown 8vo, 1*s.*

SHIRREFF (Emily). — *A SHORT SKETCH OF THE LIFE OF FRIEDRICH FRÖBEL;* a New Edition, including Fröbel's Letters from Dresden and Leipzig to his Wife, now first Translated into English. Crown 8vo, 2*s.*

———— *HOME EDUCATION IN RELATION TO THE KINDERGARTEN.* Two Lectures. Crown 8vo, 1*s.* 6*d.*

SIMKIN (R).—*LIFE IN THE ARMY :* Every-day Incidents in Camp, Field, and Quarters. Printed in Colours. Oblong 4to, 5*s.*

SIMMONDS (T. L.).—*ANIMAL PRODUCTS :* Their Preparation, Commercial Uses and Value. With numerous Illustrations. Large crown 8vo, 3*s.* 6*d.*

SINNETT (A. P.).—*ESOTERIC BUDDHISM.* Annotated and enlarged by the Author. Seventh Edition. Crown 8vo, 3*s.* 6*d.*

———— *KARMA.* A Novel. New Edition. Crown 8vo, 3*s.*

SMITH (Major R. M.), R.E.—*PERSIAN ART.* With Map and Woodcuts. Second Edition. Large crown 8vo, 2*s.*

SNAFFLE.—*GUN, RIFLE, AND HOUND, IN EAST AND WEST.* With Illustrations by H. DIXON. Demy 8vo, 14*s.*

SON OF THE MARSHES.—*WILD FOWL AND SEA FOWL OF GREAT BRITAIN.* With Illustrations by BRYAN HOOK. Large crown 8vo, 14*s.*

SOUTH KENSINGTON MUSEUM, *SCIENCE AND ART HANDBOOKS OF.* For detailed List, see page 29.

SPALDING (Lieut.-Col.).—*LIFE OF SUVOROFF.* Crown 8vo, 6*s.*

SPENCER (Herbert). — *AN INTRODUCTION TO THE PHILOSOPHY OF HERBERT SPENCER.* By Professor W. H. HUDSON. With a Biographical Sketch. Crown 8vo, 5*s.*

———— *APHORISMS FROM THE WRITINGS OF HERBERT SPENCER.* Selected and arranged by JULIA RAYMOND GINGELL. With a Photogravure Portrait of Herbert Spencer. Second Edition, revised. Crown 8vo, 3*s.*

STANLEY (H. M.): His Life, Works, and Explorations. By the Rev. H. W. Little. Demy 8vo, 10*s.* 6*d.*

STATHAM (H. H.).—*ARCHITECTURE FOR GENERAL READERS:* A Short Treatise on the Principles and Motives of Architectural Design. With a Historical Sketch. With 250 Illustrations drawn by the Author. Second Edition. Revised. Large crown 8vo, 12*s.*

———— *FORM AND DESIGN IN MUSIC:* A Brief Outline of the Æsthetic Conditions of the Art, addressed to General Readers. With Musical Examples. Demy 8vo, 2*s.* 6*d.*

——,—— *MY THOUGHTS ON MUSIC AND MUSICIANS.* Illustrated with Frontispiece of the Entrance-front of Handel's Opera House, and Musical Examples. Demy 8vo, 18*s.*

STEELE (Anna C.).—*CLOVE PINK:* A Study from Memory. Second Edition. Crown 8vo, 3*s.* 6*d.*

STODDARD (C. A.). — *ACROSS RUSSIA FROM THE BALTIC TO THE DANUBE.* With numerous Illustrations. Large crown 8vo, 7*s.* 6*d.*

STOKES (Margaret). — *EARLY CHRISTIAN ART IN IRELAND.* With 106 Woodcuts. Large crown 8vo, 4*s.*

STORY (W. W.)—*CASTLE ST. ANGELO.* With Illustrations. Crown 8vo, 10*s.* 6*d.*

SUTCLIFFE (John). — *THE SCULPTOR AND ART STUDENT'S GUIDE* to the Proportions of the Human Form, with Measurements in feet and inches of Full-Grown Figures of Both Sexes and of Various Ages. By Dr. G. Schadow. Plates reproduced by J. Sutcliffe. Oblong folio, 31*s.* 6*d.*

TANNER (Prof.), F.C.S.—*HOLT CASTLE:* or, Threefold Interest in Land. Crown 8vo, 4*s.* 6*d.*

———— *JACK'S EDUCATION:* or, How He Learnt Farming. Second Edition. Crown 8vo, 3*s.* 6*d.*

TAYLOR (E. R.).—*ELEMENTARY ART TEACHING:* An Educational and Technical Guide for Teachers and Learners, including Infant School-work; The work of the Standards; Freehand; Geometry; Model Drawing; Nature Drawing; Colours; Light and Shade; Modelling and Design. With over 600 Diagrams and Illustrations. 8vo, 10*s.* 6*d.*

TEMPLE (Sir Richard), Bt.—*COSMOPOLITAN ESSAYS.* With Maps. Demy 8vo, 16*s.*

THOMSON (D. C.). — *THE BARBIZON SCHOOL OF PAINTERS:* Corot, Rousseau, Diaz, Millet, and Daubigny. With 130 Illustrations, including 36 Full-page Plates, of which 18 are Etchings. 4to, cloth, 42*s.*

THRUPP (G. A.) and FARR (W.).—*COACH TRIMMING.* With 60 Illustrations. Crown 8vo, 2*s.* 6*d.*

TOPINARD (Paul).—*ANTHROPOLOGY.* With a Preface by Professor Paul Broca. With 49 Illustrations. Demy 8vo, 3*s.* 6*d.*

TOVEY (Lieut.-Col.), R.E.—*MARTIAL LAW AND CUSTOM OF WAR;* or, Military Law and Jurisdiction in Troublous Times. Crown 8vo, 6s.

TRAHERNE (Major).—*THE HABITS OF THE SALMON.* Crown 8vo, 3s. 6d.

TROLLOPE (Anthony).—*THE CHRONICLES OF BAR-SETSHIRE.* A Uniform Edition, in 8 vols., large crown 8vo, handsomely printed, each vol. containing Frontispiece. 6s. each.

> *THE WARDEN and BARCHESTER TOWERS.* 2 vols.
> *DR. THORNE.*
> *FRAMLEY PARSONAGE.*
> *THE SMALL HOUSE AT ALLINGTON.* 2 vols.
> *LAST CHRONICLES OF BARSET.* 2 vols.

UNDERHILL (G. F.) and SWEETLAND (H. S.).—*THROUGH A FIELD GLASS.* With Illustrations by L. THACKER Y. Crown 8vo, 3s. 6d. Picture boards, 2s.

VANDAM (Albert D.).—*FRENCH MEN AND FRENCH MANNERS.* With an Introduction, " Paris and Its Inhabitants." Large crown 8vo, 10s. 6d.

————— *AN ENGLISHMAN IN PARIS:* Notes and Recollections during the Reign of Louis Philippe and the Empire. Eighth Thousand. Large crown 8vo, 7s. 6d.

————— *THE MYSTERY OF THE PATRICIAN CLUB.* Crown 8vo, 3s. 6d.

VERON (Eugene).—*ÆSTHETICS.* Translated by W. H. ARMSTRONG. Large crown 8vo, 3s. 6d.

VON PLENER (Ernst). — *THE ENGLISH FACTORY LEGISLATION FROM* 1802 *TILL THE PRESENT TIME.* Authorized Translation by F. L. WEINMANN. With an Introduction by the Right Hon. A. J. MUNDELLA, M.P. Second Edition. Crown 8vo, 3s.

WALFORD (Major), R.A.—*PARLIAMENTARY GENE-RALS OF THE GREAT CIVIL WAR.* With Maps. Large crown 8vo, 4s.

WALKER (Mrs.)—*UNTRODDEN PATHS IN ROUMANIA.* With 77 Illustrations. Demy 8vo, 10s. 6d.

————— *EASTERN LIFE AND SCENERY.*—With Excursions to Asia Minor, Mitylene, Crete, and Roumania. 2 vols., with Frontispiece to each vol. Crown 8vo, 21s.

WARD (James). — *ELEMENTARY PRINCIPLES OF ORNAMENT.* With 122 Illustrations. Large crown 8vo, 5s.

————— *THE PRINCIPLES OF ORNAMENT.* Edited by GEORGE AITCHINSON. A.R.A. A New Edition, revised and enlarged. Large crown 8vo, 7s. 6d.

WATSON (A. E. T.).—*SKETCHES IN THE HUNTING FIELD.* A New Edition, with numerous Illustrations by JOHN STURGESS. Crown 8vo, 3*s.* 6*d.*

WATSON (John).—*POACHERS AND POACHING.* With Frontispiece. Crown 8vo, 7*s.* 6*d.*

———— *SKETCHES OF BRITISH SPORTING FISHES.* With Frontispiece. Crown 8vo, 3*s.* 6*d.*

WEGG-PROSSER (F. R.).—*GALILEO AND HIS JUDGES.* Demy 8vo, 5*s.*

WHITMAN (Sidney).—*TEUTON STUDIES;* Personal Reminiscenses of Count Von Moltke, Prince Bismarck, &c. Crown 8vo, 6*s.*

WIEL (Hon. Mrs.).—*DESIGNS FOR CHURCH EMBROIDERY.* By A. R. Letterpress by the Hon. Mrs. WIEL. With numerous Illustrations. 4to, 12*s.* net.

WILKINS (Mary E.).—*THE LONG ARM,* and other Detective Stories by other writers. **Chapman's Story Series.**

WILLIAMSON (C. N.).—*THE CARLYLE BIRTHDAY-BOOK.* Second Edition. Small Fcap. 8vo, 3*s.*

WOLVERTON (Lord). — *FIVE MONTHS' SPORT IN SOMALI LAND.* With Illustrations. Demy 8vo, 7*s.* 6*d.*

WOOD (Gen. Sir Evelyn), G.C.B., &c.—*THE CRIMEA IN 1854 AND 1894.* With numerous Illustrations from Sketches made during the Campaign by Col. the Hon. W. J. COLVILLE, C.B., and Portraits and Plans. Demy 8vo, 16*s.*

WOODGATE (W. B.).—*A MODERN LAYMAN'S FAITH CONCERNING THE CREED AND THE BREED OF THE "THOROUGHBRED MAN."* Demy 8vo, 14*s.*

WORNUM (R. N.).—*ANALYSIS OF ORNAMENT:* The Characteristics of Styles. An Introduction to the History of Ornamental Art. With many Illustrations. Ninth Edition. Royal 8vo, cloth, 8*s.*

WORSAAE (J. J. A.).—*INDUSTRIAL ARTS OF DENMARK,* from the Earliest Times to the Danish Conquest of England. With Maps and Woodcuts. Large crown 8vo, 3*s.* 6*d.*

WRIGHTSON (Prof. J.).—*PRINCIPLES OF AGRICULTURAL PRACTICE AS AN INSTRUCTIONAL SUBJECT.* With Geological Map. Second Edition. Crown 8vo, 5*s.*

———— *FALLOW AND FODDER CROPS.* Crown 8vo, 5*s.*

YOUNGE (C. D.).—*PARALLEL LIVES OF ANCIENT AND MODERN HEROES.* New Edition. 12mo, cloth, 4*s.* 6*d.*

SOUTH KENSINGTON MUSEUM SCIENCE AND ART HANDBOOKS.

Handsomely printed in Large Crown 8vo.
Published for the Committee of the Council on Education.

ANIMAL PRODUCTS: their Preparation, Commercial Uses, and Value. By T. L. SIMMONDS. With Illustrations. 3*s.* 6*d.*

BRONZES. By C. DRURY E. FORTNUM, F.S.A. With numerous Woodcuts. 2*s.* 6*d.*

COLLEGE AND CORPORATION PLATE. A Handbook to the Reproductions of Silver Plate in the South Kensington Museum from Celebrated English Collections. By WILFRED JOSEPH CRIPPS, M.A., F.S.A. With Illustrations. 2*s.* 6*d.*

DANISH ARTS.—*INDUSTRIAL ARTS OF DENMARK.* From the Earliest Times to the Danish Conquest of England. By J. J. A. WORSAAE, Hon. F.S.A., &c. With Map and Woodcuts. 3*s.* 6*d.*

DESIGN.—*MANUAL OF DESIGN.* By RICHARD RED-GRAVE, R.A. By GILBERT R. REDGRAVE. With Woodcuts. 2*s.* 6*d.*

DYCE AND FORSTER.—*HANDBOOK TO THE DYCE AND FORSTER COLLECTIONS* in the South Kensington Museum. With Portraits and Facsimiles. 2*s.* 6*d.*

EARTHENWARE. — *ENGLISH EARTHENWARE:* A Handbook to the Wares made in England during the 17th and 18th Centuries. By Prof. A. H. CHURCH, M.A. With Woodcuts. 3*s.*

ENTOMOLOGY.—*ECONOMIC ENTOMOLOGY.* By AN-DREW MURRAY, F.L.S. APTERA. With Illustrations. 3*s.* 6*d.*

FOOD GRAINS OF INDIA. By PROF. A. H. CHURCH, M.A., F.C.S., F.I.C. With numerous Woodcuts. Small 4to, 6*s.*

FOOD: Some Account of its Sources, Constituents, and Uses. By Prof. A. H. CHURCH, M.A. New and Revised Edition. 3*s.*

—————— *THE CHEMISTRY OF FOODS.* With Microscopic Illustrations. By J. BELL, Ph.D., &c., Somerset House Laboratory. Part I.—Tea, Coffee, Cocoa, Sugar, &c. 2*s.* 6*d.* Part II.—Milk, Butter, Cheese, Cereals, Prepared Starches, &c. 3*s.*

FURNITURE AND WOODWORK. — *ANCIENT AND MODERN FURNITURE AND WOODWORK.* By JOHN HUNGERFORD POLLEN, M.A. With numerous Woodcuts. 2*s.* 6*d.*

GLASS. By ALEX. NESBITT. With numerous Woodcuts. 2*s.* 6*d.*

GOLD AND SILVER.—*GOLD AND SILVER SMITHS' WORK.* By J. H. POLLEN, M.A. With numerous Woodcuts. 2*s.* 6*d.*

INDIAN ARTS.—*INDUSTRIAL ARTS OF INDIA.* By Sir GEORGE C. M. BIRDWOOD, C.S.I., &c. With Map and Wood-cuts. Demy 8vo, 14*s.*

INDUSTRIAL ARTS: Historical Sketches. With numerous Illustrations. 3*s.*

IRISH ART.—*EARLY CHRISTIAN ART IN IRELAND.* By MARGARET STOKES. With 106 Woodcuts. 4*s.*

IRONWORK : From the Earliest Times to the End of the Mediæval Period. By J. STARKIE GARDNER. With 57 Illustrations. Crown 8vo, **3s.**

IVORIES.—*ANCIENT AND MEDIÆVAL IVORIES.* By WILLIAM MASKELL. With numerous Woodcuts. **2s. 6d.**

JAPANESE POTTERY. Being a Native Report. With an Introduction and Catalogue by A. W. FRANKS, M.A., F.R.S., F.S.A. With Illustrations and Marks. **2s. 6d.**

JONES COLLECTION *IN THE SOUTH KENSINGTON MUSEUM.* With Portrait and Woodcuts. **2s. 6d.**

MAIOLICA By C. DRURY E. FORTNUM, F.S.A. With numerous Woodcuts. **2s. 6d.**

MARINE ENGINES AND BOILERS. By GEORGE C. V. HOLMES, Secretary of the Institution of Naval Architects, Whitworth Scholar. With 69 Woodcuts. **3s.**

MUSICAL INSTRUMENTS. By CARL ENGEL. With numerous Woodcuts. **2s. 6d.**

PERSIAN ART. By MAJOR R. MURDOCK SMITH, R.E. With Map and Woodcuts Second Edition, enlarged. **2s.**

PORCELAIN.—*ENGLISH PORCELAIN:* A Handbook to the China made in England during the 18th Century. By Prof. A. H. CHURCH, M.A. With numerous Woodcuts. **3s.**

POTTERY.—*FRENCH POTTERY.* By PAUL GASNAULT and EDOUARD GARNIER. With Illustrations and Marks. **3s.**

PRECIOUS STONES: Considered in their Scientific and Artistic relations. By Prof. A. H. CHURCH, M.A. With a Coloured Plate and Woodcuts. **2s. 6d.**

RUSSIAN ART AND ART OBJECTS IN RUSSIA: A Handbook to the reproduction of Goldsmiths' work and other Art Treasures. By ALFRED MASKELL. With Illustrations. **4s. 6d.**

SARACENIC ART.—*THE ART OF THE SARACENS IN EGYPT.* By STANLEY LANE POOLE, B.A., M.A.R.S. With 108 Woodcuts. **4s.**

SCANDINAVIAN ARTS. — *INDUSTRIAL ARTS OF SCANDINAVIA IN THE PAGAN TIME.* By HANS HILDEBRAND, Royal Antiquary of Sweden. With Woodcuts. **2s. 6d.**

SPANISH ARTS.—*INDUSTRIAL ARTS IN SPAIN.* By JUAN F. RIAÑO. With numerous Woodcuts. **4s.**

SPECIAL LOAN COLLECTION.—*HANDBOOK TO THE SPECIAL LOAN COLLECTION OF SCIENTIFIC APPARATUS.* **3s.**

TAPESTRY. By A. DE CHAMPEAUX. With Woodcuts. **2s. 6d.**

TEXTILE FABRICS. By the Very Rev. DANIEL ROCK, D.D. With numerous Woodcuts. **2s. 6d.**

WATER.—*PLAIN WORDS ABOUT WATER.* By A. H. CHURCH, M.A., Oxon. With Illustrations. Sewed, **6d.**

THOMAS CARLYLE'S WORKS.

THE LIBRARY EDITION.

In 34 volumes, demy 8vo, red cloth, £15 3s.
Separate volumes 9s. each, except otherwise marked

Sartor Resartus. With Portrait. 7s. 6d.
The French Revolution. 3 vols.
Life of Schiller and Examination of His Works. With Portra
and Plates.
Critical and Miscellaneous Essays. With Portrait. 6 vols.
On Heroes, Hero Worship, and the Heroic in History. 7s. 6d.
Past and Present.
Oliver Cromwell's Letters and Speeches. With Portraits. 5 vols.
Latter-Day Pamphlets.
Life of John Sterling. With Portrait.
History of Frederick the Second. With Portraits and Maps. 10 vols.
Translations from the German. 3 vols.
Early Kings of Norway; Essay on the Portraits of John
Knox; and General Index. With Portraits.

THE ASHBURTON EDITION.

In 20 volumes, demy 8vo, blue cloth, £8. Separate volumes 8s. each.

French Revolution and Past and Present. With Portrait. 2 vols.
Sartor Resartus: Heroes and Hero Worship.
Lives of John Sterling and Schiller. With Portraits and Plates.
Latter-Day Pamphlets—Early Kings of Norway—Essay on
the Portraits of John Knox. With Portraits.
Letters and Speeches of Oliver Cromwell. With Portraits and
Plates. 3 vols.
History of Frederick the Great. With Portraits and Maps. 6 vols.
Critical and Miscellaneous Essays. With Portrait. 3 vols.
Translations from the German. 3 vols.

THE HALF-CROWN EDITION.

In 20 volumes, crown 8vo, green cloth, £2 10s.
Separate volumes 2s. 6d. each.

Sartor Resartus and Latter-Day Pamphlets. With Portrait.
Past and Present and on Heroes and Hero Worship.
Lives of John Sterling and Schiller. With Portraits.
Critical and Miscellaneous Essays, Early Kings of Norway,
and Essay on the Portraits of Knox. With Portraits. 4 vols.
French Revolution; a History. 2 vols.
Oliver Cromwell's Letters and Speeches. With Portrait. 3 vols.
History of Frederick the Great. With Maps. 5 vols.
Wilhelm Meister. 2 vols.
Translations from Musæus, Tiek, and Richter.

THOMAS CARLYLE'S WORKS.—*Continued.*
THE PEOPLE'S EDITION.

In 37 *volumes, small crown* 8vo, *red cloth,* 37s. *Separate volumes,*
1s. *each. In sets of* 37 *volumes bound in* 18, 37s.

Sartor Resartus. With Portrait.
French Revolution. 3 vols.
Oliver Cromwell's Letters and Speeches. 5 vols.   With
Portrait.
On Heroes, Hero Worship, and the Heroic in History.
Past and Present.
Critical and Miscellaneous Essays. 7 vols.
The Life of Schiller, and Examination of his Works. With
Portrait.
Latter-Day Pamphlets.
Wilhelm Meister. 3 vols.
Life of John Sterling. With Portrait.
History of Frederick the Great. With Maps. 10 vols.
Translations from Musæus, Tieck, and Richter. 2 vols.
The Early Kings of Norway; Essay on the Portraits of Knox
and General Index to Carlyle's Works.   With Portraits.

CHEAP ISSUE.
In crown 8vo *volumes, bound in blue cloth.*

The French Revolution. With Portrait. **2s.**
**Sartor Resartus, Heroes and Hero Worship, Past and
Present, and Chartism.** With Portrait. **2s.**
Oliver Cromwell's Letters and Speeches. With Portrait.
2s. 6d.
Critical and Miscellaneous Essays. 2 vols. **4s.**
Wilhelm Meister. 2s.
Lives of Schiller and Sterling. With Portraits. **2s.**

SIXPENNY EDITION.
4to, sewed.

Heroes and Hero Worship.
Essays: Burns, Johnson, Scott, The Diamond Necklace.
The above three books, bound in one cloth volume, **2s. 6d.**

Thoughts on Life. By Thomas Carlyle. Selected by Robert
Duncan. With a Photogravure Portrait. Crown 8vo, 1s. 6d. ; in
paper covers, 1s.
A limited edition on Hand-made Paper, 5s.

The Carlyle Birthday Book. Compiled by C. N. Williamson.
Second Edition. Small fcap. 8vo, 3s.

CHARLES DICKENS'S WORKS.
REPRINTS OF THE ORIGINAL EDITIONS.
In demy 8vo, uniform green cloth.

The Mystery of Edwin Drood. With Illustrations by S. L. FILDES, and a Portrait engraved by BAKER. 7s. 6d.

Our Mutual Friend. With 40 Illustrations by MARCUS STONE. 21s.

The Pickwick Papers. With 43 Illusts. by SEYMOUR and PHIZ. 21s.

Nicholas Nickleby. With 40 Illustrations by PHIZ. 21s.

Sketches by "Boz." With 40 Illusts. by GEORGE CRUIKSHANK. 21s.

Martin Chuzzlewit. With 40 Illustrations by PHIZ. 21s.

Dombey and Son. With 40 Illustrations by PHIZ. 21s.

David Copperfield. With 40 Illustrations by PHIZ. 21s.

Bleak House. With 40 Illustrations by PHIZ. 21s.

Little Dorrit. With 40 Illustrations by PHIZ. 21s.

The Old Curiosity Shop. With 75 Illustrations by GEORGE CATTERMOLE and H. K. BROWNE. 21s.

Barnaby Rudge : a Tale of the Riots of 'Eighty. With 78 Illustrations by GEORGE CATTERMOLE and H. K. BROWNE. 21s.

Christmas Books. With all the original Illustrations. 12s.

Oliver Twist. With 24 Illustrations by GEORGE CRUIKSHANK. 11s.

A Tale of Two Cities. With 16 Illustrations by PHIZ. 9s.

Oliver Twist and Tale of Two Cities. In one volume. 21s.

. *The remainder of Dickens's Works were not originally printed in demy 8vo.*

THE ILLUSTRATED LIBRARY EDITION.
In 30 volumes, demy 8vo, green cloth, with Original Illustrations, £15. Separate volumes, 10s. each.

Pickwick Papers. With 42 Illustrations by PHIZ. 2 vols.

Nicholas Nickleby. With 40 Illustrations by PHIZ. 2 vols.

Old Curiosity Shop and Reprinted Pieces. With Illustrations by CATTERMOLE, &c. 2 vols.

Barnaby Rudge and Hard Times. With Illustrations by CATTERMOLE, &c. 2 vols.

Martin Chuzzlewit. With 40 Illustrations by PHIZ. 2 vols.

Dombey and Son. With 40 Illustrations by PHIZ 2 vols.

David Copperfield. With 40 Illustrations by PHIZ. 2 vols.

Bleak House. With 40 Illustrations by PHIZ. 2 vols.

Little Dorrit. With 40 Illustrations by PHIZ. 2 vols.

Our Mutual Friend. With 40 Illustrations by MARCUS STONE. 2 vols.

A Tale of Two Cities. With 16 Illustrations by PHIZ.

The Uncommercial Traveller. With 8 Illusts. by MARCUS STONE.

Great Expectations. With 8 Illustrations by MARCUS STONE.

Oliver Twist. With 24 Illustrations by CRUIKSHANK.

Sketches by "Boz." With 40 Illustrations by GEORGE CRUIKSHANK.

Christmas Books. With 17 Illustrations by LANDSEER, MACLISE, &c.

American Notes and Pictures from Italy. With 8 Illustrations.

A Child's History of England. With 8 Illusts. by MARCUS STONE.

Christmas Stories. With 14 Illustrations.

Edwin Drood and Other Stories. With 12 Illustrations by S. L. FILDES.

Uniform with above.

Life of Charles Dickens. By JOHN FORSTER. With Portraits. 2 vols.

CHARLES DICKENS'S WORKS.—*Continued.*

THE LIBRARY EDITION.

In 30 volumes, post 8vo, red cloth, with all the Original Illustrations, £12.
Separate volumes 8s. *each.*

Pickwick Papers. With 43 Illustrations. 2 vols.
Nicholas Nickleby. With 39 Illustrations. 2 vols.
Martin Chuzzlewit. With 40 Illustrations. 2 vols.   [2 vols.
Old Curiosity Shop and Reprinted Pieces. With 36 Illustrations.
Barnaby Rudge and Hard Times. With 36 Illustrations. 2 vols.
Bleak House. With 40 Illustrations. 2 vols.
Little Dorrit. With 40 Illustrations. 2 vols.
Dombey and Son. With 38 Illustrations. 2 vols.
David Copperfield. With 38 Illustrations. 2 vols.
Our Mutual Friend. With 40 Illustrations. 2 vols.
Sketches by "Boz." With 39 Illustrations.
Oliver Twist. With 24 Illustrations.
Christmas Books. With 17 Illustrations.
A Tale of Two Cities. With 16 Illustrations.
Great Expectations. With 8 Illustrations.
Pictures from Italy and American Notes. With 8 Illustrations.
Uncommercial Traveller. With 8 Illustrations.
A Child's History of England. With 8 Illustrations.
Edwin Drood and Miscellanies. With 12 Illustrations.
Christmas Stories. With 14 Illustrations.

Uniform with the above, 10s. 6d.
The Life of Charles Dickens. By JOHN FORSTER. With Illustrations.

THE "CHARLES DICKENS" EDITION.

In 21 volumes, crown 8vo, red cloth, with Illustrations, £3 16s.
Pickwick Papers. With 8 Illustrations. 4s.
Martin Chuzzlewit. With 8 Illustrations. 4s.
Dombey and Son. With 8 Illustrations. 4s.
Nicholas Nickleby. With 8 Illustrations. 4s.
David Copperfield. With 8 Illustrations. 4s.
Bleak House. With 8 Illustrations. 4s.
Little Dorrit. With 8 Illustrations. 4s.
Our Mutual Friend. With 8 Illustrations. 4s.
Barnaby Rudge. With 8 Illustrations. 3s. 6d.
Old Curiosity Shop. With 8 Illustrations. 3s. 6d.
A Child's History of England. With 4 Illustrations. 3s. 6d.
Edwin Drood and Other Stories. With 8 Illustrations. 3s. 6d.
Christmas Stories. From *Household Words.* With 8 Illusts. 3s. 6d.
Sketches by "Boz." With 8 Illustrations. 3s. 6d.
American Notes and Reprinted Pieces. With 8 Illustrations. 3s. 6d.
Christmas Books. With 8 Illustrations. 3s. 6d.
Oliver Twist. With 8 Illustrations. 3s. 6d.
Great Expectations. With 8 Illustrations. 3s. 6d.
A Tale of Two Cities. With 8 Illustrations. 3s.
Hard Times and Pictures from Italy. With 8 Illustrations. 3s.
Uncommercial Traveller. With 4 Illustrations. 3s.

Uniform with the above.
The Life of Charles Dickens. With Illustrations. 2 vols. 7s.
The Letters of Charles Dickens. With Illustrations. 2 vols. 7s.

CHARLES DICKENS'S WORKS.—*Continued.*

THE CROWN EDITION.

In 17 volumes, large crown 8vo, maroon cloth, Original Illustrations, £4 5s.
Separate volumes, 5s. each.

Pickwick Papers. With 43 Illustrations by SEYMOUR and PHIZ.

Nicholas Nickleby. With 40 Illustrations by PHIZ.

Dombey and Son. With 40 Illustrations by PHIZ.

David Copperfield. With 40 Illustrations by PHIZ.

Sketches by "Boz." With 40 Illusts. by GEO. CRUIKSHANK.

Martin Chuzzlewit. With 40 Illustrations by PHIZ.

Old Curiosity Shop. With 75 Illustrations by GEORGE CATTER-MOLE and H. K. BROWNE.

Barnaby Rudge. With 78 Illustrations by GEORGE CATTER-MOLE and II. K. BROWNE.

Oliver Twist and A Tale of Two Cities. With 24 Illustrations by CRUIKSHANK and 16 by PHIZ.

Bleak House. With 40 Illustrations by PHIZ.

Little Dorrit. With 40 Illustrations by PHIZ.

Our Mutual Friend. With 40 Illustrations by MARCUS STONE.

American Notes; Pictures from Italy; and A Child's History of England. With 16 Illustrations by MARCUS STONE.

Christmas Books and Hard Times. With Illustrations by LANDSEER, MACLISE, STANFIELD, LEECH, DOYLE, F. WALKER, &c.

Christmas Stories and Other Stories, including **Humphrey's Clock.** With Illustrations by DALZIEL, CHARLES GREEN, MA-HONEY, PHIZ, CATTERMOLE, etc.

Great Expectations and Uncommercial Traveller. With 16 Illustrations by MARCUS STONE.

Edwin Drood and Reprinted Pieces. With 16 Illustrations by LUKE FILDES and F. WALKER.

Uniform with the above.

The Life of Charles Dickens. By JOHN FORSTER. With Portraits and Illustrations.

The Dickens Dictionary. A Key to the Characters and Principal Incidents in the Tales of Charles Dickens. By GILBERT PIERCE, with additions by WILLIAM A. WHEELER.

The Lazy Tour of Two Idle Apprentices; No Thoroughfare; The Perils of Certain English Prisoners. By CHARLES DICKENS and WILKIE COLLINS. With Illustrations.

*** *These Stories are now reprinted in complete form for the first time.*

CHARLES DICKENS'S WORKS.—*Continued.*
THE HALF-CROWN EDITION.
In 21 volumes, crown 8vo, blue cloth, Original Illustrations, £2 12s. 6d.
Separate volumes, 2s. 6d. *each.*

The Pickwick Papers. With 43 Illustrations by SEYMOUR and PHIZ.
Barnaby Rudge. With 76 Illustrations by CATTERMOLE and PHIZ.
Oliver Twist. With 24 Illustrations by CRUIKSHANK.
The Old Curiosity Shop. With 75 Illustrations by CATTERMOLE, &c.
David Copperfield. With 40 Illustrations by PHIZ.
Nicholas Nickleby. With 40 Illustrations by PHIZ.
Martin Chuzzlewit. With 40 Illustrations by PHIZ.
Dombey and Son. With 40 Illustrations by PHIZ.
Sketches by "Boz." With 40 Illustrations by GEORGE CRUIKSHANK.
Christmas Books. With 64 Illustrations by LANDSEER, DOYLE, &c.
Bleak House. With 40 Illustrations by PHIZ.
Little Dorrit. With 40 Illustrations by PHIZ.
Christmas Stories. With 14 Illustrations by DALZIEL, GREEN, &c.
American Notes and Reprinted Pieces. With 8 Illustrations by MARCUS STONE and F. WALKER.
Hard Times and Pictures from Italy. With 8 Illustrations by F. WALKER and MARCUS STONE.
A Child's History of England. With 8 Illusts. by MARCUS STONE.
Great Expectations. With 8 Illustrations by MARCUS STONE.
Tale of Two Cities. With 16 Illustrations by PHIZ.
Uncommercial Traveller. With 8 Illustrations by MARCUS STONE.
Our Mutual Friend. With 40 Illustrations by MARCUS STONE.
Edwin Drood and Other Stories. With 12 Illustrations by FILDES.

THE PICTORIAL EDITION.
In 17 volumes, with over 900 Illustrations, royal 8vo, red cloth, £2 19s. 6d.
Separate volumes, 3s. 6d. *each.*

Dombey and Son. With 62 Illustrations by F. BARNARD.
David Copperfield. With 61 Illustrations by F. BARNARD.
Nicholas Nickleby. With 59 Illustrations by F. BARNARD.
Barnaby Rudge. With 46 Illustrations by F. BARNARD.
Old Curiosity Shop. With 39 Illustrations by CHARLES GREEN.
Martin Chuzzlewit. With 59 Illustrations by F. BARNARD.
Oliver Twist and a Tale of Two Cities. With 53 Illustrations by J. MAHONEY and F. BARNARD.
Our Mutual Friend. With 58 Illustrations by J. MAHONEY.
Bleak House. With 61 Illustrations by F. BARNARD.
Pickwick Papers. With 57 Illustrations by PHIZ.
Little Dorrit. With 58 Illustrations by J. MAHONEY.
Great Expectations and Hard Times. With 50 Illustrations by J. A. FRASER and H. FRENCH.
American Notes, Pictures from Italy, and A Child's History of England. With 33 Illustrations by FROST, GORDON, &c.
Sketches by "Boz" and Christmas Books. With 62 Illustrations by F. BARNARD.
Christmas Stories and Uncommercial Traveller. With 49 Illustrations by E. G. DALZIEL.
Edwin Drood, and other Stories. With 30 Illusts. by L. FILDES, &c.
The Life of Charles Dickens. By JOHN FORSTER. With 40 Illustrations by F. BARNARD and others.

CHARLES DICKENS'S WORKS.—*Continued.*

THE HOUSEHOLD EDITION.

In 22 volumes, including the " LIFE," crown 4to, green cloth, £4 8s. 6d.

Martin Chuzzlewit. With 59 Illustrations. **5s.**
David Copperfield. With 60 Illustrations and a Portrait. **5s.**
Bleak House. With 61 Illustrations. **5s.**
Little Dorrit. With 58 Illustrations. **5s.**
Pickwick Papers. With 56 Illustrations. **5s.** ·
Our Mutual Friend. With 58 Illustrations. **5s.**
Nicholas Nickleby. With 59 Illustrations. **5s.**
Dombey and Son. With 61 Illustrations. **5s.** [Illusts. **5s.**
Edwin Drood ; Reprinted Pieces ; and other Stories. With 30
Barnaby Rudge. With 46 Illustrations. **4s.**
Old Curiosity Shop. With 32 Illustrations. **4s.**
Christmas Stories. With 23 Illustrations. **4s.**
Oliver Twist. With 28 Illustrations. **3s.**
Great Expectations. With 26 Illustrations. **3s.**
Sketches by " Boz." With 36 Illustrations. **3s.**
Uncommercial Traveller. With 26 Illustrations. **3s.**
Christmas Books. With 28 Illustrations. **3s.**
The History of England. With 15·Illustrations. **3s.**
American Notes and Pictures from Italy. With 18 Illusts. **3s.**
A Tale of Two Cities. With 25 Illustrations. **3s.**
Hard Times. With 20 Illustrations. **2s. 6d.**
The Life of Dickens. By JOHN FORSTER. With 40 Illusts. **5s.**

The Illustrations in this Edition are by the same artists as in the Pictorial
Edition. See page 36.

THE CHRISTMAS BOOKS.

REPRINTED FROM THE ORIGINAL PLATES.

Illustrated by JOHN LEECH, D. MACLISE, R.A., R. DOYLE, &c.
Fcap. 8vo, red cloth, 1s. each. The five volumes, complete in a case, 5s.

A Christmas Carol in Prose.
The Chimes : A Goblin Story.
The Cricket on the Hearth : A Fairy Tale of Home.
The Battle of·Life : A Love Story.
The Haunted Man and the Ghost's Story.

SIXPENNY EDITION.

Bleak House. With 18 Illustrations by F. BARNARD.
Sketches by " Boz." With Illustrations by F. BARNARD.
American Notes and Italy. With Illustrations by A. B. FROST.
Oliver Twist. With Illustrations by J. MAHONEY.
Readings from the Works of Charles Dickens. As selected
    and read by himself and now published for the first time. Illustrated.
A Christmas Carol and the Haunted Man. Illustrated.
The Chimes and the Cricket on the Hearth. Illustrated.
Battle of Life ; Hunted Down ; a Holiday Romance. Illus.

CHARLES DICKENS'S WORKS.—*Continued.*

THE CABINET EDITION.

In 32 volumes, small fcap. 8vo, Marble Paper Sides, uncut edges, £2 8s.
Separate volumes 1s. 6d. each.
In Sets only, bound in decorative blue cloth, cut edges and gilt tops, complete
in cloth box, £2 10s.

Christmas Books. With 8 Illustrations.
Martin Chuzzlewit. With 16 Illustrations. 2 vols.
David Copperfield. With 16 Illustrations. 2 vols.
Oliver Twist. With 8 Illustrations.
Great Expectations. With 8 Illustrations.
Nicholas Nickleby. With 16 Illustrations. 2 vols.
Sketches by "Boz." With 8 Illustrations.
Christmas Stories. With 8 Illustrations.
The Pickwick Papers. With 16 Illustrations. 2 vols.
Barnaby Rudge. With 16 Illustrations. 2 vols.
Bleak House. With 16 Illustrations. 2 vols.
American Notes and Pictures from Italy. With 8 Illustrations.
Edwin Drood ; and Other Stories. With 8 Illustrations.
The Old Curiosity Shop. With 16 Illustrations. 2 vols.
A Child's History of England. With 8 Illustrations.
Dombey and Son. With 16 Illustrations. 2 vols.
A Tale of Two Cities. With 8 Illustrations.
Little Dorrit. With 16 Illustrations. 2 vols.
Our Mutual Friend. With 16 Illustrations. 2 vols.
Hard Times. With 8 Illustrations.
Uncommercial Traveller. With 8 Illustrations.
Reprinted Pieces. With 8 Illustrations.

THE TWO SHILLING EDITION.

In 21 volumes, each with a frontispiece, crown 8vo, red cloth, £2 2s.
Separate volumes, 2s. each.

Dombey and Son.
Martin Chuzzlewit.
The Pickwick Papers.
Bleak House.
Old Curiosity Shop.
Barnaby Rudge.
David Copperfield.
Nicholas Nickleby.
Christmas Stories.
American Notes.   [Italy.
Hard Times & Pictures from

Great Expectations.
Our Mutual Friend.
Christmas Books.
Oliver Twist.
Little Dorrit.
Tale of Two Cities.
Uncommercial Traveller.
Sketches by "Boz " [land.
A Child's History of Eng-
Edwin Drood and Other
Stories.

CHARLES DICKENS'S READINGS.

Fcap. 8vo, sewed, 1s. each.

Christmas Carol in Prose.

Cricket on the Hearth.

Chimes : A Goblin Story.

Story of Little Dombey.
Póor Traveller, Boots at the
Holly-Tree Inn, and Mrs.
Gamp.

CHAPMAN & HALL'S PUBLICATIONS.

ARRANGED ACCORDING TO THEIR PRICES.

52*s*. 6*d*.
Danbourg's Interior Architecture.

42*s. net.*
Dickens's Oliver Twist. Coloured Plates.

42*s*.
Burton's (Sir Richard) Life. 2 vols.
Ierrot & Chipiez's Phœnician Art. 2 vols.
———————— Chaldean Art. 2 vols.
———————— Egyptian Art. 2 vols.
———————— Primitive Greece. 2 vols
Thomson's Barbizon School of Painters.

36*s. net.*
Twelve Heads after Holbein.

36*s*.
Perrot & Chipiez's Sardinian Art. 2 vols.

32*s*.
Bonvalot's Through Heart of Asia. 2 vols.
De Falloux's Memoirs. 2 vols.
Peterborough (Earl of), Memoirs. 2 vols.

31*s*. 6*d*
Sutcliffe's Art Student's Guide.

30*s. net*.
Sandeman's Angling in Norway. L.P.

30*s*.
Griffiths' Secrets of Prison House. 2 vols.

28*s*.
Bloomfield's Memoir. 2 vols.

26*s*.
Dawson's Germany and Germans. 2 vols.

25*s. net. each.*
Jeaffreson's Middlesex Records. 4 vols.

24*s*.
Beatty-Kingston's Wanderer's Notes. 2 vls.
———————— Journalist's Jottings. 2 vls.
Elliot's Old Court Life in Spain. 2 vols.

21*s. net.*
Crawfurd's A Year of Sport.
———— Lyrical Verse.
Peok's Nema. Large Paper Edition.

21*s*.
Buffen's Musical Celebrities.

DICKENS'S (CHARLES) WORKS.
Original Edition
Our Mutual Friend.
The Pickwick Papers.
Nicholas Nickleby.
Sketches by "Boz."
Martin Chuzzlewit.
Dombey and Son.
David Copperfield.
Bleak House.
Little Dorrit.
The Old Curiosity Shop.
Barnaby Rudge.
Christmas Books.
Oliver Twist and Two Cities. 1 vol.
Greswell's South African Empire. 2 vols.
Junker's Travels in Africa. 1879—83.
———————— 1882—86.
Lilly's European History. 2 vols.
Perrot & Chipiez's Persian Art.
Ramsden's Birthday Book.
Redgrave's Water Colour Paintings.
Ribton-Turner's Vagrants and Vagrancy.
Walker's Eastern Life and Scenery. 2 vols.

18*s. net.*
Dyce's Drawing Book (Mounted)

18s.

Bingham's Recollections of Paris. 2 vols.
Crawfurd's Round Calendar in Portugal.
De Windt's Siberia as it is.
Malleson's Warren Hastings.
D'Haussonville's Madame Necker. 2 vols.
Statham's Music and Musicians.

16s.

Bradley's Geometry. 2 vols.
De Windt's Ride to India.
Harper's The Dover Road.
———— The Portsmouth Road.
———— Marches of Wales.
Kelly's Life of Cervantes.
Le Roux's Acrobats and Mountebanks.
Oliver's Vegetable Kingdom. .
Paget's (Lord Clarence) Autobiography.
Pollok's Sport and Travel.
Sandeman's Angling in Norway.
Temple's Cosmopolitan Essays.
Wood's Crimea in 1854 and 1894.

15s. *net.*

Dixon's Nests and Eggs of Birds. Col. illus.
Fyler's The 50th Regiment.

15s.

Fleming's Animal Plagues.
———— Rabies and Hydrophobia.
Perrot & Chipiez's Phrygian Art.

14s.

Bailey's Congo Free State.
Billington's Woman in India.
Birdwood's Indian Art.
Carstensen's Two Summers in Greenland.
D'Orleans' Tonkin and Siam.
Fitzgerald's Henry Irving.
Greville-Nugent's Mosques and Marabouts.
Houssaye's Comédie Francaise.
Hudson's Idle Days in Patagonia.
Lanin's Russian Characteristics.
Marceau's Reminiscences of a Regicide.
Oliver's Across the Border.
Snaffle's Gun, Rifle, and Hound.
Son of the Marshes' Wild Fowl & Sea Fowl
Woodgate's Modern Layman's Faith.

12s. *net.*

Wiel's Church Embroidery.

12s.

Dickens' Birthday Book.
Dilke's British Army.
———— European Politics.
Huntley's Travels, Sports, and Politics.
Lilly's Claims of Christianity.
———— On Shibboleths.
———— On Right and Wrong.
———— Century of Revolution.
———— Ancient Religion.
Mitre's Emancipation of S. America
Norman's Tonkin.
Roosevelt's Elizabeth of Roumania
Statham's Architecture.

11s.

Dickens's Oliver Twist. Original ed.

10s. 6d. *net.*

Lineham's Mechanical Engineering.

10s. 6d.

Bailey's Modern Methuselahs.
Bridgeman's Winters in Algeria.
Charlotte Elizabeth's Letters and Life.
Ellis's Yoruba Speaking People.
———— History of Gold Coast.
Forster's Life of Dickens.
Gillmore's Hunter's Arcadia.
Gundry's China Present and Past.
Hall's Travelling Atlas.
Stanley's (H. M.) Life and Work.
Story's Castle St. Angelo.
Taylor's Elementary Art Teaching.
Vandam's French Men and Manners.
Walker's Roumania.

10s.

DICKENS'S (CHARLES) WORKS.
The Illustrated Library Edition.
Sketches by " Boz."
Pickwick Papers. 2 vols.
Oliver Twist.
Nicholas Nickleby. 2 vols.
Old Curiosity Shop, &c. 2 vols.
Barnaby Rudge, &c. 2 vols.
Martin Chuzzlewit. 2 vols.
American Notes.
Dombey and Son. 2 vols.
David Copperfield. 2 vols.
Bleak House. 2 vols. ·
Little Dorrit. 2 vols.

10s. (*continued*).

Tale of Two Cities.
Uncommercial Traveller.
Great Expectations.
Our Mutual Friend. 2 vols.
Christmas Books.
History of England.
Christmas Stories.
Edwin Drood, &c.
Life of Charles Dickens. 2 vols.

9s.

CARLYLE'S (THOMAS) WORKS.
Library Edition.
The French Revolution. 3 vols., each 9s.
Life of Schiller.
Critical Essays. 6 vols., each 9s.
Past and Present.
Cromwell's Letters. 5 vols., each 9s.
Latter-Day Pamphlets.
Life of John Sterling.
Frederick the Great. 10 vols., each 9s.
Translations from the German. 3 vols.
each 9s.
Early Kings of Norway, &c.
Day's Racehorse in Training.
Dickens's Tale of Two Cities. Original ed.
Dilke's Art in Modern State.
Ducoudray's Modern Civilization.
Escott's Politics and Letters.
Hatton's Figure Drawing and Composition.
Jackson's Theory and Practice of Design.
Long's Dairy Farming.
Poynter's Lectures on Art.

8s.

Boyle's About Orchids.

CARLYLE'S (THOMAS) WORKS.
The Ashburton Edition.
Demy 8vo, 8s. each volume.
French Revolution and Past and Present.
2 vols.
Sartor Resartus and Heroes. 1 vol.
Lives of Sterling and Schiller. 1 vol.
Latter-Day Pamphlets and Early Kings
of Norway, &c. 1 vol.
Cromwell's Letters. 3 vols.
Frederick the Great. 6 vols.
Critical Essays. 3 vols.
Translations from the German. 3 vols.

8s. (*continued*).

DICKENS'S (CHARLES) WORKS.
Library Edition. 8s. each volume.
Pickwick Papers. 2 vols.
Nicholas Nickleby. 2 vols.
Martin Chuzzlewit. 2 vols.
Old Curiosity Shop, &c. 2 vols.
Barnaby Rudge and Hard Times. 2 vols.
Bleak House. 2 vols.
Little Dorrit. 2 vols.
Dombey and Son. 2 vols.
David Copperfield. 2 vols.
Our Mutual Friend. 2 vols.
Sketches by "Boz."
Oliver Twist.
Christmas Books.
A Tale of Two Cities.
Great Expectations.
Pictures from Italy, &c.
Uncommercial Traveller.
Child's England.
Edwin Drood, &c.
Christmas Stories, &c.
Drayson's Woolwich Professor.
Fiske's Life of E. L. Youmans.
Fitzgerald's History of Pickwick.
Hudson's Naturalist in La Plata.
Hueffer's Half a Century of Music.
Pytchley Book of Refined Cookery.
Robson's Building Construction.
Wornum's Analysis of Ornament.

7s..6d.

Andrew's Course of Scale Drawing.
Boyle's Orchid Seekers in Borneo.
Carlyle's Sartor Resartus. Library Edition.
——— Heroes. Library Edition.
De Lisle's Memoir.
De Windt's Pekin to Calais.
Dickens's Edwin Drood. Original edition.
Dixon's Migration of British Birds.
——— Birds of our Rambles.
——— Annals of Bird Life.
Forster's Life of Landor.
Harper's Drawing for Reproduction.
Hudson's Birds in a Village.
Hughes' A Week's Tramp in Dickens' Land.
Jackson's Decorative Design.
Jean's Creators of the Age of Steel.
Leroy-Beaulieu's Papacy, Socialism, &c.
Leslie's A Water Biography.
McCoan's Egypt under Ismael.

7s. 6d. (continued).

Marmery's Progress of Science.
Muntz's Raphael.
Pratt's Sciography.   .   *
Reid's Present Evolution of Man.
Robinson's Italian Sculpture.
Scott's Republic as a Form of Government.
Stoddart's Across Russia.
Vandam's Englishman in Paris.
Ward's Principles of Ornament.
Watson's Poachers and Poaching.
* Wolverton's Sport in Somaliland.

7s.

Burchett's Linear Perspective.

6s. 6d. net. -

Dyce's Drawing Book (Selection mtd.)

6s. net.

Nelson's Wood Working Positions. (*Large*).

6s.

Aïdé's Elizabeth's Pretenders.
Bailey's From Sinner to Saint.
Bos's Agricultural Zoology.
Church's Food Grains of India.
Cooper-King's George Washington.
Courtney's Studies at Leisure.
———— Studies New and Old.
De Bovet's Three Months in Ireland.
De Koninck's Chemical Assaying (Iron).
Dixon's Nests & Eggs British Birds. Vol. 1.
———,   Ditto.   Vol. 2.
———— Jottings about Birds.
———— Migration of Birds.
———— Idle Hours with Nature.
Douglas's Physiography.
Ducoudray's Ancient Civilization.
Ellis's South African Sketches.
Fane's Autumn Songs.
Gore's The Scenery of the Heavens.
Griffith's Criminals I have known.
———— Chronicles of Newgate.
———— French Revolutionary Generals.
Grinnell's Story of the Indian.
Henry's Queen of Beauty.
Hunt's A Hard Woman.
———— The Maiden's Progress.

6s. (continued).

Hutchinson's Creatures of Other Days.
———— ———— Extinct Monsters.
Lavelaye's Political Economy.
Le Conté's Evolution.
Lee's Life of General Lee.
Lineham's Street of Human Habitations.
Lloyd's Sketches of Indian Life.
Low's Table Decoration.
Macdonald's Ocean Railways.
Malleson's Prince Eugene of Savoy.
Mallock's The Heart of Life.
Meredith's Lord Ormont.
———— One of our Conquerors.
———— Diana of the Crossways.
———— Evan Harrington.
———— Richard Feverel.
———— Harry Richmond.
———— Sandra Belloni.
———— Vittoria.
———— Rhoda Fleming.
———— Beauchamp's Career.
——— .—— Egoist.
———— Shagpat and Farina.
Peek's Nema and Other Stories.
Pilling's Land Tenure.
Puckett's Sciography.
Spalding's Life of Suvóroff.
Reid's Life of W. E. Forster.
Swift, his Life and Love.
Tovey's Martial Law.   [2 vols.
Trollope's Warden and Barchester Towers.
———— Dr. Thorne.
———— Framley Parsonage.
———— Small House Allington. 2 vo's.
———— Last Chron. of Barset. 2 vols.
Whitman's Teuton Studies.

5s. net.

Dyce's Drawing Book.
Raphael's Cartoons and Drawings.

5s.

Boyle's The Prophet John.
Burchett's Practical Geometry.
Character in the Face.
Carlyle's Thoughts on Life.
Craik's English of Shakespeare.
Crawfurd's Dialogues of the Day. .
Cumberland's South Africa.
Daly's Ireland in the Days of Swift.

5*s.* (*continued*).
DICKENS'S (CHARLES) WORKS.
Crown Edition.
Pickwick Papers.
Nicholas Nickleby.
Dombey and Son.
David Copperfield.
Sketches by " Boz."
Martin Chuzzlewit.
Old Curiosity Shop.
Barnaby Rudge.
Oliver Twist and Two Cities.
Bleak House.
Little Dorrit.
Our Mutual Friend.
American Notes, Italy, and England.
Christmas Books and Hard Times.
Christmas Stories and Others.
Great Expectations and Uncommercial.
Edwin Drood, &c.
Uniform with the above.
Life of Dickens.
The Dickens Dictionary.
Lazy Tour of Two Idle Apprentices, &c.
Household Edition.
Martin Chuzzlewit.
David Copperfield.
Bleak House.
Little Dorrit.
Pickwick Papers.
Our Mutual Friend.
Nicholas Nickleby.
Dombey and Son.
Edwin Drood, &c.
The Life of Dickens.
Das's Sketches of Hindoo Life.
Delille's Some French Writers.
Drayson's Earth's Past History.
Foster's Round the Crooked Spire.
Fouqué's Undine.
Francatelli's Royal Confectioner.
Gordon's Letters from the Crimea.
Gore's Planetary and Stellar Studies.
Hartington's New Academe.
Hudson's Philosophy of Herbert Spencer.
Lloyd's On Active Service.
Maitland's Hethia Hardacre.
Maspéro's Egypt and Assyria.
Maude's Five Years in Madagascar.
O'Grady's Toryism and Democracy.
O'Connor's Some Old Love Stories.
Rae's Austrian Health Resorts.
Robinson's Bee Farming.

5*s.* (*continued*).
Roland's Dairy Farming.
—— Poultry Keeping.
—— Tree Planting.
—— Stock Keeping.
—— Drainage of Land.
—— Root Growing.
—— Grass Lands.
—— Market Gardening.
Ross's Early Days Recalled.
Schauermann's Wood Carving.
Seeman's Mythology of Greece and Rome.
Seton-Karr's Ten Years' Sport and Travel.
Simkin's Life in the Army.
Ward's Elementary Ornament.
Wegg-Prosser's Galileo and his Judges.
Wrightson's Agricultural Practice.
—— Fallow and Fodder Crops.

4*s.* 6*d.*
Aflalo's Sea and the Rod.
Duckitt's Hilda's " Where is it ? "
Griffin's Great Republic.
Leslie's Sea Boat.
Maskell's Russian Art.
Mill's Advanced Physiography.
Moltke's Poland.
Seton-Karr's Bear Hunting.
Tanner's Holt Castle.
Younge's Parallel Lives.

4*s.*
About's Social Economy.
Adam's Building Construction.
Baker's The Beam.
Bentley's Songs and Verses.
Brackenbury's Frederick the Great.
Breakfasts, Luncheons, and Ball Suppers.
DICKENS'S (CHARLES) WORKS.
Charles Dickens Edition.
Pickwick Papers.
Martin Chuzzlewit.
Dombey and Son.
Nicholas Nickleby.
David Copperfield.
Bleak House.
Little Dorrit.
Our Mutual Friend.
Household Edition.
Barnaby Rudge.
Old Curiosity Shop.
Christmas Stories.
Hozier's Turenne.

4s. (continued).

Lamennais's Words of a Believer.
Malleson's Marshal Loudon.
Midgley's Plant Form and Design.
Poole's Saracenic Art.
Riano's Spanish Arts.
Stoke's Irish Art.
Walford's Parliamentary Generals.

3s. 6d. net.

Crawfurd's Lyrical Verse.

3s. 6d.

Angel's Geometry.
Boyle's From the Frontier.
Bromley-Davenport's Sport.
Buckland's Log Book of a Fisherman.
CHAPMAN'S STORY SERIES.
  The Long Arm. By M. E. Wilkins.
  In a Hollow of the Hills. By Bret Harte.
  At the Sign of the Ostrich. By C. James.
Courtney's Constructive Ethics.
DICKENS'S (CHARLES) WORKS.
  Charles Dickens Edition.
Barnaby Rudge.
Old Curiosity Shop.
Child's History of England.
Edwin Drood, &c.
Christmas Stories.
Sketches by "Boz."
American Notes, &c.
Christmas Books.
Oliver Twist.
Great Expectations.
The Life of Dickens. 2 vols., 3s. 6d. each.
The Letters of Dickens ,, ,,
  The Pictorial Edition.
Dombey and Son.
David Copperfield.
Nicholas Nickleby.
Barnaby Rudge.
Old Curiosity Shop.
Martin Chuzzlewit.
Oliver Twist and Two Cities.
Our Mutual Friend.
Bleak House.
Pickwick Papers.
Little Dorrit.
Expectations and Hard Times.
American Notes, Italy, and England.
Sketches and Christmas Books.
Stories and Uncommercial.
Edwin Drood, &c.

3s. 6d. (continued).

Life of Dickens.
Dickens (Mary) Cross Currents.
Escott's England.
Harrison's Decoration of Metals.
Hope's The Vyvyans.
Hovelaque's Science of Language.
Humphry's Cookery up to Date.
Jokai's Pretty Michael.
————— Midst the Wild Carpathians.
Lacordaire's Conferences.
Laing's Human Origins.
————— Problems of the Future.
————— Modern Science.
————— Modern Zoroastrian.
Lefevre's Philosophy.
Leslie's British Privateer.
Letourneau's Sociology.
————— Biology.
Little's Waif from the Waves.
Mallock's A Human Document.
Meredith's One of our Conquerors.
————— Diana of the Crossways.
————— Evan Harrington.
————— Richard Feverel.
————— Harry Richmond.
————— Sandra Belloni.
————— Vittoria.
————— Rhoda Fleming.
————— Beauchamp's Career.
————— Egoist.
————— Shagpat and Farina.
Mill's Quantitative Analysis.
Muddock's Star of Fortune.
Murray's Economic Entomology.
Official Handbook of Cookery.
Pushkin's Queen of Spades.
Renan's Recollections of my Youth.
Robert's (Morley) In Low Relief.
Russell's Miss Parson's Adventure.
Sexton's First Technical College.
Simmond's Animal Products.
Sinnett's Esoteric Buddhism.
Steele's Clove Pink.
Stories from *Black and White.*
Tanner's Jack's Education.
Topinard's Anthropology.
Traherne's Habits of Salmon.
Underhill's Through a Field Glass.
Vandam's Mystery of the Patrician Club.
Veron's Æsthetics.
Watson's Sketches in the Hunting Field
————— British Sporting Fishes.
Worsaae's Danish Arts.

3*s.*

Bell's Chemistry of Foods. Part II.
Carlyle's Birthday Book.
Church's English Porcelain.
———— English Earthenware.
———— Food.
DICKENS'S (CHARLES) WORKS.
    Charles Dickens Edition.
Tale of Two Cities.
Hard Times and Pictures from Italy.
Uncommercial Traveller.
    Household Edition.
Oliver Twist.
Great Expectations.
Sketches by "Boz."
Uncommercial Traveller.
Christmas Books.
Child's History of England.
American Notes, &c.
A Tale of Two Cities.
Gardner's Ironwork.
Gasnault's French Pottery.
Gower's Practical Metallurgy.
Holmes's Marine Engines and Boilers.
Industrial Arts : Historical Sketches.
Sinnett's Karma.
Spencer, Herbert ; Aphorisms from.

2*s.* 6*d.* net.

Dyce's Drawing Book. Standards I—IV.
Nelson's Wood Working Positions.
Lineham's Directory of Schools, &c.

2*s.* 6*d.*

Adam's Machine Construction. (Elem.)
———— ,, ,, (Advan.)
Aveling's Mechanics.
———— Chemistry.
———— Magnetism and Electricity.
———— Light and Heat.
Bell's Chemistry of Foods. Part I.
CARLYLE'S (THOMAS) WORKS.
    The Half-crown Edition.
Sartor Resartus & Latter-day Pamphlets.
Past and Present and On Heroes.
Lives of Sterling and Schiller.
Critical Essays. 4 vols., 2*s.* 6*d.* each.
French Revolution. 2 vols., 2*s.* 6*d.* each.
Cromwell's Letters. 3 vols., 2*s.* 6*d.* each.
Frederick the Great. 5 vols., 2*s.* 6*d.* each.
Wilhelm Meister. 2 vols., 2*s.* 6*d.* each.

2*s.* 6*d.* (*continued*).

Translations from Musæus, &c.
Cromwell's Letters. 1 vol, blue cloth.
CHAPMAN'S STORY SERIES.
The Long Arm. By M. E. Wilkins.
In a Hollow of the Hills. By Bret Harte.
At the Sign of the Ostrich. By C. James
The White Feather. By Os. Crawfurd.
Church's Precious Stones.
Craik's Outlines of the English Language.
Cripp's College and Corporation Plate.
De Champeaux Tapestry.
DICKENS'S (CHARLES) WORKS.
    The Half-crown Edition.
The Pickwick Papers.
Barnaby Rudge.
Oliver Twist.
The Old Curiosity Shop.
David Copperfield.
Nicholas Nickleby.
Martin Chuzzlewit.
Dombey and Son.
Sketches by "Boz."
Christmas Books.
Bleak House.
Little Dorrit.
Christmas Stories.
American Notes and Reprinted Pieces.
Hard Times and Pictures from Italy.
Child's History of England.
Great Expectations.
Tale of Two Cities.
Uncommercial Traveller.
Our Mutual Friend.
Edwin Drood and Other Stories.
    Household Edition.
Hard Times.
Earl's Dinners in Miniature.
Engel's Musical Instruments.
Fortnum's Maiolica.
———— Bronzes.
Frank's Japanese Pottery.
Hatton's Elementary Design.
Hildebrand's Scandinavian Art.
James's Handbook to Perspective.
Kempt's Convivial Caledonia.
Maskell's Ivories.
———— Dyce and Foster Collection.
Mill's Alternative Physics.
Nesbit's Glass.
Newcy's Elementary Drawing.
Pollen's Gold and Silver-smith's Work.

2s. 6d. (continued).

Pollen's Ancient and Modern Furniture.
Radical Programme.
Redgrave's Manual of Design.
Rock's Textile Fabrics.
Ryan's Egyptian Art.
Sanders' Bent Ironwork.
Statham's Form and Design in Music.
Thrupp's Coach Trimming.

2s.

Agricultural Science Lectures.
CARLYLE'S (THOMAS) WORKS.
French Revolution.
Sartor, Heroes, Past & Present, &c. 1 vol.
Critical Essays. 2 vols., 2s. each.
Wilhelm Meister.
Lives of Schiller and Sterling.
Crawfurd's The White Feather.
DICKENS'S (CHARLES) WORKS.
Two Shilling Edition.
Dombey and Son.
Martin Chuzzlewit.
The Pickwick Papers.
Bleak House.
Old Curiosity Shop.
Barnaby Rudge.
David Copperfield.
Nicholas Nickleby.
Christmas Stories.
American Notes and Reprinted Pieces.
Hard Times and Pictures from Italy.
Great Expectations.
Our Mutual Friend.
Christmas Books.
Oliver Twist.
Little Dorrit.
Tale of Two Cities.
Uncommercial Traveller.
Sketches by "Boz."
Child's History of England.
Edwin Drood and Other Stories.
Fane's Helen Davenant.
Fleming's Practical Horse Shoeing.
Gonner's Political Economy.
Gore's Astronomical Lessons.
James's Perspective Charts.
Jokai's Pretty Michal.
Pushkin's Queen of Spades.
Robert's (Morley) In Low Relief.
Smith's Persian Art.
Underhill's Through a Field Glass.

1s. 6d. net.

Dyce's Drawing Book (Selection).

1s. 6d.

Brock's Elements of Physiology.
Carlyle's Thoughts on Life.
DICKENS'S (CHARLES) WORKS.
The Cabinet Edition. 1s. 6d. each vol.
Christmas Books.
Martin Chuzzlewit. 2 vols.
David Copperfield. 2 vols.
Oliver Twist.
Great Expectations.
Nicholas Nickleby. · 2 vols.
Sketches by "Boz."
Christmas Stories.
Pickwick Papers. 2 vols.
Barnaby Rudge. 2 vols.
Bleak House. 2 vols.
American Notes, &c.
Edwin Drood, &c.
Old Curiosity Shop. 2 vols.
Child's History of England.
Dombey and Son. 2 vols.
A Tale of Two Cities.
Little Dorrit. 2 vols.
Mutual Friend. 2 vols.
Hard Times.
Uncommercial Traveller.
Reprinted Pieces.
Gorst's An Election Manual.
Jopling's Hints to Amateurs.
Little's Waif from the Waves.
—— Broken Vow.
—— Child of Stafferton.
Mill's Elem. Physiographic Astronomy.
——Quantitative Analysis (Intrody).
Sanders' Bent Ironwork.
Shirreff's Home Education.

1s.

Breakfast and Savoury Dishes.
CARLYLE'S (THOMAS) WORKS.
People's Edition.
Sartor Resartus.
French Revolution. 3 vols., 1s. each.
Cromwell's Letters. 5 vols., 1s. each.
On Heroes.
Past and Present.
Critical Essays. 7 vols., 1s. each.
Life of Schiller.
Latter-day Pamphlets.
Wilhelm Meister. 3 vols., 1s. each.

1s. (*continued*).

Life of Sterling.
Frederick the Great. 10 vols., 1*s.* each.
Translations from Musæus, &c. 2 vols.
1*s.* each.
Early Kings of Norway, &c.
Thoughts on Life.
Dawson's Julius Cæsar.

DICKENS'S (C.) CHRISTMAS BOOKS.
A Christmas Carol. Red cloth.
The Chimes. ,,
Cricket on the Hearth. ,,
The Battle of Life. ,,
The Haunted Man. ,,

DICKENS'S (CHARLES) READINGS.
Christmas Carol. Paper Wrappers.
Cricket on the Hearth. ,,
Chimes. ,,
Little Dombey. ,,
Poor Traveller, &c. ,,
Hatton's Guide to Estab'mt. of Art Schools.
Little's Waif from the Waves.
—— Broken Vow.
—— Child of Stafferton.
Moltke's Poland.
Radical Programme.
Sexton's Home Work in Inorganic Chemy.

9*d.*

Redgrave's Manual of Colour.

6*d.*

Brewer's Conjugation of French Verbs.
CARLYLE'S (THOMAS) WORKS.
Sartor Resartus.
Heroes and Hero Worship.
Essays: Burns, Johnson, &c.
Chapman's Magazine (Monthly).
Church's Plain Words about Water.
DICKENS'S (CHARLES) WORKS.
Oliver Twist.
American Notes and Pictures from Italy.
Bleak House.
Readings from Dickens.
A Christmas Carol, & The Haunted Man.
The Chimes and Cricket on the Hearth.
The Battle of Life, Hunted Down, &c.
Dyce's Drawing Book Text).

2*d.*

Brewer's Conjugation of French Verbs.

A LIST OF CATALOGUES ISSUED BY

CHAPMAN & HALL, Ltd.

TO BE HAD ON APPLICATION.

MODERN SCIENTIFIC PUBLICATIONS AND OF WORKS ON ART,
Technology, and other subjects, including those published by Messrs. WILKY & SONS of New York, classified under subjects, authors, and titles.

A CLASSIFIED CATALOGUE OF BOOKS published by CHAPMAN & HALL, Ltd., with Index to subjects and authors.

THE COMPLETE WORKS OF DICKENS, CARLYLE, MEREDITH,
Laing, &c., with specimen of type, illustrations and size of pages.

MODELS, EXAMPLES, DIAGRAMS, CHEMICAL AND PHYSICAL
Apparatus, Mathematical Instruments, &c., including those issued under the authority of the Science and Art Department, South Kensington, for use in Technical Schools, Science and Art Classes, &c., &c

MECHANICAL MODELS, AND MODELS OF MACHINE AND
Building Construction, &c., being a Selection from the list of Polytechnisches Arbeits-Institut, J. SCHRÖDER, A.-G., Darmstadt.

BOOKS, PORTFOLIOS, INSTRUMENTS, COLOURS, &c., suitable for
Art Prizes, and as examples for use in Schools of Art and Art Classes.

BOOKS, INSTRUMENTS, APPARATUS, TOOLS, &c., suitable for Prizes,
for Grammar Schools, Evening Continuation Schools, &c.

MODERN WORKS ON SCIENCE AND TECHNOLOGY, classified under
authors and subjects, with Index. Issued annually. Twenty-fourth Edition. Demy 8vo, 1*s.*